THE WARR

Garrick lunged at _____ _____ him take the offensive, _____ _____ _____ precise pattern. And when she _____ _____ _____ontal swing from her right, he came ba_____ _____ lunge.

When next he lunge_____ he stepped aside as before. As he moved past, she pushed the tip of his sword down with her own. She slid her sword down the edge of his, toward the ground, whirled around, and arced her own blade in a circle. The sharp edge caught him in the shoulder, biting deeply. Blood stained the blade when she pulled it free.

The tip of his blade grabbed at the ground, throwing him off balance. He stumbled, nearly losing hold of the handle of his weapon. Now, he looked surprised.

In two paces, she reached him. With a sweep of her leg, he was flat on the ground. His sword lay within reach of his hand. Elissa kicked it away, then stood with a foot on either side of him. She turned the sword and gripped the handle with both hands, prepared to plunge the tip into his heart . . .

THE
WINTER
QUEEN

DEVIN CARY

ACE BOOKS, NEW YORK

THE WINTER QUEEN

This is a work of fiction. Names, characters, places, and incidents are
either the product of the author's imagination or are used fictitiously,
and any resemblance to actual persons, living or dead, business estab-
lishments, events, or locales is entirely coincidental.

An Ace Book / published by arrangement with
the author

PRINTING HISTORY
Ace edition / December 1999

All rights reserved.
Copyright © 1999 by Cary Osborne.
Cover art by Yvonne Gilbert.
This book may not be reproduced in whole or in part,
by mimeograph or any other means, without permission.
For information address: The Berkley Publishing Group,
a division of Penguin Putnam Inc.,
375 Hudson Street, New York, New York 10014.

The Penguin Putnam Inc. World Wide Web site address is
http://www.penguinputnam.com

Check out the ACE Science Fiction & Fantasy newsletter
and much more on the Internet at Club PPI!

ISBN: 0-441-00681-7

ACE®
Ace Books are published
by The Berkley Publishing Group,
a division of Penguin Putnam Inc.,
375 Hudson Street, New York, New York 10014.
ACE and the "A" design are trademarks
belonging to Penguin Putnam Inc.

PRINTED IN THE UNITED STATES OF AMERICA

10   9   8   7   6   5   4   3   2   1

Dedicated to the memory of Robert "Kim" Pugh. He was a good writer, a great critiquer, and a wonderful friend. He is loved. He will be missed.

1

Two priests prayed in a monotone. The male members of the court, including an uncle and cousin, stood stoically. The son and daughter were bewildered, looking from their father, lying white and still in the bed, to their mother, standing at her husband's side.

"Your majesty, you are dying," Patriarch Dathan said close to his king's ear. "You must name a regent to lead your son, to help him rule, until he comes of age."

Ethelred shook his head side to side. Did he not believe he was dying?

Lord Geoffrey motioned for Dathan to move aside and took his place on the side of the bed.

"Your majesty, Dathan is right," he said. "And you know I rarely agree with him about anything." A smile flitted across the king's lips. "Your death is imminent. Please do this for your son. Who would you have as regent?"

Ethelred tried to focus on the face of his marshal. Behind him stood all of the likely candidates for the position.

"Would you have Dathan, sire?" Geoffrey took hold of the patriarch's arm and the older man took a step forward. "Your uncle, Roric, or cousin, Randall?" The two of them moved closer. "Lord Witram? Or Lord Luther?"

The king lay silent and still, his eyes looking only at Geoffrey's face. He will choose the marshal. Everyone must see that.

His arm rose slowly. His index finger with the royal signet ring extended, pointing. "Elissa," he said hoarsely. Everyone stared at him a moment, then turned toward his wife, the queen.

A look of dismay or horror showed on every adult face in the room—except for Geoffrey's. He looked surprised, yet delighted. This choice spoiled everyone's plans.

The king's hand dropped back to the bed, his eyes open but lifeless. The king was dead.

Elissa took Geoffrey's place on the edge of the bed, myriad emotions running through her at breakneck speed. It had happened so fast. There was so much to do—and too much to fear.

Dear gods, she had not loved her husband, but she was certain she would miss him. For nine years Ethelred had been the only stable thing in her life. He had been kind and they had even shared amusing moments together. Now that he was gone, everything would be thrown into turmoil, especially his kingdom. Who would save the kingdom for her children?

He had named her.

Geoffrey, Marshal of Albor, touched her shoulder. He spoke softly.

"My queen, it is over. Plans must be made."

She looked up at him, and the grief in his eyes almost crushed her. Geoffrey had been the king's one true friend. Surely he would help to ensure the succession of his friend's son.

"I know," she said.

She touched her fingertips to her mouth then pressed them against the lips of her husband. He was still warm to the touch. She wished for the all-consuming grief that should be hers, but that she could not pretend to feel; he deserved true grief. It would have to be enough to comfort her children, who would be inconsolable once they understood their father would never . . .

She stood, whispered to the nurse to take the children to their room, and followed Geoffrey into the hall. Behind them came the king's uncle and cousin. The marshal led the way to the Privy Council chamber, a room into which she had seldom been invited. All of the councilors, except the marshal and Lords Roric and Randall, had awaited news of the king's health there.

Elissa sat in the chair at the head of the table as Geoffrey indicated she should do. Her thoughts were still very much on Ethelred. He had been a good father, a good husband, and a good king. And that counted for a lot, especially in this place where most men thought women existed only for their pleasure. Now Edgar must learn to be a good king, and hopefully a good man, in his father's place, but not without a struggle.

Geoffrey stood behind his chair while Roric and Randall took their places. His wide hands gripped his chair back so that his knuckles turned white. His head was bowed, his breathing came almost in gasps. Elissa suspected he fought back tears. He cleared his throat and looked up, surveying the assemblage with red-rimmed eyes.

"Fellow councilors," he began and cleared his throat again. "Our king is dead. He passed quietly a few moments ago."

They all muttered sorrowfully, looking from one to the other shaking their heads. Whether they were truly saddened by Ethelred's passing or only feared for their exalted places at court, Elissa did not know. She knew little of them except for the things her husband had told her. He had said much at times, but only as a way of venting his frustrations. Although a woman's counsel was neither sought nor valued in Albor, he had often listened when she ventured an opinion, and once or twice had done as she suggested.

Patriarch Dathan rose, his expression as sanctimonious as ever.

"I will set the priestesses to preparing the final meal," he said.

For a moment, the meaning of his words escaped her. As realization came to her, Elissa gasped.

"Not for my son," she said coldly. "He will not take part."

"It is his duty, my queen," Dathan said. "The king's sins must be eaten. The sins of the father are passed to the son."

"Edgar is only five years old," she protested. "He does not understand."

"It is time for him to understand. The nearest male relative must perform this duty. And if there is a son, it falls to him."

"He will not do it!"

Panic and fear were about to take hold of her and she could not let that happen. These men thought a woman incapable of rational thought. She could not reinforce that belief. Her arguments must be as logical and succinct as possible.

"Our gods require it and you will not go against this," Dathan was saying. "You are a mere woman . . ."

"I am the queen," she said with as much haughtiness as she could muster. "Mother of the future king and the one chosen to act in his name."

Those who had not witnessed the final moments looked confused by her words. She looked to Geoffrey, her one possible ally in the Council, for support, but he looked away. All right. She would be alone in this fight.

"Prepare the meal, Patriarch," Geoffrey said after a long silence. "Someone will eat it. Meanwhile, we must move on to other arrangements."

Dathan resumed his seat, but the look he gave her did not bode well. A widow for less than an hour and already she had made an enemy. If she was to ensure Edgar's ascension to the throne, she needed these men as allies, not enemies. Could she somehow reconcile herself to this ceremony, even though it went against everything she believed?

"We must order a sarcophagus and funerary items. Lord Luther, if you could see to those arrangements," Geoffrey said.

The ancient one nodded his head. He was the largest landholder in the kingdom, had outlived four wives and thirteen of his children, but still he went on, more fragile each year.

Organizing the basilica, the mourners, and necessary ornaments would be done by Randall, Ethelred's cousin. Dathan would, of course, make all other religious arrangements. Geoffrey was in charge of seeing that the body was guarded and properly prepared. Other duties, including organizing hunting parties to feed those who would come for the funeral, were meted out according to the man's position or length of time within the council or relationship to the king himself. Roric, Ethelred's uncle, would oversee everything.

In the end, Geoffrey turned to her.

"Do these arrangements suit you, your majesty?" he asked.

From the stern expression in his eyes, she knew he expected her to acquiesce. Since nothing more had been said about the meal, she could do so.

"Yes, Marshal, they do."

"Good." He turned from her to the other councilors. "Those of you who were not there when our king died should know one thing. As her majesty said, with his dying breath, he named his wife and queen to act as regent for their children."

Those who had been there shook their heads. Those who had not began to splutter and fume.

"It will not happen," Dathan nearly shouted. "A woman cannot be named regent for the heir to the throne."

"Why not?" Elissa asked. "Wives are named by their lords to rule domains under all sorts of conditions."

"But this is the future king we speak of," Dathan said. "A woman is not fit to rule an entire kingdom."

"My husband, the king, thought I was, my lords. Will you go against his wishes?"

"Fah," Lord Witram blurted out. "He was out of his head with fever and pain. No one can believe he meant it."

"I believe he meant it, my lords," Geoffrey said. "One month after the funeral, we will name the regent. In doing so, we must consider the king's wishes, traditions, and the charters. We have much work. I suggest we now concentrate on the funeral, which lies before us.''

''Yes, let's,'' Dathan said. The others nodded, having regained their somber expressions and mumbling their agreement in appropriately subdued tones.

''Thank you, gentlemen,'' the marshal said, ending the meeting.

Geoffrey rose and the others followed suit. Everyone waited as he escorted the queen from the room, then scattered to be about the business of organizing the funeral, sending retainers home to spread the sad news, and fetching other family members for the upcoming services. He walked with her as far as the door to her chambers, and started to turn away.

''Lord Geoffrey, please come in,'' she said. ''I would talk with you.''

''I have . . .''

''I know. You have much to do. But please. For a moment.''

He bowed his head in acceptance and opened the door for her to precede him. The chambermaid stood waiting for her, having heard the door open in time to prepare herself.

''Clara, leave us for the moment,'' Elissa said. ''I will ring when I need you.''

The maid nodded and left through the door they had entered. Elissa sat in the chair nearest the fireplace and motioned for Geoffrey to seat himself in the one nearest her. She sat forward in the chair, soaking up heat from the fire. It was always so cold in this castle, sometimes even in the summer, and this particular fire was never allowed to go out.

She had been born in Morrigan, the warmer south, and lived there until Ethelred brought her to Winfield to be his queen.

Geoffrey sat calmly.

''My lord, I never sought to be named regent for my son during his minority,'' she said.

The marshal smiled.

"It was not the first time Ethelred said something in this vein, although I thought that he was merely teasing me," she said. "You know the forces that are struggling within the court. I am sure he would have named you years ago, had he known what lay in the future. But there was so little time. So little warning."

"But your majesty . . ."

"I will step aside if you will accept the position and responsibility, Lord Geoffrey. The others respect you and will often be guided by you. These next few years will be dangerous times, and my inexperience would be a liability."

"That may be true, your majesty." He stood and started pacing between her and the fireplace. "As dangerous as those years will be, I would like to see our king's wishes followed. My accepting that responsibility would only cause a great rift in the Council, and might end with someone else being regent."

"If someone else is named—other than you or me—my son will be bent to his will. He will become that man's disciple, probably abandoning everything good his father accomplished in his short reign. I will not let that happen!"

The marshal stopped pacing and stood before her, hands on his hips.

"True, your husband did many good things for the people of this land. I do not want to see them all destroyed either."

She looked up at him, prepared to plead, cajole, whatever was necessary to convince him that he should take the role of regent. However, she could see in his eyes that nothing would sway him. She looked down at her hands, folded in her lap, and nodded.

"Thank you, my lord, for hearing me out," she said. "Now, I know you must be eager to get back to your duties."

She looked back up and thought there was a trace of worry in his eyes. She smiled at him. It was a winning smile, or so she had been told many times, and he smiled back.

With a few words of condolence and reassurance, he left.

The fire crackled, bringing her attention back to it. So many times she had sat in the same place, doing the same thing, while she awaited Ethelred's return from an inspection of one of the forts or a hunting trip. He was often gone for days at a time and the castle seemed lonely without his masculine warmth and ready smile. It had always seemed that he was due back any moment. Usually Geoffrey was with him. More than once she wished he had been with the king on that day, when life was irretrievably changed.

She shook off the memory and stood up. At twenty-five she suddenly felt old, and more afraid even than the first day she walked into the castle. Then, it was all strange and forbidding. Now, it was familiar and forbidding. And it was so far from everything she had grown up with.

That Ethelred had named her regent was incomprehensible, in spite of that one night they had discussed the subject. It was one of those nights when he came to her bed and lay close to her, their bodies pressed against each other for comfort. It was the first time she had understood that he also felt very alone in this world of theirs.

Earlier that day, word had come that one of Lord Luther's sons had died of a fever. He left a widow and three small children to Luther's care.

"What would happen to our children if I should die?" Ethelred had asked as she caressed his arm lying across her. "I have no father to leave in charge of them. I do not trust my uncle—his son is too ambitious. Nor Dathan, who would make a priest of him. They will all fight to possess my son."

"What about Lord Geoffrey? He is strong, young, and your best friend."

"If a king can have a best friend. No," he said and rolled over onto his back. "Geoffrey is a good man and would make a fine regent, but he would be the worst choice of all. Choosing him would cause the jealousy the other nobles feel for him to erupt into violence. I fear that would tear my kingdom apart."

"Why talk of this now, Ethelred? You are young and strong

and will live to see our children grow up and take care of themselves.''

"The news today . . ." he began, then fell silent. "You would make a very good diplomat, my love. I know," he said with a laugh. "I'll name you regent. No one could find fault with that.''

"Me? A woman? *Everyone* would find fault with that. I'm very sure it's never been done before.''

He had laughed quietly at that. More than once he had made a decision just the opposite of what his councilors expected, simply because they had told him, ''It's never been done before.''

Until now, she had thought Ethelred could not have been serious about going against this particular tradition. Now that the decision was made, it was what she wanted for her children and herself.

But she not only had to make it happen, she also had to ensure that her regency would last until her children were grown. And a means to accomplish that had occurred to her.

She moved to the desk and, using the key on her chatelaine, unlocked the top drawer on the left side. From there she took out a sheet of paper with her feather crest embossed at the top. She desperately needed a friend to help secure her position as regent. Someone who would support her and her children, who might even need her as much as she needed him. She started writing and soon the paper was covered with her fine hand-writing.

Returning to her chair at the fireplace, she turned the sheet so that light from the fire illuminated the writing. The idea of sending a letter had occurred to her when she realized that, with the king dead, she no longer had a safe position in this court. Although Geoffrey seemed adamant about obeying Ethelred's wishes, she would need help from someone whose position depended on her.

She read it over one last time: *Your majesty,* it began. *My husband, Ethelred, king of Albor, has died. I am left with his two children to raise and protect. You have two unwed sons.*

Please, send me one of your sons and I will marry him and he and I will be regents for my son. I am but a weak woman in need of a man's guidance, and I promise to be a good wife and make your son happy. She signed it, *Elissa, Regina, Albor.*

With a sigh, she returned to the desk, and folded the paper. On the outside she wrote, "To His Majesty King Verald, Ravelin." She fetched a burning twig from the fire and melted the wax onto the edge, pressing the wax with the ring from her finger. The feather seal on it matched the one at the top of the paper.

She rang the silver bell on the desk, and Clara appeared immediately.

"Fetch Tommy," Elissa said. "I have an errand for him."

Clara bobbed a curtsey and disappeared again. Tommy was devoted to her and would let no one but the addressee see the letter, she was sure of that. At least six days for him to get to Ravelin, a couple of days there, and six days for the return trip. Perhaps longer. But he must make it back before the period of mourning was over.

Elissa went into her children's rooms, checking to be sure they slept quietly. A wild desire to move them into her own room had to be beaten down for the hundredth time. She must protect them at any cost, but in some ways there was so little she could do. She was, after all, only a woman.

However, there were things she could do as a woman that no one in the capital even dreamed possible. And it was concerning these that she prepared to write another letter to her uncle in the south.

2

"Concentrate, girl!"

Elissa looked up, angry words on the tip of her tongue. She was practically gasping for breath both in anger and frustration at not being able to summon the image of the goddess. She could not delve into the inner self, where there was danger of getting lost, if she could not summon the Lady's protection. Without that protection, she could not move things with her mind. Without mastering that ability, she could not progress to the next stages.

The work was hard—she had forgotten how hard. And the lack of respect from her uncle, who had arrived just the day before, was beginning to wear. Worst of all, thoughts of the trial Edgar was about to face were distracting.

Damn! So many things at once. And every thought of the letter she had sent to Verald, the king of Ravelin, she pushed down roughly. An answer could not possibly come for some time. If the son was sent, the timing would depend on how large a party he decided to bring and the winter weather. She did not delude herself with hopes of an eager suitor who would risk all for love of her. She only hoped for a prince who was eager to join her in ruling.

Deward sighed and dropped into a chair.

"Elissa . . ." he began.

"I know," she said. "I should not even have thought of trying to start today. There is no way I can concentrate until after the trial this evening."

"Right at sundown?"

"Yes. That's the tradition. It's barbaric!"

She crumpled to the floor in front of the fireplace and wrapped her fur robe around her. Surely, it was colder than any other winter she had spent in the north.

"I know you disapprove," Deward said. "I disapprove. It *is* barbaric. But it is the custom of their people, both Ethelred's and Edgar's. If Edgar is to rule Albor, he must start by winning the people to his side. That includes the nobles and leaders of the country."

"I never thought you would defend this."

He shook his head. "You're acting like a headstrong, spoiled little girl."

"I am not!"

"Elissa, you must do whatever is necessary to win the powerful to your side. This final meal is a symbol only. It will have no lasting effect on the prince."

"What about this?" She waved her hand aimlessly in the air, meaning the skills of mind and magic she was practicing. "They don't approve of what they consider witchcraft. And this they would place under that heading."

"I know," Deward said and rose from the chair. He moved to the table on one side and poured himself a goblet of mead. "Meeting too often here in your rooms is not very safe. We will have to be very careful."

"They can't mind my uncle visiting."

"Too often, and they will begin to talk about us. Some of the time, you will have to practice on your own." He sat back down. "You are right, however. Today is not a good day to begin."

"I *am* glad that you are here, Uncle. I needed my own family in these days."

She stood and leaned down to kiss his forehead.

He smiled and nodded. "I'm glad to be here."

She laughed out loud and poured herself some mead. He went to one of the windows beside the fireplace and stood looking out for a time. Elissa drank from the goblet, feeling the warmth of the honey wine move from mouth, down her throat, settling in her abdomen. It relaxed some of the tension that had seized her for days, and that would return when the effects of the mead were chased away by further events.

"The sun will set soon," Deward said. "You should go to your son now."

"Yes, I know." She took another swallow and set the goblet on the table. "How do I prepare a child for this ordeal?"

"You tell him that it is a step to becoming a man. That his father will rest better in the hereafter thanks to him. Tell him that the food will be the best he has ever eaten—all of his favorites will be there. And lastly, you tell him that you love him very much and nothing will change that."

"Yes."

He turned from the window and smiled. "It is only a ceremony, niece. Nothing more. It changes nothing. Not him. Not you. Neither the future nor the past."

She nodded. He was right, of course, and she had made too much of it.

"I must go," she said, and wrapped the robe tighter around her. "I wish you could be there."

"You will be fine. And so will Edgar."

She smiled and slipping the latch on the door, opened it, and swept down the hall toward her children's room.

The chamber was normally one of the king's sitting rooms, but now every piece of furniture was gone in order to accommodate all who needed to attend. In the center sat a low bier on which lay the body of the king. He had been dressed in his finest official garments, including the circlet which he would wear as a symbol of his royal blood even in the grave. A lone chair sat beside the bier.

Dozens of candles brightened even the most distant corner. The attendees wore their finest clothes, many with gold and silver cloth and jewelry reflecting the light.

When Elissa entered behind her son, a murmur rose from the crowd. She had chosen to wear a black gown with a white veil, the traditional garments of mourning for her people. Her long, auburn hair hung loose—another tradition. This and leaving Ethel in her rooms were small victories, in spite of the girl's heartbreak at not being included. For the court, the princess's presence was expected, but not essential.

The path through those assembled closed up behind them. Edgar walked toward the chair, his little back ramrod straight. She had felt such pride as he listened and accepted what she told him like a little man, and as he became the center of attention, that sense of pride returned. He was truly a worthy successor to his father.

However, as he drew near the bier, he hesitated. He stopped and turned to look at her, his stern expression tinged with fear. Elissa smiled and nodded once. He took a deep breath and turned to stand in front of the chair. As he did so, Patriarch Dathan approached the opposite side of the bier. He wore his most official robes of red and gold, a tall hat on his head, and a staff chased with gold in his hand. The colors accented the ruddy color of his narrow face and contrasted sharply with his shoulder-length grey hair. Beside him, Gerrold, Ethelred's personal religious advisor, looked very plain in his dark gold and blue robes.

Dathan glared at Elissa as she took her place behind her son. It was customary for the sin eater to sit alone as he partook of the foods, but she had insisted on being allowed to stand with him. He was only five years old, after all, and the religious leader was convinced by the other councilors that since she had withdrawn her objections to the ceremony altogether, this one concession meant little.

Edgar stood with his little hands clasped in front of him. Resisting the temptation to comfort him was hard, but she must. Dathan raised his hands for silence, although everyone was already quietly awaiting the beginning of the ceremony.

"Today we honor our king," he began. "He has died before his time. Yet even so, he too is not without sin. As Edgar partakes of the foods that have been prepared..." A door opened and servants began filing in with dishes filled with all sorts of foods. "...the gods will visit the sins of the father upon his son." The servants began placing the dishes on the bier around the body. Steam rose from each, filling the room with wonderful aromas. "In this way Ethelred will find the eternal rest in the afterworld to which he is so entitled. One day, Edgar's son will do the same for him. This is our way. And it is good."

"It is good," everyone echoed. Someone's stomach growled loudly and Dathan frowned. Elissa was glad the veil hid her smile.

"Now, young Edgar, eat," Dathan commanded.

Edgar approached the bier and reached out to the nearest dish: a small venison roast, already sliced. He must eat once from every one, sitting down only when he grew tired. Elissa counted. There were thirty-two, one for each of the thirty-one years her husband had lived, plus one for the sins of Ethelred's father and all who had gone before.

He ate from the second, the third, and sat down. He chewed slowly as she had told him. A servant brought a goblet of water and he took a single swallow, also as she had instructed. It was going to be a long evening.

All of the privy councilors were assembled except for Lord Luther, who had been too fatigued. He must be replaced soon, Geoffrey thought, knowing everyone would agree, but no one actually dared suggest it to him. The old man was too much of a fixture in the chamber and too bullheaded to ever offer to retire. Keeping active might actually be one of the things that kept him alive these days.

Geoffrey looked up and realized that everyone was looking at him expectantly. He cleared his throat, leaned forward, and pressed his hands together on the tabletop. With a glance at the empty chair at the head of the table, he began.

"Patriarch Dathan asked us to meet tonight to discuss the selection of a regent to lead our kingdom and teach our new king his responsibilities."

They had all grumbled when told about the planned meeting. It was late, the boy had eaten slowly, and everyone was tired. No one was concerned that Edgar had been a bit pale when he finished, except the queen, of course, and her solicitations on his behalf had been tiresome.

"I do not think that we should wait long to make this decision," Dathan said in his most officious voice. He had a rich baritone, which was most helpful when he addressed a congregation of worshippers or priests. "We must think of what is best for our country. To delay could put us in peril."

"From whom, Patriarch?" Roric asked. "Our northern border with Ravelin has been secure for more than a generation. The others even longer."

"During that time, my lord, Albor was led by mature kings," Dathan said.

"But how do we make such a decision?" Randall asked. "If my cousin had only made a legitimate provision . . . But he did not have the foresight to make a will."

"No one expected him to die so young," Geoffrey pointed out.

"Who do you think Ethelred would have named, had he been in his right mind, Lord Marshal?" Randall asked.

Within the Council, the king's cousin was Geoffrey's greatest enemy, constantly goading him in meetings, a practice that had angered the king on more than one occasion. Even then, Randall's jealousy would not let him stop.

"He named a regent, my lord," Geoffrey said. "It is up to the Council to either confirm her or choose someone else. After due consideration."

"Well, it must be one of us, of course," Dathan said. "We cannot let a decision made in the throes of death make a mockery of this kingdom."

Everyone nodded agreement except Geoffrey. Elissa was politically inexperienced, it was true, but the king had named

her. Someone would have to come up with a very good reason
to reject her, as far as he was concerned. Shortly after the birth
of the heir apparent, he had suggested that Ethelred name
someone, even hoped he might be the one. However, they had
waited too long. Now was not the time to try to convince these
men that the royal widow should be given the chance, with
their guidance, of course. That moment would come later.

"It should be a blood relative of the king," Roric announced.

"You mean you or your son?" Witram asked. He was dis-
tantly related to the royal line through his mother.

"Who else," Randall shouted. "Who is better suited?"

"Perhaps someone with the interests of the kingdom uppermost in his mind," Geoffrey suggested. "To me, that
would mean someone without an interest of his own in oc-
cupying the throne."

Randall glared at him and Roric stiffened.

"It was a mistake to try to resolve this issue tonight,"
Geoffrey said. "We are all tired after today's ceremony and
all the preparations. We must consider this more carefully. The
last thing we should do is decide hastily."

"Geoffrey is right," Witram said. "This is too important
a decision. Albor has prospered under Ethelred's leadership. I
do not want to risk destroying the good things that have happened. Besides"—he smiled around at the others—"tradition
says we wait no less than a month for mourning before we
can officially consider the question."

Geoffrey slapped the top of the table. "Then we will ad-
journ for now," he said. "I will notify everyone of the next
meeting."

Witram and Quincy grumbled about having wasted their
time as they rose to leave. Roric and Randall spoke quietly to
each other a moment. Dathan looked angry, not having gotten
the support he seemed to have expected. Geoffrey stood aside,
letting the others file out. Roric was the last. He stopped beside
the marshal.

"Don't think for a moment we will let you or the queen

be named regent, Lord Marshal,'' the royal uncle said. ''This will be kept in the family.''

''As you say, my lord,'' Geoffrey said and smiled.

Roric stared at him for the space of several heartbeats, turned on his heels, and stalked away. Geoffrey watched until the man disappeared around a corner, then shook his head. What did he think to accomplish by threatening him? As marshal of the kingdom, he had accumulated vast wealth and power rivaling that of any other house. The king had been generous not only rewarding his service, but also making him independent of the others.

However, as strong as his position was, he must attempt to avoid any internal fighting. That would make Albor susceptible to invasion from outside, and that must not happen. In spite of Albor's comparatively small size, it occupied an important geographic position, with the most and the best harbors on the southern coast. One of those was the only harbor that remained open during the entire winter.

Now, he said to himself as he made his way toward his own apartment, *a plan must be made to have Flissa named regent.* He opened the door and entered his sitting room. A ewer of ale sat with several goblets on the large table against the right wall. That was standard when he returned from a Council meeting to relieve the inevitable stress.

He poured some of the amber liquid into a goblet and sat in one of the chairs near the fireplace. The conversation with the queen played over and over in his head. What she had said about raising the young prince in his father's image made sense. However, there was no way to convince the Council that responsibility should be placed in a woman's hands. Any woman's.

Right?

He got up to stir the fire with the poker and sat back down.

As difficult as that might be, Ethelred had made his choice clear. They might eventually accept her, as long as she would follow their advice.

That would not eliminate the serious problem of competition among the Council members, but it would give them a reason to work together. Something in their own interests.

He felt a sudden need to reassure the queen of his belief in Ethelred's choice.

Edgar moaned in his sleep. In the other bed Ethel had finally cried herself to sleep. She had been so put out about not being allowed to attend the ceremony. Now that it was over, it did not seem as bad a thing as imagination had made it.

Elissa sighed and took another swallow of mead. She looked down into the goblet and swirled the liquid. This was one of the best things the north had created, she decided, although the nobles usually relegated it to the peasants, preferring wine and sometimes ale. She had first drunk it at her wedding. Drinking mead together was one of the rites that had bound her to Ethelred and both of them to the people. Did anyone remember that some of the rituals from her own beliefs had been used, too?

Going to bed was tempting, but she was not sleepy and either of her children might awaken. Their world had been turned upside down. But they were children and their minds and hearts were still flexible. May the Lady grant that she be allowed to help mold their futures.

She rose, and went to her own room to fetch her book. The cover was soft leather with gold lettering. The subject was a history of Albor, a gift from Ethelred. She caressed the front cover as tears came to her eyes. Grief began to set in. She had loved him after all, and that surprised her. It had always seemed that she had only accepted his kindnesses. But now she missed their nightly talks, when he would tell her the events of the day, what he intended for the morrow, and ask about her day. As dull as it must have seemed to him, he had always listened patiently and she had always intended to keep her recitation short. However, she was a person full of wonder at even the simplest things and he had found that charming.

She smiled through the tears that spilled down her cheeks. Clearly, she had not managed to protect her heart as her mother had warned her to do.

"These kings born in the north are never satisfied with just one woman," Siobahn had said. "Don't let yourself fall in love with him. He will only break your heart."

Her father had said, "What an honor for our family—the king marrying my daughter. That will bring us honor and reward."

He had pushed her into the marriage, although not unkindly. He believed it was in her best interests. Since she did not love another, and seeing the palaces and capital city in the north were exciting prospects for a sixteen-year-old, she had not objected. That the king was quite handsome and kind made the acceptance easier.

She started toward the door, meaning to return to the children's room to read for a while, when the door of her sitting room burst open. Lord Randall rushed in from the hall. With a cry, she backed away.

"Hush, woman," he said. "I have come for you."

He closed the door. She felt the blood drain from her face and she swayed a moment.

"What do you mean?"

"Your husband is dead. You have needs."

"My needs are none of your concern, my lord."

"Fah," he said with a wave of his hand, and she realized that he was drunk. "You need a man to take care of you." He tried to snap his fingers and moved toward her.

"My lord, you are married," she said, moving to stay out of his reach. "Please return to your apartment."

"Not yet," he said and grabbed for her.

She sidestepped, but he was not so drunk that he had lost all agility. He lunged, grabbed her wrist, and pulled her to him, twisting her arm behind her back. He nosed her hair.

"You always smell so good," he said.

All of the anger and grief gathered from their hiding place within her. She pushed against his chest with her palms, leaning back so that she could see his face. He leered down at her.

"I like a woman with fire," he said.

"I'll give you fire!"

Rage exploded into a vision of flames engulfing the man

before her. Randall's leer turned to a look of surprise. Sweat popped out on his forehead and he cried out. He released her and stepped back.

"What sort of witchcraft is this?"

His expression turned to fear as he shook his hands to cool them.

"It is in your mind, my lord. Your drunken mind took the word 'fire' and expanded it. You are burning up from the inside. I can almost see the flames behind your eyes."

"You witch!" he shouted.

The door burst open once more. This time Geoffrey rushed in.

"Your majesty, what . . ."

Randall rushed at her, oblivious of the intrusion, both hands reaching for her throat. Geoffrey grabbed him, spun him around, and hit him with his fist. The royal cousin dropped to the floor, out cold.

Elissa swayed, closed her eyes against the darkness that closed in. She had come close to setting a man on fire. In front of a witness.

Strong hands caught her and helped her to a chair. In another moment, a cold wet cloth was being pressed against her face. She opened her eyes and saw Geoffrey kneeling before her. His expression of concern turned neutral as soon as he realized she was all right.

"What happened here?" he asked brusquely.

"Lord Randall was drunk and broke in," she said shakily. "He professed his . . . desire and attacked me."

Geoffrey nodded and stood up. He showed no signs of having seen her retaliation. Randall moaned. Would he remember much of what had happened? If he remembered about the fire, would that be dismissed as ravings from a drunken mind? Would it be advisable to make up some explanation now to tell the marshal, just in case?

"I'll send for his retainers to get him back to his apartment," Geoffrey said. "Are you sure you are all right?"

"Yes, I am fine."

He started toward the door. "I'll be right back," he said.

She sat looking at the man lying on the floor. Several times in the past, she had caught Randall looking at her with a strange expression on his face. At first, she had thought he lusted after her, but later, she realized that it was not she he wanted, but what she represented. She was queen, Ethelred's wife, and he was dangerously jealous of his cousin, the king.

Geoffrey returned with two men dressed in the livery of Randall's house. Without a word or a glance around, they stooped to pick up their lord, but he began struggling.

"Take your hands off me," he shouted.

They got him to his feet in spite of his struggles. He pointed at Elissa with a shaking hand.

"She burned me," he said. "She's a witch."

"You're drunk, my lord," Geoffrey said. "Take him and get him into bed."

The two men began leading their master out. He muttered all the way to the door, where he shouted, "Witch!" one more time. Soon, he disappeared from sight and sound.

"Thank you, my lord," she said. "He was like a madman."

She told him what had happened, although assigning the perception he was on fire to Randall's own drunken imagination. Geoffrey nodded understanding and expressed concern over the possibility of future attacks.

She agreed it was possible, then asked, "Was there something you had come to see me about?"

"Yes, but it can wait until tomorrow."

"All right. I need to check on my children."

She stood up and he bowed slightly.

"Send for me if anything else should happen," he said.

"Thank you, my lord. I will."

Their eyes met and she saw such honesty in his gaze that suddenly Elissa knew why the king had trusted him.

3

The day dawned grey and cold. New snow fell in small flakes, a promise of heavy fall for the rest of the day. Randall wakened, saw the grey light beyond the window, and pulled the covers over his head. He moaned when the movement hurt his head until everything settled back into place. Sleep descended, and he had just begun to dream when a sharp noise broke the blessed silence.

"Out of that bed, you sluggard," his father's voice roared. The previous sound must have been the door slamming open. "The funeral begins in an hour."

"It can go on without me," Randall mumbled.

"Did you say something?"

With that, Roric jerked the covers off the bed. Randall shivered in spite of his flannel nightshirt. His body servant appeared from the next room and stoked up the fire in the fireplace, adding more logs. In a moment, it was blazing and warming the room.

"I said I'm not going," Randall shouted. Pain shot through his head from ear to ear and he pressed his hands against his temples. His jaw hurt too, but he could not remember why. "Give back the covers."

"Benjamin, bring mulled wine for your master," Roric shouted.

"Don't shout, Father. My head hurts enough."

"Serves you right for drinking the night away. And you had better eat something. It's going to be a long day."

Randall's stomach churned at the mention of food. "It is too early to eat anything," he said.

"The next meal won't be served until midafternoon. You will need your strength to carry your cousin to the chapel."

Randall groaned again. He was one of eight pallbearers who were to transport Ethelred's body from the room where it had lain in state to the sarcophagus in the chapel. So were his father and the rest of the members of the Privy Council. After the funeral, a meal would be served in the great hall, then everyone would march back into the chapel for another service to send the dead on his way and pray for guidance for his heir.

It *was* going to be a long day.

Benjamin returned with a pitcher of warmed wine and some bread and cheese on a trencher. He put them on the table set against the far wall, poured wine into a goblet already on the table, and gave it to Randall. The latter sat up and swung his feet over the side of the bed as he took the goblet. He downed half of the sweetened wine, warmth spreading quickly through much of his body.

"My lord?" the servant said to Roric. The older man shook his head and Benjamin retreated to his own room where he was still within hearing.

"What in the world set you off last night?" Roric asked. "And where did you get that bruise on your jaw?"

He sat in one of the straight-backed wooden chairs near the table. Randall reached up to tentatively probe the soreness with his fingertips.

"I was angry."

"At Geoffrey?"

Randall nodded. He held his feet toward the fire, its warmth moving that far, as he tried to remember.

"We will be rid of him once one of us is named regent," Roric said.

"And when will that be?"

"Within the month, I hope. For practical reasons it might be sooner. Once our neighbors learn of Ethelred's death, some of them may decide it is an opportune time to invade. Can you imagine what they might think if the queen is actually named regent? Every one of them will invade, each trying to take a part of Albor for itself."

The queen. A memory started forming in Randall's mind, something he had wanted to be sure to tell his father. About the queen. Last night. He shook his head.

"What is the matter?" his father asked.

"Just trying to remember something that happened last night. About the queen."

"You saw her last night?"

"Yes."

"Where?"

"I can't . . ." He snapped his fingers. "In her rooms."

"What were you doing there?"

"I don't remember." But he did. He remembered kicking in the door to her sitting room.

Randall stepped into his slippers, grabbed up the blanket from the floor, and wrapped it around himself. He walked to the window, looked out a moment, then paced back and forth. He reflected on the memory of last night, beginning with kicking down the door. That part would anger his father and he must keep it from him, if possible. The rest was too important to just let go, however, and he would take the risk.

At least, he thought it was important.

After he burst into the room, he had grabbed Elissa. That, too, he must keep to himself. But that was when it happened. He had his hands on her arms, holding her. And it was as if he suddenly burst into flames on the inside.

Roric stood suddenly. "You had best get dressed," he said. "We have to assemble in just a few minutes. Tell me later, after you have remembered it all."

Randall nodded. That would give him time to create a lie, or decide on a half-truth about the less important aspects of the event. But his father and the rest of the Council must know that their queen was a witch, practicing her black arts in this very palace.

"May the gods bless this man. He was a father to his people. A loving husband. A wise leader."

Dathan stood at the head of the bier, seven monks and priests flanking him, all dressed in their best finery. They acted as intermediaries between the people and the gods, whose names Elissa could not at that moment remember. She was a follower of the goddess, the Lady of the forest. However, here in the palace, she could practice her beliefs only in the privacy of her room, even though Ethelred had permitted some of her rites at their wedding as a way of alleviating any concerns she or her people might have.

The patriarch droned on, enumerating the many fine qualities of the late king. In the afternoon ceremony, he would offer blessings and guidance for the son of the deceased who, although not yet crowned, was his father's acknowledged successor.

As the widow, Elissa stood at the foot of the bier with her children. Her mourning attire had once more caused a murmur among the crowd. For other funerals, she had dressed like the rest: in her finest clothes. But for her husband, she felt compelled to wear the black gown and white veil which in her beliefs showed the greatest respect and sense of loss. However, she had chosen to follow the court when dressing the prince and princess. They were of their father's people and must respect their traditions.

The funeral had gone on for some time and those same well-garbed children were beginning to shift from one foot to the other. Elissa placed a hand on a shoulder of each. Ethel looked up at her. A tear had traced its way down the child's cheek. The poignancy of that face brought tears to her own eyes, the wife's eyes, the queen's eyes.

By the Lady, she no longer knew who she was. Her husband's death could take away her total identity if she allowed it. Yes, she had to admit it. Seeking to be named regent was due in part to her own ambition, her own need to remain someone. Giving up all leadership to her son once he was grown was one thing. Giving up everything to someone else who would guide him was quite another.

Standing near the head of the bier, Randall suddenly looked up. Their eyes locked and she knew he remembered. Whom did he intend to tell? His father, of course. Who would, in turn, tell the patriarch, who would declare her a witch. However, Geoffrey knew Randall had been drunk, had actually manhandled the queen. No, he did not know that. He had come in too late to see Randall actually gripping her arms. Everyone would question why either one of them was in her apartments at such a late hour.

Dathan droned on as she imagined what the look in Randall's eyes meant. He and his father would do anything to be rid of her. He might even lie and say she had invited him to visit her.

Her only protection was Geoffrey. But whom would he believe in the light of day? His determination to follow the king's wishes by no means meant that he was her friend. And without friends at court, she had no way to win.

Dathan was now enumerating the many talents and skills of the deceased.

"He was a good son, striving to please his parents. When young, he worked hard at his studies: reading, writing, science, mathematics, all taught by learned tutors. He learned how to govern from his father. In all of these he excelled."

Mathematics? Elissa thought. *He hated that and left such work to others.* But writing. For the first time in a year or more, she remembered the poems he had written in their early days together. Sometimes, he had read them to her at night when he came to her room. They ranged from lyrical to brutal accounts of battle and were as good as any others she had heard.

Finished with the intellectual side, Dathan turned to the physical.

"Our king was an excellent warrior. He wielded every weapon with precision and confidence."

The greatest exception being the axe, Elissa recalled. It had vexed him that he never could find the balance point of that weapon no matter how much he practiced. He had finally given it up, concentrating instead on those weapons which he used easily, admitting to her that he realized for the first time there were limits to what he could master. He wanted to be perfect, hated giving up, but hated wasting his time even more.

With an effort, she brought her attention back to the words of the patriarch.

"Ethelred excelled at wrestling, was a good swimmer and horseman."

She started visibly, but Dathan went on. How could he have said that? She remembered too well the page coming into the great hall as she instructed the cooks on the evening's meal.

"Your Highness," he had said breathlessly as he drew near. "I seek the Lord Marshal."

His young face was pale, his lips trembled, and there were tears in his eyes.

"What is wrong, Jonathan?" Cold fear gripped her heart. The lad had gone out with the hunting party that morning. She had counted on their bringing in a boar or deer for dinner.

"Uh, highness . . . I was sent to fetch the marshal."

"Tell me! Has something happened to the king?"

The lad backed away from her and she realized she had raised her fists and stepped toward him.

"I mean you no harm, but I must know. Is my lord husband all right?"

He looked pleadingly at the cooks standing behind her. Not finding any sign of assistance there, he had dropped to one knee.

"What has happened?" she said more gently.

"There was an accident, highness," he said. A tear spilled down his left cheek. "His horse . . ." He swallowed hard and looked down. "... it stepped into a hole or something. When it fell, it threw his majesty over its head. The fall broke the king's back." He looked up, tears now streaming from his eyes. "The king is dying." The last word broke on a sob.

"No, you must be mistaken."

"I wish I were, highness."

He closed his eyes tightly, trying to block out the memory. Her knees buckled, but she stiffened and managed to stay on her feet.

"Lord Geoffrey is in the stables, I believe," she said. "Run and fetch him, please. I will go with him to bring my husband home."

"Yes, Highness."

Jonathan ran as she had commanded. She wished that was the last she remembered of that day. However, every moment, every action was etched into her memory. The wait until the horses were saddled. The ride into the forest, the coldness of the afternoon. The silence as they passed among the trees. The silence of the men who flanked the still form. The purple cloak covering him that contrasted so sharply with the white snow.

With muted voices instructing and guiding, a sling was tied between two horses. Gently, they lifted Ethelred and placed him in it. He cried out, but did not regain consciousness. The trek home was long and slow. Within three days, the king was dead.

She must see her uncle soon, she thought, bringing her mind back to the present. He must know what happened the night before between her and Randall.

The service dragged on. After the patriarch, every person who had been related to or had known the king had something to say. She realized that instead of helping her children stay still, she was leaning on their shoulders. She moved her hands, clasping them in front of her, trying to concentrate on the voices, the words.

Suddenly, it was over. Everyone had spoken and Dathan was moving out of the room. Behind him came his priests, then the body, carried on the wooden platform of the bier. She and the children were next, followed by his family, then the rest of the nobility of Albor. The best and the worst. Everyone was here, even Lord Luther, supported on either side by two of his several grandsons.

Slowly, the cortege made its way to the chapel. Candles were lit, the priests chanted for several minutes, Dathan said a prayer, and they were dismissed for the meal.

Elissa settled the children in their room with a large dinner and went to her own rooms to sit and rest her legs and feet. The chapel had benches, thank goodness, and the afternoon and evening ceremonies would be observed sitting down.

"Clara, as soon as you've finished here, I want you to find my uncle and ask him to come see me before we return to the chapel."

"Yes, Your Highness."

Naked, Elissa shivered. She pulled the robe Clara held for her around her body with alacrity, grateful for its soft lining. The slippers felt good on her sore feet, too. Clara poured some mead and warmed it with the poker heated in the fire, then left on her errand.

While she waited, Elissa ate some of the bread, cheese, and boar's meat. Hunters had been sent to kill enough game to feed the influx of people who would stay in the castle for several days. It had been a long day and the food tasted good. She ate sparingly, though, not wanting to become so sated that she would become sleepy during the afternoon's ordeal.

She heard a knock on the door and Deward entered. His dark blue pants and shirt were much more somber than the garb of the mourners in the chapel. He smiled, and momentarily chased away all gloom.

"How has it gone, niece?"

"Well, I suppose," she said and could not stop the sigh that followed. He took a seat opposite her. "I'm tired and the children are tired. But I need to speak with you about something else."

"Something serious, it would seem."

"Yes. The longer I think on it, the more seriously it looms."

She told him of her encounter with Randall the night before. He said nothing, only pursing his lips once before she told of her own reaction. She finished and he sat deep in thought.

"Dammit, Elissa!" He burst out and hunched down in the chair, anger furrowing his brow. "Perhaps he was too drunk to remember."

"I saw him in the chapel. From the look he gave me, I am sure he does remember."

"Was Geoffrey convinced that he attacked you?" His voice was stern.

"I thought so at the time. But now I can't help wondering what he might think if Randall tells him some tale."

"Most people can be convinced that he was too drunk to remember," Deward said. "We must continue your training as soon as possible. You must learn control before another an incident can occur."

Elissa nodded, feeling once more like a little girl being chastised for carelessness. For all these years she had hidden both her magical talents and her skills with weapons, both of which she had begun learning as a child. Now, this one slip could undo everything. The renewed training, after so many years, had awakened power but little control.

"Did your maid see anything last night?" Deward asked suddenly.

She shook her head. He leaned forward and patted her hand.

"It's all right, niece," he said. "We will handle this. It is a small incident. But please, be more careful until we complete your retraining."

She nodded, determined that she would be.

Elissa held her daughter's hand. It was one way to try to prevent Ethel from showing or voicing her anger. In this chapel ceremony, only Edgar was acknowledged as the child of the king. The princess had no position other than as sister to the heir to the throne. However, she must be shown that she did have value. The daughter of this king would not be married off to the first prince or lord who asked.

Another reason she must be named regent for her children. Both of them.

Her hand suddenly tingled, and Elissa resisted the temptation to drop Ethel's hand. Fear rose in her throat, strangling her momentarily. That tingling was caused by power rising. She was sure of it. As if there were not problems enough, Ethel may have power, too. But that was impossible. She was not born with the caul over her head or any of the other signs. And her father was a northerner, a nonbeliever. The birth of a child of power was not supposed to be possible unless both parents were believers.

I must have imagined it, Elissa thought. *It simply could not happen.*

She returned her attention to the ceremony, keeping an eye on her son, standing as proudly as he could in spite of the exhaustion she knew he felt. Poor boy. There would be troubles aplenty in the months and years to come. And he must understand that his mother was best suited to help lead him, for if he did, others might be easier to convince.

She surreptitiously looked around at those faces within view. Randall stared at her, but she had sensed that for some time. He could not seem to keep his eyes off her. He was going to be a constant problem, he *and* his father. Was there some way to win their loyalty and friendship? Well, one of the two would be enough.

Dathan was too entranced with his own voice and the role he was playing to pay any more attention to her. The possibility of his warming to her cause was even less likely than gaining the support of the other two. The Privy Council had been divided into two factions: one led by the uncle and cousin, the other led by the king and his marshal.

Geoffrey was her best hope. Perhaps her only hope among the nobles. She should have trusted him and forgotten about sending the letter to Verald. Perhaps the king of Ravelin would think her request was a joke, or even a trap—anything, as long as he didn't send her a husband.

～ 4 ～

King Verald was as big around as he was tall, with a round fat face, part of which was hidden by a nearly black mustache. His dark hair was cut in the military style—one length, down to his ears—but it was curly and refused to hang straight. He watched Tommy as the messenger moved toward the throne, picturing him as a mouse straying into the cat's realm. In his hand, he held the letter from Queen Elissa.

Tommy reached the short dais on which the throne sat and bowed deeply. He handed the letter up.

"Have you read this?" Verald asked, lifting the sheet of paper toward him.

"No, sire. It was sealed when it was given to me."

"Have you any idea what it says?"

"No, sire."

"What sort of woman is this queen of yours?"

Verald sat back in his throne and crossed his legs as he broke the seal.

"She is a good, honest woman, sire. Beautiful beyond compare. And greatly saddened by the recent death of her husband, the king."

"When did he die?"

Tommy told him the date and described the events of his death. "He will have been buried in the chapel by this time," he added.

The king studied the letter a moment, tapping a forefinger against his lips. The message was clearly even more important than he had first believed. Not to mention surprising.

"I will give her message some thought," Verald said at last. "Meanwhile you will consider yourself our guest. Timothy," he said, turning toward the chamberlain who had led Tommy in. "Arrange for quarters for our guest."

"Yes, your majesty."

"I will send for you when I have a response."

"Thank you, sire," Tommy said and bowed. He followed the chamberlain out of the audience chamber.

Sometime later, King Verald still sat on his throne. Two men stood before him, one talking with much arm waving. The quiet man was not of Ravelin. His clothes did not seem to suit him. He was usually dressed in Alboran clerical robes.

Deep inside lay the roots of power and those of control. Both must be found, activated, before anything else was possible. Elissa had turned inward in search of them, delving deep within her own personality. Suddenly, she could not breathe. Memories of her birth came out of the darkness, when the caul covered her face and she could not even gasp for air.

She struggled as if to swim to the surface. Air! She must have air!

Hands gripped her arms, soothing words came out of the void. But she could not breathe.

"Elissa, come back," Deward said. "You've done enough for today. Come back to the light, Elissa."

He spoke soothingly, calling her name over and over. Slowly, she rose into the light of the Lady. She gasped for air as the strands unwound. She opened her eyes to find Deward wiping sweat from her forehead.

"I couldn't breathe," she gasped. "Something was over my face and I could not get it off."

"Memories of your birth." He wiped the rest of her face and handed her the cloth.

"Yes. It was the caul, but I knew that only in the back of my mind. All I cared about was breathing." She sat up straighter and blotted her throat. "I was sure I was going to die."

"It could have killed you at birth; it could have killed you now. However, being born with the caul is one source of your powers."

"I know. I was told that years ago." She got up and poured some water from the pitcher on the sideboard. "Is it possible for a child born without a caul to have similar power?"

Deward shrugged. "Power comes to us in many ways. Yes, it is possible."

She had tried to dismiss the memory of the surge from Ethel during the funeral services, but could not. Staying in the castle could prove very dangerous for her daughter.

"I want Ethel to go south to our people and I want you to take her, Uncle."

"Why is that?"

She described what had happened in the chapel. "I won't have time to instruct her in ways to control the urges. She needs instruction."

"Yes, she does. I don't think she will like the idea of being sent from court, though."

"No, she will not. And I am not happy with the thought of losing her company. But she is a princess and she still has much to learn about duty."

He agreed and they planned to speak on the subject again in the next few days. It was late and Deward excused himself. Once he had left for his own room, Clara appeared to help her get ready for bed. Elissa stood in front of the fire, yet shivered as she stood naked waiting for Clara to put her nightgown over her head. The soft material slithered down, caressed her arms, warming with the heat from the fire. The maid pulled a small bench in front of the fireplace and Elissa sat down. While her hair was braided, she stared into the fire.

Loneliness descended over her, much as the birth caul had. Once Deward left, she would have no friends still at court. Two days after the funeral service, Geoffrey received word that his wife was ill. Citing that and a need to get away for a while, he had left the castle for his own lands.

Randall and Roric were home too, for a time. Dathan was visiting some outlying monasteries, and Lord Luther had returned home for the remainder of the mourning period. There had been whisperings that he would die there at last, and leave his place in the Privy Council to a younger man.

Everyone wanted something, including her. Waiting for word from the north was wearing. Trying to design some plan for winning the place of regent was equally exhausting. For several nights she had slept little, as attested to by the dark circles under her eyes. Everyone probably attributed that to her bereavement, and that was a part of it, too. But fear for her children occupied her thoughts most often.

Clara finished her hair and Elissa sent her off to bed. She lingered in front of the fire awhile longer. The bed would be cold and for the moment she felt warm enough.

Memories of another warmth came unbidden. Of strong hands helping her to a chair. The concern in Geoffrey's eyes when he had rescued her from Randall.

She stood abruptly and walked away from the heat, wanting to feel cold. She had been a widow less than two weeks and already she was lusting after another man. A married man. But such a brave and honest man. The king had sworn by Geoffrey's loyalty with never a moment's regret. She must never allow their relationship to become personal.

Elissa slid beneath the covers, stiffening at the chill. That and speculations on where Ethel had come by any powers kept sleep at bay. She tossed and turned, going from cold to warm as the down comforter captured her body's heat.

She slept sometime before dawn, awakening when the sun was halfway toward noon. It had snowed again during the night. She propped herself up with two more pillows and pulled the covers up under her chin, looking out the window at the sparkling whiteness. It was beautiful, but the silence was unsettling sometimes.

She called for Clara, who appeared with a tray. She put it on the table, then she built up the fire. When it blazed again, she took Elissa's robe to the fire to warm it. After a moment, she brought it to the bed, and Elissa slipped from beneath the covers and quickly put the robe on.

"What is happening in the castle this morning?" Elissa asked. She poured water from a large pitcher into a bowl and washed her face and hands. The cold water jolted her system but did not quite bring alertness.

"Everything is quiet this morning, majesty," Clara answered. She set the tray on the small bench and placed it in front of the chair. "With so many gone from the capital, it's boring."

Elissa sat down and looked over the fare. There was fresh bread, cheese, a bit of sausage, dried apple, and a goblet of mulled spiced wine. Nothing sparked hunger within her, but she had to eat something. The wine was warm going down and that comforted her. She picked at the food while Clara straightened the bedcovers and checked the fire.

"I'll call you when I am ready to dress," Elissa said.

"Yes, majesty."

The maid disappeared through the little door into her own small bedroom, closing it behind her. Elissa sat picking at the food and feeling as if she had drunk too much the night before. There was so much to do and she had no idea how to go about most of it. One of the most important things for today was to work on her powers with Deward.

By the Lady, she would miss him when he returned home. Oh, and Ethel. Her throat closed at the thought of sending her daughter away. How could she bear it?

"Clara," she called, turning away from such thoughts.

The maid appeared and helped her dress. Last were her shoes, and when she had slipped them on, she felt at a loss as to what to do next. It was true that with so many gone from the castle, there was less to do for others. Less to think about.

Still, she must check the kitchen and set the tasks for the servants. The empty rooms should be cleaned out thoroughly and the dining hall was in a bad state. Before leaving her rooms, she set Clara to sweeping her sitting room.

She stopped first in the children's room. Both were up and giving Nurse a hard time. They wanted to go out and play in the snow, but Nurse argued that it was too cold and they would get soaking wet. She, herself, did not like the cold and at her advanced age that was understandable.

"Nurse, have one of the girls take them outside," Elissa said. "I would prefer that you do some cleaning in these rooms. They're a shambles."

Nurse looked both relieved and chagrined, but was happier to be staying inside. She immediately started getting out the children's warm coats and boots, while they both hugged their mother and thanked her. She inquired about their breakfast, pleased that they both had good appetites. Especially Edgar, who had not eaten much for two days after the sin-eating ceremony.

She left, their laughter and shouts following her all the way to the head of the stairs. It was wonderful to hear them like that after so many somber days.

On the way to the kitchen, she stopped in the dining hall, making note of the many things needing done there: The tables could use a scrubbing, the rushes on the floor needed to be changed, and the ashes in the fireplace should be discarded. More wood needed to be brought in, too, and candles replaced in the chandeliers overhead and in the sconces on the walls.

The kitchen itself was a flurry of activity. To one side was the long table where the servants ate their meals. The other side of the room was dominated by an immense fireplace with all of the ironwork necessary for cooking for dozens, sometimes hundreds of people.

Opal, the head cook, was first to see the queen enter. "Majesty," she said with an awkward curtsey.

"Good morning, Opal."

"Do you want everyone gathered, majesty?"

"Yes, please."

She banged on a pot with a metal spoon and quiet descended almost immediately. She called for everyone to gather round.

Elissa proceeded to set their tasks, beginning with the dining room. Those already assigned work set off. Ensley, the steward, listed those still in the castle when she inquired. Many more were gone than she had known, and she felt a bit put out that most had not said goodbye or asked her permission to leave. She was still queen, after all, and most of them would have heard that Ethelred named her to be regent. Perhaps they were afraid of even the appearance of taking sides in the coming power struggle.

She dismissed such thoughts and assigned servants to cleaning the vacated rooms and apartments. Several things she could not do since the castle and the city were still in mourning, but they could not all be done at once anyway.

Having set as much in motion as she could, she left the kitchen. In the dining room, work was proceeding. The servants moved quietly, still respectful of the sorrow that had invaded their home. Yes, it was their home, too, Elissa thought, and Ethelred had been their king. Would these subjects object to her ambitions, or did they care? No doubt, they did not want to get caught in the struggle either.

The enormity of what lay ahead overwhelmed her, and she had to lean against a table to keep from collapsing to the floor.

"Majesty, are you 'right?" one of the women asked from a distance. All work ceased as they all looked at her.

She took a deep breath and straightened. "Yes, Mary. I'm fine." She smiled reassurance and left the hall with as much strength as she could muster.

Outside, she leaned against the wall of the hallway until the strength she had pretended to possess returned. She had intended to return to her rooms to practice, but decided that now was not the time. Maybe she should go riding instead. Even with the snow so deep, a road or two would be cleared for business that must always continue.

On the way to her rooms to change, she stopped in the children's room. They were gone, and Nurse looked up from her mending and smiled. Elissa smiled back and decided to check on them on her way to the stables.

Clara heard her enter, and quickly laid out her riding clothes and heavy cloak as instructed. Elissa loved the cloak of heavy red velvet and white ermine trim.

While the maid went to have her horse saddled and the escort called, Elissa made her way toward the side exit that led to the stables. The children should have been in that part of the grounds but she did not see them. Nor were they around the next corner.

A warning started to ring in her heart and she set off for the stables. If she had to search, it would be easier on horseback. Her horse was saddled and ready. She had ridden her horse, Schuy, almost daily ever since coming to Winfield and she loved the mare dearly. Usually, she brought a treat but today she had forgotten and the horse snuffled her disappointment.

Grey, Tommy's assistant, was already in the saddle along with three guardsmen.

"I can't find the prince and princess," Elissa said as she let the stableman give her a leg up. "We'll search the grounds for them."

Grey touched his forelock, and he and the others followed her out. Clouds rose before them as their exhalations condensed in the cold. The horses sensed the tension and moved with alacrity. After making a full circuit of the grounds, she pulled up where the children should have been playing. Here, as everywhere, the snow was so stirred up that individual footprints were impossible to make out. Deward came running across the courtyard from the castle. He had not bothered to put on his winter cloak, and as he ran toward her, he wrapped his arms around himself.

"Elissa," he called. "They have been taken."

She knew who had been taken without asking. She also

knew how he had discovered what now appeared to be a kidnapping.

"By whom?"

"I'm not sure," he panted as he drew up beside her. "It
has not been long. You can catch them if you hurry." He
handed her one of Ethelbert's swords in its scabbard, then
pointed toward the main gate. "Go quickly."

Deward was a teacher, not a warrior, and he knew she had
once been trained to use a sword.

"Call up the guard," she told him. She slipped the sword
into the loops made into her saddle and spurred Schuy toward
the gate. The mare stumbled in the slick snow, caught her
footing, and bounded off. She was a good northern horse with
broad hooves that worked well in the snow.

"Your majesty," Grey called from behind.

She did not look back, and in moments, other hoofbeats
followed. There was no time to waste. If she and the four men
with her could catch the kidnappers, they could stall them until
more guards caught up.

5

Freezing wind burned her face. It kept pushing back the hood, preventing the fur trim from protecting her cheeks and forehead. The road was treacherously slick and Schuy occasionally stumbled. Elissa could not take the time to stop and tie the hood in place with its drawstring. However, in a short stretch of less dangerous road, she took one hand from the reins, pulled the hood back in place, and held it tight under her chin.

The smooth, packed snow on either side of the road would clearly show if the culprits left the road. No sound came out of the snowy silence all around.

The sounds of her own party consisted of snow crunching under hoof and the heavy breathing of their mounts. Even those seemed muffled. They reached the top of a hill just in time to see a lone rider round a turn ahead. Although he was not dawdling, he seemed not to be in a hurry either. If he was one of the kidnappers, he clearly did not expect anyone to be following so soon. She signaled for the guards behind her to speed up and started to spur the mare to run faster, but Grey came up beside her, grabbed the reins, and pulled Schuy to a stop.

"Majesty," he said, panting. "Might it not be dangerous

if we come up on them too fast? We don't know how many they are.''

"There is no way to take them by surprise.'' Anger clipped her words. Or was her mouth so cold that the words could barely escape from between her lips?

"Just before that turn''—he pointed ahead—"a narrow lane leads to the left. It rejoins the road farther down. It's a shortcut of sorts.''

"But the snow will be deeper there. We cannot make good enough time to get ahead of them if we have to plow through deep snow.''

"We'll have to check, but there is a chance it's been cleared. It leads to a store of firewood used by several farmers. They may have been up there to retrieve wood.''

"What do you suggest, then?'' Elissa asked.

"You and two of the men follow them, and let them see you. Maybe if they see only three are following, they will turn and fight.''

"You are assuming there are more than three of them.''

"There have to be.''

Elissa shrugged. She was not sure she agreed with him, but this was not the time to stand and argue.

"Keep out of their reach,'' he warned. "But if they stop or slow down, that will give us more time to get around in front of them.''

She nodded. It was better than any plan she could come up with. Of course, if he and Jonas took a bad spill, the only hope remaining was for the other guards to catch up fast.

They reached the turnoff and Grey ordered the two named to go with her to protect her at all cost. "Stay just out of reach,'' he said, then started up the narrow path.

She watched the mare's breath crystallize in the cold air and remembered the path. It was steep in places, narrow, but it was a much shorter route. The two men with her looked grim but determined as she motioned for them to follow her. It suddenly struck her that not one of them had protested her, a woman, leading them or insisted that she turn back. Perhaps they did not feel they had any right to do so. Still, it was interesting.

They spurred their mounts to go as fast as they dared on the treacherous road. She looked back once, but Grey and Jason had disappeared into the forest of bare trees.

Once they rounded the turn, the main road ran straight for a mile and five horsemen were in sight nearly halfway down its length. They rode single file and there was no way to see where the children might be. However, the serving girl's skirts seemed to be visible on the back of one of the horses. They had probably taken her to keep the alarm from being raised too soon. So far, they showed no awareness they were being followed.

Elissa pressed on, determined to get close before they reached the next hill. The pounding of hooves seemed louder now and she prayed to the Lady that the kidnappers would soon hear. They were within a tenth of a mile when the rider in the rear turned in the saddle and spied them. He put his gloved hand to his mouth and shouted to his companions.

Suddenly a figure tumbled from a horse and rolled into the ditch on the right side of the road. The riders spurred their horses into a gallop.

"Stop!" Elissa shouted. "The queen commands it." They quickened their pace.

She rode past the maid just picking herself up in the ditch. "Start back to the castle," the queen called, hoping the girl was all right, but not daring to stop to see.

They rode on. The kidnappers galloped to the top of the small hill and down to another level part of the road. The pursuers followed, neither gaining nor losing ground. Surely, the kidnappers realized that they could not get cleanly away. She would keep behind them until they either turned and fought or gave up.

Just then, two riders reined in and turned to face the way they had come. Their horses stamped, their wide eyes reflecting the tension of their riders. Sword steel glinted in the weak sunlight. Elissa and her companions slowed, drawing their own swords. Closer now, she thought she recognized one of the men. He served Lord Witram.

"Let us pass and you will be pardoned," she said as she pulled up.

"We have our orders, majesty," one of the men said. "Turn back now and no blood need be shed."

"Those are my children. They must return to the castle with me."

"Then we fight here," the same man said and spurred his horse forward.

The two guardsmen spurred forward, too, getting between her and the attackers. The clang of steel striking steel broke the silence yet sounded as muffled as did the rest of the world. She sat watching a moment, Schuy prancing under her. Her protectors, two young, ordinary guardsmen, faced two experienced campaigners. They were all gallant and ready to die for those they served.

The road was not a wide one and the portion cleared of snow was even narrower. She needed an opening to slip through and continue the pursuit. She tried very hard to concentrate enough to use her powers, but she had to work on keeping her seat.

An opening finally came and Elissa spurred her horse forward and between combatants, then galloped after the other kidnappers. The sounds of battle continued behind her for some ways, but this time, she resisted the temptation to look back.

Her hands were cold now, even in the thick gauntlets, and she had trouble holding the edges of the hood together around her face. She tried to ignore the cold, concentrating on the figures ahead, who had gained some distance after the delaying action. She tried to catch a glimpse of her children. They must be riding in front of their captors and shielded from her sight by the men's larger bodies. However, that also meant they were getting the brunt of the wind.

"Please don't let them get too cold," she prayed aloud.

Again, the last rider turned and saw her pursuing. He reined in hard and the horse slid to a stop. He turned to face her. She slowed Schuy to a walk, stopping within a few feet of the man.

"Please don't make a fight of this," she said. Her mouth was so cold that the words came out slightly slurred.

The man spread his hands to either side, indicating he had no choice in the matter, and drew his sword.

"Majesty," he said. "I have no wish to harm you. You are mother of the king-to-be. You are a woman. And you are queen. Why not turn around, go back to the castle, and leave this matter to men who know about such things?"

She raised her own sword. It had been years since she handled one, but its weight felt good, and her hand gripped the handle naturally.

"Those are my children. That is what I know. And Lord Witram cannot have them."

"He only intends wedding the young prince to his granddaughter. Is that so bad?"

"No, if it were done well. But this is done badly. And I will not allow it."

"Then I have no choice."

"Neither do I."

He spurred his horse at her. She sat very still, willing Schuy to be calm so that she would have one good swing of her sword. When the man came up beside her, he turned his horse into hers. The startled mare pranced sideways, lost her footing, and went down. Elissa kicked out of the stirrups, landing on her back on the hard-packed snow.

He halted his horse a short distance away, and seeing her on the ground, stepped down. She scrambled on all fours to reach the sword, getting tangled in the cloak in the process. He must have believed that she had no idea at all how to handle a sword, for he gave her time to pick it up.

She tossed back the hood, wishing there was time to take off the cloak. They closed the gap between them.

"Please majesty, go back."

She lunged, sword held high, bringing it down toward his

head. He raised his own, easily deflecting the blow. She swung again, fearing that her cold hands might lose their grip on the handle. He deflected the blow, swung at her halfheartedly. She barely managed to deflect his blade. Her mind raced, trying to come up with something within her powers that would help her swordplay. When he had handed her the sword, Deward had been telling her that more earthly methods should be used, or he might have simply been accepting the fact that she did not have the necessary skills.

They swung back and forth, she trying with all her might, he with an indifferent wariness. Clearly, he thought he could dissuade her with the sword if not with words. Then, quite suddenly, she got a lucky stroke in, cutting his right upper arm. He shouted in surprise and stepped back. The expression on his face turned stern.

"So, your majesty. You will not be deterred." She held her sword at the ready, her elation at drawing first blood dying. "It is time to put us both out of our misery."

The pounding of hoofbeats suddenly sounded from behind her. She dared not turn to see who it was, but her adversary smiled and she knew it was not her guardsmen.

He lunged, swinging wide as if to cut her in two at the waist. She stepped back, but her left foot slipped and she went down, out of harm's way. In her confusion, she thought she heard hoofbeats coming from both directions. The man stood over her, a smile on his face.

"I am sorry, your majesty. But you just had to follow."

He raised the sword. As he swung it down, she rolled aside. The tip of his blade hit the ground where she had been lying. With a curse, he raised the sword again. She rolled again and his blade caught her cloak. She now rested against the bank of snow on one side of the road. He stood in her way of rolling back. This time he would have her.

He raised the sword the third time, a look of confidence on his face. It was all she could see. She wanted to close her eyes but could not get past the fascination of death descending on her. Blood roared in her ears. The blade began its slow descent.

And stopped.

An expression of surprise crossed his face as he tried even harder to finish the downward arc. Suddenly, he jerked out of her field of vision. Hoofbeats surrounded her. Horses' legs became a forest through which she could not see. She rolled into a ball, making herself as small as she could. New sounds came from overhead: more steel striking steel, horses snorting and crying out, and men shouting.

She levered herself carefully into a sitting position. The man she had faced lay very close beside her, his eyes open and unseeing. His blood stained the hem of her cloak.

Grey and Jason must have come. But what of her children? Where were they?

"Protect the queen!" someone shouted.

Too many horses milled around. All she could see were their legs. She pushed backward with hands and feet, into the clean snow on the side of the road. With more distance between herself and them, she finally got to her feet and surveyed the melee.

Grey and Jason were among the combatants as well as the two kidnappers who had dropped back to face her earlier. Geoffrey was in the middle of the action, astride his big chestnut stallion. Two of his men were with him. Off to one side, she spied Jason. On the horse with him were Edgar and Ethel, frightened, but seemingly uninjured.

She stifled a cry with the back of her hand at the sight of them unharmed. Silently, she thanked the Lady for sparing them and returning them to her.

Geoffrey leapt from his horse and placed the tip of his sword at the throat of the man he had just knocked from his horse.

"Yes, I yield," the man gasped.

Elissa skirted the combatants as they began sorting themselves out, and ran to her children. She gathered both into her arms and, kneeling, hugged them to her as tightly as she could.

"Mother, you're hurting me," Ethel protested, but Elissa held them a moment longer.

"Thank the Lady you are all right," she said.

They smiled at her, but fear still tinged their eyes.

"It was an adventure, was it not, Mother?" Edgar asked in his bravest voice, and she assured him it was.

"Jason," Geoffrey's voice called from just behind her. "Take the children and safeguard them. We'll be ready to return to the castle shortly."

She turned to thank him for the rescue, but the thunderous look on the marshal's face stilled the words on her tongue.

Turning away, Elissa sought out Grey to find out what happened after he had left her.

Shortly after they had returned to the main road, he said, they had come upon Geoffrey and explained to him what had happened. Geoffrey, coming from the opposite direction, had encountered no one so they knew the culprits were caught between them and the queen.

Joining together, they had to equal the number of kidnappers. It was not long before they came face to face with the remaining three men, who had possession of the children. They turned back at a gallop and the pursuit began.

"What a terrible sight it was when we spied you on the ground, majesty," Grey said. "I was so afraid you were wounded or even dead. We rode like wild men, then."

There had not been time for the lives of the children to be threatened and the fight took only minutes. The wounds were few among the rescuers, and they were soon all remounted and returning to the castle. On the way, they found the two guardsmen Elissa had left behind. One of them was dead, the other badly wounded. He was so young and brave. She hoped he would survive.

Farther on, they came upon the serving girl, limping along the road. One of the men took her up onto his horse. The rest of the ride seemed to take forever, even though the wind was at their backs.

Elissa, wearing her warmest undergarments and gown and wrapped in a thick wool shawl, shivered over and over. The fire blazed but it seemed to have no effect on the chill that had settled in her bones.

By the time they had gotten back to the castle, the wet cold from rolling around in the snow had soaked clear through to her skin. Although her teeth were chattering, she first saw to her children. Once she was sure they were warm and safe in the care of their nurse, she made her way to her own rooms.

Clara had scolded and fussed as she helped remove the wet garments, worrying over whether the stains could ever be removed. Not only had the cloak been stained with blood, mud, and snow, but her gown had suffered too. Elissa had ordered the maid to place a table in front of the fireplace for the wash basin as she started disrobing.

She had stood naked for a time, checking to see if any of the blood had been her own. However, not a mark could she find. That in itself was a miracle.

Now bathed and dressed in dry clothes, she stood as close to the fire as she dared, drinking warm mead, and awaiting Geoffrey's arrival. His expression had not changed during the silent ride back. The first words he spoke were to order the prisoners into the dungeon beneath the castle. Then he had turned to her.

"Your majesty," he had said through tight lips. "As soon as I have seen to the prisoners, I will join you in your sitting room. There are things we must discuss."

She wanted to assume that his anger was because she had gone out to rescue the children herself, but something told her that was not the case. She had no idea what else it might be.

A knock came on the door, and with a nod from her, Clara opened it. The lord marshal strode into the room, heading straight to the side table to pour himself a goblet of the mead.

"Clara, you may go," Elissa said. When the maid closed the door behind her, she said, "My lord Geoffrey, please be seated and tell me what has you so upset."

He glared at her, but sat down in the large chair facing the fireplace. She took the other chair, assuming a relaxed posture. Silence remained between them for several minutes. Both stared into the fire, and she stole glances at him out of the corner of her eye.

"Are you mad, woman?" he asked suddenly, but without looking at her.

"If you are angry about my pursuing the kidnappers . . ."

"That is not the issue at the moment."

"Then please tell me, what is the issue?"

He stood abruptly and set the goblet on the mantel of the fireplace. He gripped the old wood and turned his head toward her.

"Did you really believe that no one would ever find out about your treason?"

"My what?" She leapt to her feet. "Sir . . ."

He pulled a folded paper from inside his tunic and handed it to her. She opened it, then felt all the blood drain from her face. It was a copy of her letter.

"How did you get this?" she asked as she collapsed into her chair.

"The question is, why did you send it? The Council will be deciding on a regent soon. If knowledge of this treachery gets out, do you think there is a chance you would be named regent? You will be lucky if they don't cut off your head."

Her hand went to her throat. But in a moment, anger replaced fear.

"You did not let me know, sir, that you intended to honor my husband's wishes to have me named regent. You spoke of tradition and how a woman had never held that position before. Then you spoke of honoring the king's wishes. You moved from one side to the other, leaving me to feel that I was on my own. If none of you would help me, I determined to find someone who would."

"Do you have any idea what you have caused here?" he countered. "Verald may now be considering invading Albor because your letter has convinced him that we are leaderless, divided. You probably do not know that he has always wanted to gain control of our southern ports. His, you see, are closed during the winter."

"Yes, I knew that. My husband often discussed things with me. I took a chance writing to Verald, and I knew that, too. But I will do anything to keep my children out of the clutches of their great uncle and cousin. My son will end up with nothing if they gain control of the throne. And my daughter will be sold to the highest bidder no matter where her heart might lie."

Tears came to her eyes but she fought them back. This was an argument—and possibly a man—that would not be won by a woman's tears, no matter how honest they might be.

"If you were allowed to, would you still want to marry one of Verald's sons?" He began pacing in front of the fireplace.

"No, I would not. In fact, I hope that he will decide it is either a hoax or a trap."

Geoffrey continued to pace, clearly deep in thought, and she held her tongue. As much as she might resent it, this man now held her future, and that of her children, in his hands. He came to a stop directly in front of her.

"Your servant, Tommy?"

She nodded.

"He is being detained in Verald's castle right now."

"Oh, no."

"He is in no immediate danger, but might be in the near future."

"You do have a man in their court, then?"

He nodded. "As do others," he said. "I had already decided to help you in gaining the regency, your majesty. Truth to tell, this letter of yours might make it even more imperative. We must keep anyone else from discovering its existence, or perhaps more importantly, from proving that you sent it."

"How can we possibly do that if there are other spies in their court?" He would not look at her. "You're going to steal the letter?"

"If it disappears, who is to say what happened?" He sat back down in the large chair next to her. "I will get word to your man to get out of there. He carried a message there; let's see if he can bring it back." He took a swallow of the mead. "For now, we have other problems closer to home. What are we going to do about Witram?"

6

Twilight had descended and the room was dark and cold. The lone man sat looking out the window at the snow-covered landscape. It looked as bleak as he felt.

The door creaked open and a shaft of light sliced across the stone floor.

"My lord . . ."

"Go away."

A pause, and the light went out as the door creaked shut. Silence closed back around him as if it had never been interrupted.

How long would it be? Lord Witram kept asking himself. The disaster had occurred two days ago. How long before troops appeared demanding his surrender? When they did appear, he had not the manpower to oppose them. Oh, he could barricade himself in the castle and withstand a siege for several months. Possibly a year. In the end, he would be overcome and the lot of his family and retainers would be the worse for it.

None of the neighboring lords would help. His messengers had all returned with negative replies.

He had gambled for much and lost. His advisors had warned against such a move, but he had thought with everyone gone from the capital that it would be easy. How could anyone know that the queen herself would pursue the kidnappers? If she had not, even meeting Geoffrey on the road might not have put the scheme in jeopardy, since there would have been no one to tell him what was happening.

However, if it had been his own children who were abducted, Witram certainly would not have waited this long to act. Even though it would take more than two days for troops to be sent this far, a messenger demanding his surrender and return to court could have arrived yesterday.

The same thoughts round and round, over and over. No matter how long he pondered his predicament, no course of action came to him that might save his family and himself. Perhaps he was expected to present himself at the capital for punishment. And what could that punishment be other than death?

The door creaked open again and he covered his eyes against the brightness of the light.

"I said go away," he growled.

"My lord . . ."

"No!"

"My lord, a messenger has arrived from Winfield." His chamberlain spoke rapidly to prevent being interrupted. "You said if one came, you wanted to see him."

"Yes, I do," he said, nodding his head. "Light some candles, too."

"Yes, my lord."

The door stayed open and in moments several servants scurried in with tapers to light the candles in wall sconces and in holders on the mantel. For eyes accustomed to no more than twilight for several days, the light was unbearably bright. He kept his hand over his eyes, listening to the sounds around him, looking up only when silence returned. His eyes watered and he wiped them on his sleeve. Damned if he would let this messenger think he was crying over his fate!

A man entered, dressed in royal livery. This was not just a servant, Witram realized, but one of the royal retainers. The man bowed then stood waiting for permission to speak.

"What news do you bring?" Witram asked.

"My lord Witram," the man began reciting. "The action you took in the capital at Winfield was treason of the worst sort. Your men not only took the royal children by force, they also threatened and attacked Elissa, our queen, on the main road.

"These actions have created anger and consternation in our kingdom at a time when we should all be thinking of the good of the land in memory of Ethelred, our late king. Therefore . . ."

Here it comes, Witram thought.

". . . you will leave your home tonight and present yourself in Winfield as soon as possible. Once there, you will declare your support for the regency of Queen Elissa during the minority of her son, Prince Edgar. You will express this support in the Privy Council and to any others in authority of any kind within the kingdom.

"To ensure your continued compliance with these terms, you will read and sign the written confession now being presented to you." The messenger handed over a folded piece of paper. "Our messenger will bring it back to us and it will be kept under lock and key, only seeing the light of day should you prove false."

He unfolded the paper. On it, the kidnapping was described in detail along with his involvement. It also stated that a signed confession had been obtained from one Alfred, retainer of Lord Witram, who led the kidnappers in their attempt, but no word on whether he or the men with him were now alive or dead. Alfred's signature, then, was just added insurance for his compliance.

He looked up at the messenger. "Is that all?"

"These terms are sent you by Her Majesty, Elissa, Regina, queen of Albor, and Geoffrey, lord high marshal," the man said, completing the message.

Witram sighed. He was being given a way out. But supporting a woman as regent . . . Geoffrey was clearly in favor of this, for whatever reason. Probably because he believed he would control the kingdom, using the queen as a figurehead.

Even this message and confession must be at Geoffrey's instigation.

Having the lord marshal in charge was not such a bad thing, especially for the country. He had worked hand in glove with Ethelred—everyone knew that.

"Cecil," he shouted. The chamberlain appeared through the doorway. "Feed this man and give him whatever he needs for his return to Winfield. Bring me pen and ink, then have my horse made ready and instruct my son and my equerry to prepare to ride with me. I will be off to the capital shortly."

The man bowed and followed the chamberlain out. Soon pen and ink were brought and more candles for the same table. Witram read through the confession once more then signed. He folded the paper and sealed it with wax from the candle, impressing the seal with his signet ring, making it as official as it could possibly be. And as damning.

He sat back in the chair, contemplating this strange turn of events. For the moment, both he and his family were safe. Perhaps the prince would even marry his granddaughter one day. For now, though, he must be content with watching events unfold over the next few months.

"I am just not sure this is a good idea," Geoffrey said.

Elissa sighed and tried to relax. With her uncle's help, she had been trying to convince Geoffrey of the wisdom of sending Ethel south to live with her family there. Doing so was the best possible way to protect the princess from further danger.

The marshal was afraid it might give the wrong message to those nobles who opposed the queen's being named regent. News of the kidnapping had been successfully quashed, but sending Ethel away would certainly rouse suspicions.

"I am certain everyone will accept that she is having difficulty dealing with the death of her father and needs time away from court to recuperate," Elissa said.

"What does she say about it?"

The queen looked to her uncle, but he had said nothing in support of her decision or about anything else. He simply nod-

ded. He agreed with the decision when Elissa told him and
had further agreed to escort the princess.

"She has not been told. However, she is only a child and
will obey her mother." Knowing Ethel, the possibility of the
last statement being true was slim at best. "If she is out of
harm's way, we can concentrate on other matters more fully,"
she continued. "She can be well protected there and no one
else need know exactly where she is staying. I would send
Edgar if I could, but I know that he must stay here in the
capital so that he is visible to those who will one day obey his
orders. But I don't want to leave both of my children in open
danger."

"When do you propose sending her?"

"By the middle of next week. Word will be sent ahead to
prepare for her stay. It will take a few days to organize the
trip as befits a princess. Everyone will assume that she is going
to Malvern. However, once her party arrives there, the escort
will be sent back here and she will be taken to her real destination."

"What about the servants who will accompany her? Will
they stay with her or return to the castle?"

"We will send only as many as she will need with her. I
don't want anyone coming back here who knows her
whereabouts, except Deward, of course."

Geoffrey looked over at the queen's uncle sitting farther
away from the fireplace.

"You are returning?"

"Yes," Deward said, speaking for the first time. "It should
not be surprising to anyone that the queen would want someone from her own family with Ethel. And since Elissa's father
is too ill to make the trip, I am the most likely candidate."

"But it will be just you and your servants or retainers?"

"Yes. We certainly don't want anyone thinking there is a
possible coup under way to replace one family with another."

The marshal looked chagrined, as if the same possibility
had occurred to him. He fell into thought, his brow knit, his
fingers tapping on the arm of the chair.

Elissa waited impatiently. She was tired of having to justify every suggestion and idea she had. She could only hope that one day he would recognize her intelligence, and think of her as a partner more than as a woman. However, she must live down his belief that her letter to King Verald was treasonous, and that would take some time.

"All right," Geoffrey said at last. "Maybe it is a good idea. Particularly since she is a child and will want to tell everyone about her adventure with the kidnappers. Few people need know about that, especially with Witram due here tomorrow. If he has signed that confession and agrees to work with us, we do not want anyone knowing what leverage we used to convince him to cooperate."

"Agreed," was all Elissa said. He had come to the same conclusion she had.

"How do we keep Edgar from telling everyone?"

"I have already told him it was a test, but that he must tell no one," she said. "Edgar loves secrets."

She cast a glance at Deward but his expression did not change. The truth was, the night before, he had cast a spell of sorts over the boy. Edgar was still at an impressionable age, but as Ethel was older and might have powers of her own, trying the same with her was not advisable. Sending her away was not only the best way to keep word of the kidnapping from getting around, it was also the best way to safeguard her. After she was away for some time, Elissa even hoped that she might be more or less forgotten.

"I would suggest that we try to get her ready to go by Monday," Deward said, startling the others. "It might not be wise to wait any longer. Keep the child busy making her own preparations, and for goodness sake, don't tell her it's for her safety. Give her a reason to want to go."

"Like what?" Elissa asked.

Her uncle shrugged. "What would make her happiest? Having her own castle to rule? She has to prepare for her own wedding? She need not be told that years must pass first. Or something mysterious. She is being sent on a mission for the crown."

"She's only seven, Uncle."

"Then you think back to yourself at that age and come up with something that might have convinced you to leave."

Nothing came to mind immediately. The only thing that ever convinced her to leave home was marrying the king and seeing the capital. He was right that Ethel should be made eager to go somehow, but nothing had occurred to her.

They agreed to start planning details for the trip the next day. Talk then turned to the expected arrival of Lord Witram.

None of them doubted he would take their offer, which might be naive, Elissa thought. The man was not without his own ambitions for himself and his family. Although a member of the Privy Council, his family as a whole was not much honored throughout the country. His was an old family which may have reached its natural end. Only one son had been born to the old lord, and the granddaughter was said to be Witram's pride and joy. Debts and bad political decisions had diminished their landholdings over the past few generations. Marrying the girl to the heir to the throne would have improved their economic and political position, even if it would not perpetuate the family name.

They agreed they would all meet with Witram when he arrived next morning and Deward and Geoffrey soon left. Elissa sat silently for several minutes, trying to convince herself that she must practice her magic. However, she was too tired and gazing into the fire reduced ambition to contentment. Presently she rallied what alertness remained and called for Clara. The maid appeared quickly and helped her mistress prepare for bed. The last thing was to braid her long hair, something Elissa always enjoyed.

"Rouse me just before first light, Clara," she instructed later as she sat before the fire in her nightdress and robe.

"Yes, majesty."

Clara removed the pins that held the thick auburn hair in a knot on top of her head. Then she brushed it with the boar's bristle brush Ethelred had given Elissa for a wedding present.

The braiding took some time since her hair reached below her waistline.

Fatigue and contentment combined with the pleasure of having someone work with her hair, and Elissa relaxed. Her eyelids lowered time and again. When Clara had finished, it was all she could do to get into bed. For once, she let the maid help her slip between the cold sheets. Even that shock did not rouse her. Soon, Clara was gone and the only sound was the crackling of the fire.

As Elissa's mind drifted, a solution suddenly came to her. Ethel would be sent south to learn her adult responsibilities in a smaller castle more suited to her training. Every girl wanted to learn what she saw her mother do on a daily basis, and she was certainly old enough for that.

She had been asleep only three hours when she was awakened by a bad dream. As soon as her eyes opened, the details began to fade, but not their effects. Her heart pounded and her breathing was rapid. She sat up, cold air taking her breath away momentarily. Her first inclination was to burrow back under the covers, but she was too restless to be able to sleep.

She threw the covers off, grabbed up her robe, and stepped into the fleece-lined slippers. Making a dash for the fireplace, she held out the robe, letting the heat in the embers warm it, and flung it around her shoulders. She stirred the ashes and embers until they blazed and added a couple of logs. Hugging the robe around her, she stepped to the window by the fireplace and looked out.

The moon was nearly three-quarters full in a sky filled with stars. Their light reflected off the snow that lay everywhere. Black skeletons of trees swayed in the wind which beat at the windows. That was one of the sounds from her dream, although realization brought no other memories. Remembering would chase away the unease it had caused, but there was nothing left other than the sound.

Her stomach growled and there was one thing she could remember: She had not eaten much the day before. Perhaps something could be found in the kitchen.

Moving as silently as she could, Elissa opened the door to the hallway and slipped out into greater darkness. She moved toward the back stairway, in the opposite direction of her room. The slippers made little noise against the stone, yet she almost tiptoed in her efforts to move silently, even though there was hardly anyone left in the castle to waken.

The stairway ended in a corner of the kitchen. One large window let in the moonlight, and the room was coldly bright. Only a few red embers glowed among the ashes of the great cooking hearth. It was darker in the large pantry but she was able to find a large wheel of cheese on one of the shelves and a bowl of dried apples. It was a little harder to find a knife, but she knew where they were kept, and being very careful not to cut her hand, she felt for the one she wanted.

Quickly, she cut a hunk of cheese from the wheel, placing it in a smaller pewter bowl along with some of the apples. Leftover loaves of bread were kept on shelves next to the cheese. She found one less stale than the others and cut a piece from it. Too hard to eat as it was, the bread would be passable once she soaked it in wine. She found a ewer of wine and took it and her bowl into the main kitchen. As she filled her goblet, a noise at the main door startled her and she tiptoed to a dark corner.

A figure came into view, and even in the dark she recognized him. His height. The confident way he carried himself when he moved. Her breath caught in her throat. He spotted her snack on the table, and slowly went over to it. He reached out his hand as if to touch the goblet but hesitated. Instead, he looked around. She shrank farther into the corner.

"Your majesty," he said and bowed slightly. "Don't let me keep you from your food."

"You startled me, Lord Geoffrey," she said and felt herself blush.

"There is no need to fear me."

His voice was soft and warm. Reassuring. She stepped out of the shadows.

"Probably not. However, recent events have raised my level of caution."

"That isn't a bad thing."

She moved to the table to stand beside him. His scent came to her and his sleeve brushed against hers. She shivered.

"Would you care to share the food?" she asked, her voice a trifle shaky. "In the dark I think I cut off a bit more than I really need." He looked at the plate she held, but said nothing. "This was all the wine there was, but it's a full goblet."

"Thank you," he said. "Where shall we eat it?"

She started to suggest her own sitting room, but that would not be wise, considering the feelings that were being roused within her.

"There may still be a fire in the great hall," he suggested.

The hearth was raised in there, and when she sat down, the stones from which it was built were warm against her buttocks and thighs. The fire warmed her back. She placed the bowl and goblet between her and Geoffrey as much to keep them from touching as to share. They ate in silence awhile and Elissa wondered if he felt the tension between them as much as she did.

"That was a very good idea you had about Lord Witram," he said with his mouth full of cheese and bread.

"You would have thought of the same thing eventually."

"Perhaps."

She watched the light from the fire play across the side of his face, leaving the other side in shadow. He glanced at her, their gazes locking a moment before he broke off another piece of bread. He stuck a piece of dried apple in his mouth, followed it with some cheese, then took a sip of wine, careful to place his lips on the same place as before.

"I still don't understand why you chose to support me as regent, Lord Geoffrey."

He shrugged. "Because you could be the one unifying figure, something that everyone could rally around. Especially if there is an invasion. Your pursuit of the kidnappers would convince everyone of your courage if we could tell them. But we can't." He scooted backward and brought one foot up onto the hearth. "Did you know that there are legends of warrior queens?"

She laughed. "No, I never heard such a thing."

"It's true." He wiped his mouth on his sleeve. "In other lands, of course. I had a tutor whose specialty was foreign history and mythology. I was never sure which was which when he told me stories. He probably wasn't sure either."

She offered him the last swallow of wine, but he refused it and she drank it down.

"What sort of woman would make a good warrior?" she asked. "And how could she possibly hope to beat a man in combat?"

"I suppose they were very large women."

She could not tell if he was joking or not until he smiled suddenly. She laughed then, but part of her mind was working, a concept planted by him.

"I'm not so large," she said.

"No, but not all warriors are."

"Are you trying to tell me that I should learn to be a warrior?"

"It isn't impossible." He stood and looked into the fire. "You showed that you know something about using a sword, and given the right incentive, you aren't afraid to. I do wonder if the councilors and soldiers would be more willing to follow you if you could actually lead them in battle."

"An interesting idea. We must give it more thought." She stood and straightened her cloak around her. "I would need a teacher."

"Your husband's arms instructor is still in the capital."

"Caedmon?"

He looked over at her in surprise. "I didn't know you knew him."

"Ethelred was still taking lessons when I first arrived in the palace. Later, he practiced regularly, but Caedmon no longer taught him. I had the feeling there had been a falling out between them, but never knew what it was."

"No one did, except the two of them. With most men, it's usually women or money."

He averted his eyes quickly and she knew that he feared he might have said too much. However, she had always been sure that her husband never visited another woman after their wedding. It would have been accepted by everyone if he had, of course. But while there had been some women before her, he was among the rare men who where faithful to their wives.

"Can you find him?" she asked.

"He isn't difficult to find."

"Tomorrow, perhaps. After we talk to Lord Witram."

"Certainly, your majesty." He straightened and bowed. "For now, I will say good night."

"And to you, my lord. Please be sure to have me notified as soon as Lord Witram arrives."

"Of course."

He started out and had gotten halfway down the dining hall when he turned back. He stood looking at her a moment, smiled, and walked away, disappearing into the deeper shadows at the other end of the room. She thought of how his blond hair had caught the light from the fireplace, and of the strong grace of his hands. Her heart pounded and she pressed a hand to her breast as if to slow its beating.

"He's married," she whispered to herself. "I must learn to control these feelings or all will be lost."

She gathered up the plate and goblet and took them back to the kitchen. She returned to her floor by the back stairs, stopping in her children's room. Softly, she sat on the edge of Ethel's bed and tucked the covers around her small body.

She did not look forward to telling the child about her upcoming trip south. Not only because the girl might be full of resentment, but also because she would be missed terribly. Yet it must be done for her own protection.

Elissa stood and went to look down on her son. He lay on his side, serene in sleep. How like his father he looked.

∽ 7 ∽

Snow fell on the other side of the window. There was no wind and the tiny flakes fell straight down. Thousands of them made the air look foggy and everything else in the landscape white. Even the dark tree skeletons wore white costumes that settled about their branches and limbs until the next breeze swept the snow away. She felt closed in even though she knew all of the doors would open, and trapped in spite of the fact that the nearest roads and lanes would be swept periodically.

Geoffrey sat in the other chair, patiently instructing her as they waited for their next visitor. He was clearly pleased with how things had gone with Lord Witram.

So why had gloom settled about her after his lordship left? She could think of nothing that had been said, no gesture, that would have dimmed her spirits. Witram had been contrite when he entered and surprised when they did not ask for an explanation of his actions. Instead, Elissa simply asked him if he would support her efforts to be named regent. He had agreed. She then asked him to make every effort to gain Lord Quincy's support for the same. Again, he had agreed.

She and Geoffrey thanked him for coming and for his co-operation. Then they *invited* him to stay in his apartment in the palace for the time being.

"Of course," he said.

The look of relief he had worn faded somewhat, but she had smiled encouragement. He rose, bowed to her, and left the sitting room. Out in the hallway, two guards waited to escort him to that apartment. They would be with him throughout his stay.

It was still morning, and since the next visitor was not due until after noon, Geoffrey was taking advantage of the free time. He was determined that she should learn as much as possible about every aspect of the kingdom, from its economy to politics to the most prominent families. The last two subjects were hopelessly intertwined. Every noble family wanted its own position in the government, even if some of those positions were strictly honorary. To some, power was everything; to others it was appearances.

"Lord Luther will always be a problem until the day he dies," Geoffrey said. "And everyone fears he may never die. But he will not voluntarily relinquish his place in the Privy Council; you can count on that. It's not the power or even appearances that are important. For him, it is a matter of tradition. I doubt that he can remember a day when he was not on the Council. He is also jealous and does not want any of his sons or grandsons to best his record of longevity."

"Are there no provisions for asking a councilor to leave?" Elissa asked.

"Only in the case of treason or the commission of a crime. The charter for the Council was written with such language as to assure that no one person, not even the king, would have the power to summarily dismiss anyone without real cause. They are there to advise him, even against his will."

He stood. "It's time for lunch right now. Would you like to continue while we eat, or would you prefer a break?"

She had opted for a quiet lunch, but invited him to eat with her. He declined, saying he had some things he should check on, but that he would return before Caedmon was to make his appearance. After he left, she summoned Clara, ordered lunch for herself and the children, and went into their room.

When Elissa walked in, their tutor and nurse were gone and Ethel and Edgar were arguing. As soon as they saw her, they quieted.

She sat in one of the chairs and asked what the fight was about. They both spoke at once and in the end she could make little sense of it. Clearly, neither of them was sure. They only knew that once more the other had committed some grievous error and should be punished. Nurse opened the door and, on seeing the queen, curtsied and went back out. Elissa set each of her children a task for the afternoon which would keep them both occupied and out of each other's hair. Lunch arrived and she stayed and ate with them. All during the meal, they remembered things they wanted to show her.

Ethel pulled a piece of embroidery from a chest, eagerly displaying her work. Although it showed some flaws due to lack of experience, the quality of the work was surprisingly good. Elissa praised it, pointing out the parts that were done especially well.

Not to be outdone, Edgar showed her the long strips of leather he was braiding together. When complete, it would be the reins for the horse he was getting on his sixth birthday, he announced proudly. The work was done sloppily, yet she managed to find good points to praise. She encouraged him to keep at it, since his birthday would be here before he knew it.

"It takes forever," he whined. Elissa remembered her own eagerness for birthdays at that age and smiled.

"You're such a baby," Ethel teased.

"I am not!"

Their mother quieted the argument before it could get started by announcing that it was time for them to be about the tasks she had set them. She would have liked to stay and hear them read, but it was nearly time for the arms instructor to arrive. She kissed both children and sent them off, nodding to the guards who now followed them everywhere.

Her own sitting room was empty when she returned. She stirred the fire to greater life then moved to a window and looked out on the bleak landscape. Snow is beautiful, she reminded herself. Geoffrey returned and they spoke, but could not seem to find anything to actually talk about.

This meeting with Caedmon was a big step and they both knew it. Reaction within the court would probably be negative at first and ways must be found to convince everyone that it was a good idea for their queen, and regent, to be trained to fight.

Someone knocked on the door and Clara went to open it.

Elissa turned in her chair to see the newcomer while Geoffrey rose to greet him. The arms instructor was short but powerfully built, with upper arms that were nearly as big around as her thighs. His legs, also short and powerful, were bowed slightly. She had never seen him dressed in anything but leather and today was no exception.

Clara took his cloak and hat and disappeared into her own room.

"My lord," Caedmon said to Geoffrey with a slight bow of his head.

"It's good to see you again, Master Caedmon," Geoffrey greeted him. He turned with a hand on Caedmon's arm and they walked toward her. "I don't believe you have met our queen." They rounded the chairs and stopped in front of her. Caedmon bowed more deeply.

"It is good to finally meet you," she said.

He looked directly into her eyes. There was a wariness in his that did not surprise her, given the estrangement between him and her husband. And a curiosity that must stem from his being summoned to the castle.

Geoffrey moved a chair for him where he would be facing away from the fireplace. It was decided earlier that Geoffrey would tell the arms instructor what they wanted and she looked to him to begin.

"I don't know what rumors may be floating around out there," he said, waving his hand vaguely toward town. "With

Ethelred's death, it is necessary to name a regent to act in his place. Queen Elissa intends to be named to that responsibility and I am employed in that endeavor.''

Caedmon's eyes widened and he looked from the lord marshal to her in disbelief.

"We realize that because she is a woman it will be difficult to get everyone's agreement,'' Geoffrey went on. "Part of this disagreement will be based on her inexperience in areas such as the martial arts. She has had some training with a sword, by the way,'' he added. Caedmon's left eyebrow went up as he registered that bit of information.

"There are outsiders who might believe our country is weak because we don't have a king,'' Geoffrey said. "If our country should be invaded, we must be prepared to repel them. It is traditional for our armies to be led by our king or our prince. Since Prince Edgar is only five years old, he obviously cannot. However, if named regent, our queen can.''

"Would it not be better for you to lead the army in her stead?'' Caedmon asked.

"In some ways, yes.''

"It doesn't seem wise to take this other path. If someone does decide to invade, they'll probably come this next spring. Not enough time to get her fully trained. Hell, we'd have to build up her muscles first.''

"I am stronger than you think, Master Caedmon,'' Elissa spoke up. "I realize that I might not be as strong as you think necessary. But I am willing to work hard to build my strength.''

"Would you be willing to cut that lovely hair of yours?'' He folded his arms across his chest.

"My hair?'' One hand went up to touch her auburn tresses.

"Why do you think warriors always wear short hair? So the enemy can't use long locks for a handle.''

"I could wrap it up and put a helmet over it.''

He indicated surrender by moving his hands to either side. "Then you aren't willing to make the sacrifices necessary to becoming a true warrior.''

Elissa realized that, to him, the discussion was over. He might feel that cutting her hair was a practical necessity, but he had also issued a challenge to her determination and found it wanting. And she remembered from what Ethelred had told her, that Caedmon expected total obedience in matters of training.

"I will cut my hair if you think it necessary," she said.

Geoffrey looked over at her in surprise, but not as surprised as Caedmon looked.

"You will?" he asked.

"Yes," she said. "I am not doing this on a whim, Master Caedmon. I am doing this because I feel it is right for my children and for my country. I take this very seriously, as I am sure you will."

He placed a finger against his cheek and pondered a moment. When he spoke again, it was with another challenge.

"And how do you propose dressing for this training?" he asked. "I'm sure those skirts will get in your way."

Elissa looked down at her lap, realizing that he was right. How could anyone fight in a skirt and petticoats?

"Something will be arranged," she said. "Either I wear men's clothing or something of mine must be modified to suit the purpose."

He grinned then. "This might work after all," he said.

"I will agree to your provisos," she said, "but I have one of my own."

"Oh?"

"Never shout at me when I do something wrong. Do not chastise me as if I were a child, or even a man. Tell me what I have done wrong and what I must do to correct it in a reasonable tone and manner. I will not be bullied."

He pondered again, looking from her to Geoffrey, who sat in surprised silence.

"When do you want to start?" Caedmon said suddenly.

For the next half an hour they discussed the logistics necessary for her training. Caedmon insisted on two hours every day along with her practicing every evening on her own. As her strength increased, the lessons might be extended to three hours or more, but it was best not to tire her too much in the beginning.

The problem of where to train was not so easily solved. All three agreed that keeping it all secret at first was an absolute must. Geoffrey hit on the idea of her taking Edgar to Caedmon's academy for his first lessons. One of Caedmon's best pupils would teach him in a downstairs classroom of the school, while the master himself would teach Elissa upstairs. She would have to leave clothes there and change each time. And they would have to be careful that Edgar did not know. He was only a child and already had one big secret to try to keep.

As for when the lessons would take place, Elissa insisted that she could not start until after Ethel had left for the south. She wanted to spend as much time as she could with her children over the next few days. The very day her daughter departed, she would present herself at the school. At first, Caedmon tried to argue that she should start immediately.

She reminded him that arrangements for clothes still had to be made. How to make them or alter them without anyone knowing was her problem. Elissa thought she might be able to solve that with Ethelred's clothes, which were still in his storage chests. Although not an accomplished seamstress, she could sew well enough to alter the garments to fit her.

"Be sure you don't delay," Caedmon said as he departed.

"I will not," she replied.

Although just past midafternoon, the clouds had darkened outside, bringing early twilight and possibly more snow during the evening and night. She and Geoffrey sat in silence, both contemplating the tasks ahead of them. He looked worried and Elissa wondered what concerned him.

"My lord," she said. "Is there something in this that makes you doubt we will succeed?"

He turned from staring into the fireplace and studied her face a moment. He placed the tips of his fingers together and sighed.

"How do you think you are going to get away with cutting your hair?" he asked. "You know that most men view a woman's long hair as evidence of her beauty and faithfulness. There will be an uproar."

"Now you object?" she said with more than a hint of humor. "During the entire discussion you said nothing."

"You seemed determined to make the arrangements on your own."

"Do you think Caedmon would have agreed to teach me if I had refused that condition? It was a test to see how determined I am in this. He knows well what men think of a woman's hair, and I am quite sure he shares that same opinion. So, I passed that test and he was satisfied. He probably was quite right that it is necessary for the reason he gave, too."

"Maybe. But if this is all to be done in secret at first . . . how will you keep your shorn hair a secret?"

The solution came to her in a flash.

"I will simply take my hair and have it made into a hairpiece. They aren't an uncommon thing. Many women who can afford it have pieces to add to the volume of their own hair."

"And how will you do that in secret?" he asked, leaning forward in his chair.

"I'm not sure yet. I can't take the hair myself, and with Tommy away, there is no one I can trust to keep it secret. My uncle is here now, but the connection might somehow be made to me. Perhaps you or someone you trust could take it."

"That's possible," he said. "My lady wife being ill, I might even say it was a gift for her. To make it easier for her to style her hair or something."

A pang of jealousy hit her in the pit of her stomach. She had no right to feel that way, but could not help it. Much of the time, it was easy to pretend that he was free.

"I am sorry," Elissa said. "I have not asked how Lady Meryl was when you were home."

"She has been ill for some time now," he said, and a cloud passed over his face.

He loves her, Elissa realized. With arranged marriages so

common among the nobility, love was such a rare thing that she had let herself hope Geoffrey's marriage was no different.

"But that is not our concern at the moment," he said abruptly. "I will make some kind of arrangement to have this hairpiece made once your hair is cut. But who will cut it?"

"As for that, I am at a loss. I certainly cannot go to one of the barbers. Nor to one of the hairdressers here in the castle or in the town. Or to anyone else who knows me."

She thought of Tommy again, but only heaven knew when he would return to Winfield.

"Deward," she said at last. "He has cut hair before. Surely, he can do mine."

"All right, then," Geoffrey said and smiled. "Little obstacles, but solved ones."

"Yes. And now it is nearing dinnertime and I must be with the children this evening. It is time I told Ethel about her upcoming trip."

"I don't envy you that task," Geoffrey said. He stood and stretched with his arms overhead.

"I do wish it was not necessary," she said. "I also wish I was certain that she will be safe there. In some respects, I would feel better if I could keep an eye on her."

"She will be safer there than anywhere else," he reassured her. "And you will be too busy to keep an eye on either of them, I fear."

She stood and turned away from him. The urge to go to him for comfort was strong, but with his wife ill, there was even more reason to resist this temptation.

"I do hope so," she said, referring back to her daughter. "My family will do everything they can, I know. And if we can keep her location a secret, I will feel much better."

"Nothing is sure," he said, starting toward the door.

"Thank you, Geoffrey," she said. "For everything."

"You are welcome, your majesty." He bowed, then left the room.

Elissa stood staring at the closed door for several minutes. Yearning flowed through her and she thought how ridiculous it was. He was the man who had agreed to help her, and that was why she found him so attractive. Nothing more. Nothing less.

She shook her head and went to the children's room, but stood with her hand on the latch.

The immediate task of telling Ethel she was going away filled her with dread. Her mother's instinct begged her to keep her only daughter near. Ethel would feel that Edgar was being favored again, unless the reasons could be presented convincingly enough. But no matter her reaction, it had to be done.

Having reinforced her resolve, Elissa pushed the door open and stepped into the large bedroom. She put a finger to her lips, silencing Nurse's welcome.

She had always wished that her room and the children's were joined by a door, but Ethelred had insisted on this arrangement. It had been his room as a child: near enough to his mother's for her to visit often, but separated enough to give them both privacy. Between them were Clara's room and the children's privy. She had often been glad of that privacy, although putting them together in the same room while they were still children had been her idea and the king had relented on that score. She knew they comforted each other on those dark nights when all manner of noises could be heard.

This evening, Ethel sat on her bed working on a piece of needlework. Edgar sat on the floor, arranging the small metal soldier figures that had belonged to his father. The image of Ethelred standing just inside the door, watching this play, came to her in a flash. It had pleased the father to see his son following in his footsteps, even this much.

"Maman," Ethel said when she looked up and saw her. Her smile faded as she studied her mother's face, and Elissa smiled instantly to chase away the girl's fears.

Ethel smiled in return. "You scared me, Maman," she said. "I thought you looked just like you did when Father was hurt."

Edgar looked up, momentarily apprehensive. When he saw his mother's smile, however, he beamed at her, too.

"Do you mind if I join you for dinner tonight?" she asked.

"That would be fun," Ethel said. The look in her eyes hinted that she suspected something.

"All right," Edgar said, and he returned his attention to his soldiers.

Elissa walked over to the chair nearest him and sat down. She leaned down and studied his arrangement of the figures.

"Who are they fighting tonight?" she asked.

"Barbarians," he answered without looking up.

"Are you winning?"

"I always win."

"Oh, I see."

She watched for a while longer, then moved to sit at the foot of Ethel's bed.

"May I watch?"

Ethel nodded but kept her eyes on the piece of linen and silk thread she worked with. It was a new project that Nurse had assigned her. As she worked at making her stitches small and precise, she stuck her tongue out between her lips.

Clara arrived with two serving girls in tow bearing dinner trays. Everyone bustled about, arranging the dishes on the table. Clara and the servants were soon gone and the children set to eating with good appetites. Elissa picked a bit from their dishes, but she had little appetite. Clara had thought to include a ewer of warm mead and she drank some of that. Nurse hovered about, making sure her charges did not drink too much of the watered and sweetened wine.

Before long, their appetites sated, the children sat back in their chairs and took one last drink from their goblets. Edgar belched and everyone laughed. Then, very soberly, Elissa told him that was not very good manners. He grinned sheepishly, as if secretly proud of his sounding off so loudly in spite of her chiding.

"Well," Elissa said. "Now that you both are full of yourselves . . ." She reached over and tickled Edgar in the ribs. He squirmed and giggled. "There is something I must talk with you about."

Nurse sat in a comfortable old chair in her corner, a piece of mending in her lap. Her fingers flew with the needle, but it was well known that she could work and listen at the same time. In this case, it was just as well, for the news affected her too.

"This is a very grown-up matter, so you must pay close attention." The children quieted and looked at her solemnly. "This has to do with you, Ethel, but it affects us all." Ethel's expression became wary and Elissa hurried on. "Now that you are nearly eight years old, it is time that you received your womanly training. It is customary among my people in the south to send daughters to relatives for this."

She explained how learning to manage servants was an important part of that training and it had been further decided that a smaller household would provide a more manageable venue. She went on with all of the positive reasons she could think of, saying how proud she was of Ethel, and how exciting such a journey would be. She would also meet more relatives than she even knew she had.

"But, Maman," Ethel said in a quavering voice. "I don't know any of them."

"You know your great-uncle Deward. He is such a fine man, and most of our relatives are like him."

Edgar looked from one to the other, not yet sure that this was good news, or how he felt about being left without his daily companion.

"The weather is much warmer down there and the people are friendly. Although your grandmother is dead, your grandfather will welcome you with open arms. You will find some of the customs strange for a while, but it won't take long to become accustomed to them."

"Strange how?" Ethel asked, her interest piqued.

"Well, my dear, my people have not always been part of Albor. At one time, we were an independent nation called Morrigan, and our customs have not changed much since then. In fact, my marriage to your father was intended as another means of joining our peoples together."

"Am I like them?"

"No, dear, you are a child of the north, your father's people. But you will learn to fit in. Just as I did here."

She told of her childhood and of her parents, who were minor nobility in Morrigan. Many of the higher nobility and the former royal family had died in the short war of annexation Ethelred's grandfather, King Edwin, had waged for one month. Being a small kingdom, Morrigan never had a large military force, and the surprise attack had not left much time to hire mercenaries.

She had learned the history of her own small country with resentment at its being forced to become just another province of Albor. She had even felt some of that resentment at the prospect of marrying a northern prince. However, the chance for adventure had overcome that, and she hoped a similar desire for adventure would help Ethel accept this immense change.

For a long time she wove tales of the different vegetation, animals, and styles of houses Ethel would find. Elissa spoke of the warmth of the sun, even at this time of year, and about all of the butterflies that lived there when winter descended on the north. She described the sandy beaches along the coast, so different from the northern rocky ones.

"Are there any unicorns?" Ethel asked.

Elissa laughed, realizing that she had perhaps painted too magical a picture.

"No, my love, there are no unicorns. As far as I know, they are mythological and have never lived in this world. But there are goats with horns."

"How long will it take me to get there?"

"I would say seven or eight days. It will be a long journey, but you will have many people to take care of you and keep you safe."

"How long must I stay?"

"A year. Perhaps two."

Tears welled up in the child's eyes and her lower lip trembled. Elissa scooted her chair back, held out her arms, and

Ethel came to her. She folded her only daughter in her arms, holding her to her breast for a long moment. Across the table, Edgar sniffed and she held out an arm to him. He came to stand on the other side of her and she held on to him.

"I know you will miss her," she whispered against his hair. "We both will." He sniffled, but stood very still.

Elissa picked them both up and moved to Edgar's bed, which was nearer. She sat down and placed Ethel in her lap still holding Edgar close on one side. Ethel held out a hand to her little brother and he took it in his smaller one.

"I will miss you too," she said in a soft voice.

8

In the early morning darkness, Elissa lay in her bed, unable to sleep. At the first hint of dawn, the caravan would assemble to escort her daughter to the south. It was probable she would not see the girl for a year or more, depending on how fortune would handle the coming spring and summer.

In spite of the sadness the parting brought, she would gladly send Edgar with his sister if she thought he would be safer. However, the heir to the throne must make appearances. Everyone had to know that he was alive and well. She only hoped they would be able to keep him that way.

The attempted kidnapping had served as a reminder of how vulnerable her children were. That realization had brought both nightmares and moments of panic when she would rush to make certain they were safe.

The past few days had been spent in mending and packing Ethel's clothes, supervising the gathering of food, and making all of the other arrangements for a princess's travel. She left the task of choosing guards to Geoffrey with only a moment's hesitation. She had to trust someone, after all.

Just yesterday, letters were sent to all of the privy councilors at their residences, telling them of the move of the princess to her mother's former home for her womanly training. Other lords were also notified, but no one was told soon enough for them to launch a protest or, worse, an effort to overtake her. By the time they got the letters—any of them—she should be safely out of everyone's reach.

Deward had volunteered to select horses and arrange for their trappings and the baggage that would carry everything. He commandeered a small wagon and found wide wheels that would make it pull easier in the snow.

Ever since Elissa's talk with both of her children about the forthcoming journey, Ethel's spirits had slowly risen. All little girls eagerly await the day they can begin to emulate their mothers, and Ethel was no exception. She had often admired the chatelaine worn around her mother's waist bearing keys and small tools, emblems of the mistress of castle or house.

Edgar's reaction had been just the opposite. As the day for his sister's departure approached, he had become withdrawn and ill behaved. From what he had said, and her own instincts, Elissa knew that he was unhappy at being left on his own. But he was also jealous of what must seem a big adventure. Training with the sword would soon occupy his mind and energy.

When she was not working on arrangements for the trip, she and Deward worked on her other skills. With everything going on around her, she found it difficult to concentrate and little progress had been made. However, she had moved an object without touching it, for the first time. Only a small coin, to be sure, but it had felt like a huge accomplishment after so many failed tries.

Just last night he had warned her that she must continue to practice after he had left. They had discussed written instructions, but that was too much of a danger. If they were found, Dathan would happily use them to discredit her. Instead, her uncle repeated over and over the spells she should practice while he was gone. That he would be gone nearly a month, was difficult for her to bear.

She propped herself up on her elbows and looked out the window. In the darkness beyond, it might be snowing again, but she could not be sure. A large, white shadow flashed across the window. Her heart leapt. It was a ghost, perhaps the spirit of Ethelred. Would he disapprove of what she was trying to do?

She waited for the shadow to return, but nothing further happened. What if it were an owl in its winter plumage? That would be even worse than a ghost. Owls presaged death.

She lay back on the pillows. No use in trying to sleep now. But it was too cold to get up and there was little she could do this early in the morning. She could practice, but her eyes kept looking at the window, hoping and fearing the shadow would reappear. By the Lady, she might as well get up. Lying there with her mind racing around everything was torture. She could find *something* to do, something that she could focus on to the exclusion of all other considerations for a while.

Sitting up, she grabbed the robe from the foot of the bed and slipped her arms through the sleeves. It fell around her as she slipped from beneath the covers and quickly put on her slippers. She moved to the fireplace and poked the fire back to life.

With a taper from the mantel, she lit several candles around the room, two of them on the desk. There she saw her lists of things to do. She sat in the chair and read it over one last time. On the very first page was an item that she had nearly forgotten in the rush of the past few days, a most important item.

Opening the center drawer of the desk, she found the key to her jewel box. She retrieved the box from the large chest that held her gowns, unlocked it, and quickly found the item she sought.

Ethelred had bought it himself. That was a loving and kind gesture, especially since Ethel was only two at the time.

Elissa held it in her hands, the silver glinting in the candlelight. Ethel's very own chatelaine. This would be her New Year's gift, something for her to open on the trip south. Something to make her stay there more pleasant and special, and appropriate to the reasons being given for her going.

Out of the same chest, Elissa found a small piece of yellow

silk and a length of deep green cord. Closing the jewel box, she locked it and replaced it in the chest. From a smaller chest, she took a small square of gold brocade. Carefully, she placed the chatelaine in the center of the silk cloth and folded it into a roll, tying the two ends together in a single knot. This small package she placed in the center of the brocade, folding it into a square package which she tied around with the green cord.

She put her hands in her lap and studied the finished piece. Ethel would love the gold cloth and would want to open it immediately. Elissa would insist that she wait until New Year's Day. Maybe it would be best simply to have Deward give the package to Ethel at the appropriate time.

Sudden tears stung her eyes and this time she let them stream down her cheeks. Better to cry now rather than later, in front of everyone.

The horses stamped their impatience in the cold air. The wagon was loaded with food and clothes chests and folded tents. Everyone was assembled to either depart or cheer them on their way. All except Edgar. Nurse searched for him even now, but the chances of finding him in time were slim. He had a positive knack for not being found when he did not want to be.

Elissa had told her daughter of the New Year's gift and showed her the package. As expected, she had wanted to open it immediately, but Elissa gave it to Deward with the proper instructions. He had smiled evilly at Ethel as he deposited the disputed item in his saddlebags and the two engaged in teasing each other about who was in charge.

The guards mounted their horses. Just as Elissa started to embrace her daughter, Edgar suddenly ran up. Tears had stained his little cheeks and his eyes were red. He stood awkwardly for a moment with his hands behind his back.

"Oh, Edgar," Ethel said, a tear now showing in her eye. "I'm glad you are here."

He held out a small, crudely wrapped package.

"You can't open it now," he said. "It's for New Year's."

Ethel took it in her gloved hand.

"I'll wait," she promised.

The boy rushed to his sister and they embraced. Tears came to Elissa's eyes as well, and she fought them back with difficulty. The two parted and Ethel kissed her brother on the forehead. Deward lifted her into Elissa's arms and the two embraced for a long moment.

"I love you," Elissa whispered against her daughter's ear. "Make me proud," she added.

"I love you, too," came Ethel's response with a small catch in her voice.

They kissed each other's cheek and Deward took hold of Ethel and placed her in the saddle of her horse. For the first part of the trip, she would ride there. It was part of the pomp of their departure and she had insisted that she was grown up now. However, for most of the trip, she would ride with Deward for safety and warmth.

Geoffrey came forward, picked up Edgar and wrapped his own cloak around the boy. Deward and Elissa hugged each other tightly.

"Have a safe trip," she said. "Come back to me soon."

"I will, niece. Keep practicing and watch yourself."

She nodded as they parted and he stepped up into his saddle. With a wave, the party started off. Everyone called out farewells. It would be a long trip for them, but they should leave the snow behind within about four days.

As the party passed through the gate, Edgar shouted, "Let's go up on the wall walk." Geoffrey set him down and he ran inside. The marshal looked over at Elissa and they both smiled and followed rapidly.

"Geoffrey, forgive me for not remembering, but do you have any children?" she asked.

"No, my wife has had several miscarriages. The physicians believe they damaged her heart."

"I'm sorry," she said.

They made their way up the main staircase, following the sound of Edgar's footsteps.

"I must find out if anyone in the castle has children. Edgar needs one companion, if not several, to play with."

"I'll inquire. Surely, there are one or two."

They had reached the top of the staircase. The door leading out to the wall walk stood open and frigid air blasted through it. When they stepped outside, the wind was numbingly cold. Elissa thought immediately of her daughter, astride her horse, subjected to such cold. Deward would keep an eye on her, but still she worried.

They joined Edgar at the wall and Geoffrey lifted the boy so he could see better. They watched until the travelers reached the first small grove of trees. They would be in sight for some time, but Edgar already shivered.

"Time to go," Elissa said.

"Not yet," Edgar protested.

"Yes, young sir. You are shivering as it is. Time to warm you up."

Geoffrey carried him to the doorway and set him down. Edgar ran down the stairs and once more they followed.

"Has Lord Witram been in touch with his friend?" she asked.

"Yes. Quincy was very surprised, but it would seem he is willing to listen to Witram's arguments. He has always been led by his friend's judgement and we hope he will be now."

They reached the second floor and stopped on the landing.

"You are meeting with Caedmon tomorrow?"

"Yes, for my first lesson."

"Everything is ready?" he asked, referring to her hairpiece, clothing, and sword.

"Yes, everything. Edgar is excited about starting his training. I believe a few people have expressed surprise that I intend going with him to his lessons, but since they already think me strange, they have accepted it."

"Do you want me to accompany you?"

"It isn't necessary. That might draw attention to us."

He nodded. "I will take my leave then, your majesty," he said and bowed. "Oh, I sent word that Tommy was to return to you. I hope that he will also bring the information we expect."

That was certainly welcome news. She had missed her equerry, even though he was often complaining and lazy. But above all else, he was loyal.

"I am glad to hear that," she said.

"With the weather as bad as it is, though, it will take him several days to get here."

"Should we send an escort to meet him and make sure he arrives safely?"

"I think not, considering the reason he went to Ravelin in the first place."

Elissa felt herself blush. "However, the news he may carry would surely outweigh all else."

Geoffrey grew thoughtful for a moment. In the distance, Edgar called to her, probably from his room.

"Let me think about it," the lord marshal said. "It might be a good idea at that."

They parted and she went to Edgar's room to see what he wanted. As it turned out, he wanted to move all of Ethel's things out and claim the room as his own. Elissa could not bring herself to do that just yet and put him off.

"Right now," she said, "why don't you lie down for a short nap? You were up early and have a big day tomorrow."

His little face brightened at the reminder of his first sword lesson. He agreed with a smile that almost erased the grief she felt at parting from her daughter. Elissa made her way to her own rooms, and once her hands had warmed, she turned to the mirror hanging on the wall. It was another gift from Ethelred and a very expensive luxury. Now, however, she was interested only in making sure that the hairpiece was firmly pinned in place. It had been difficult to convince Deward to cut her auburn hair that had grown to her waist in a thick mass. He could not understand the necessity of doing something that might alienate all those she was trying to win to her side.

"The hairpiece will keep them from knowing until we are ready," she had said. "Lord Geoffrey is going to take it to a wigmaker in the town with some story about its being for his wife."

"Geoffrey? Are you sure about him?"

"Who else is there, Uncle? I need his support to become regent. He knows these people, from the privy councilors down to the blacksmith. No one else wants me to do this. To them, I am only a woman who will always be in the way. Perhaps to him, too. It may even be that he wants to rule through me." Deward looked at her in surprise. She put her hand over his. "I am not fool enough to think he does not have his own ambitions. But I also believe that he wants what is best for my children and his country."

"He has no feelings for you?"

"I suppose he thinks of me as a tool. One that needs some honing, to be sure, but a tool that he can use to accomplish what he has in mind. His goals are similar enough to mine for us to work well together. Eventually."

He had picked up the razor then, looking from it to her. He started to cut the first piece so that her hair would be shoulder-length, but she stopped him. "Like a warrior's," she said. He nodded and proceeded to finish the job quickly.

When she first looked in the mirror, she was horrified. That night, alone in her bed, she had cried herself to sleep.

The next morning, she told Clara that she had cut her hair off in a fit of grief. She asked the servant to tell no one, nor that she intended having the shorn locks done up in a hairpiece in hopes of hiding what she had done. Clara agreed, in spite of her own look of horror. For the next three days she had helped Elissa pin the hairpiece in place so skillfully that no one was the wiser. As a reward, Elissa had given her a pair of pigskin gloves the girl had admired. However, she knew how servants gossiped, and that one day word would get out. She could only hope that it would not become common knowledge until she was ready to let people know herself.

Alone, she went to the chest and pulled out the clothes she

had worked on all week. Ethelred had been a man of medium height, but strongly built. Since she was tall for a woman, there had been no need to shorten anything. However, it had been necessary to take everything in, and she had blessed her mother for teaching her the rudiments of sewing.

The linen breeches were still loose fitting, which would give her room to move. The shirtsleeves were a bit long, but she could manage them with wristbands. Beside these, she laid out stockings and an overtunic. She would wear her chemise under it all. Then came an old pair of her own boots. Last, she laid two short swords in their scabbards over everything. They were Ethelred's practice swords. If anyone asked, she would say they were for Edgar, and since that was true of one of them, the lie would be easier to say.

All of these things would be left at Caedmon's practice hall.

She folded everything carefully, then bundled the items in a piece of wool, tying it all together. Her one worry was how she would get the hairpiece back in place after practicing. Maybe she would not even have to wear it to Caedmon's. A simple hat would hide her short hair.

She tried to sit and relax a moment in front of the fire before practicing the word spells that Deward had left for her, but fear and excitement once more overrode everything. Tomorrow she would see if there was a chance of getting away with this part of the plan. However, once it was an accomplished fact, another possible objection would be overcome. Little by little, things were coming into place.

She closed her eyes and pushed everything out of her mind. Her breathing became regular and deep. The Lady of the forest appeared. She glowed with a soft green light. She was beautiful, yet not too dazzling to look upon. Her expression was benign.

Please protect me, Elissa said.

The Lady's left hand reached out and light spilled from it, wrapping around Elissa. It enveloped her from her feet to the top of her head, caressing her skin as a feather would. She smiled at the feeling of comfort, and once the cocoon of light was complete, she opened her eyes.

On the hearth, she had placed the short remains of a white candle. It lay on its side, the burnt end of the wick pointing toward her.

"Candle," she whispered to get its attention. "Candle, turn."

It lay perfectly still.

"Candle, turn."

In her mind's eye she pictured it turning slowly but the real one merely sat.

"Candle, turn."

The one in her mind seemed to balk and she concentrated harder. She felt rather than saw the slightest movement. She repeated the command, concentrating on the image of the candle turning. Repeated again and again. Something deep inside her said, "Give up. It will not happen today." But she persisted, blocking out that thought and everything else that distracted.

"Candle, turn."

It did, a quarter of a turn. Thrilled, she concentrated and turned it another quarter turn. And again, until it had turned back to where it started. She had the strange sensation that she was now watching the candle from above, but concentrated on making it turn the full circle in one full motion.

In a distracted way, she felt sweat trickle down her sides, but she spoke to the candle, over and over. And it turned a full circle. Again! She must do it again.

Suddenly, the protective cocoon trembled. Her concentration was lost. However, she must return the cocoon to the Lady, with her thanks. It seemed as if she floated to the floor before the light unwrapped from around her, and threaded its way back to the Lady's hand. Elissa bowed and the image disappeared. She was back in her sitting room again, bathed in sweat, her heart racing. She had almost pushed too far this time; almost beyond her endurance. Deward had warned her to be careful about that. But it was so tempting. She would remember in future.

Now, it was time to bathe and check on the staff. Then in the evening, she must deal with dinner and getting Edgar to bed. What else did she need to do to prepare for tomorrow? The clothes were ready. The sword. Edgar's clothes and weapons were ready . . .

Stop. It was an important day, but everything had been done. For now, she must go on as if everything were ordinary—in a life that had been turned upside down.

⌒ 9 ⌒

The day was sunny for a change, although new snow had fallen again in the night. The glare was blinding and Elissa pulled her hood closer around her face. The wind had died down and the cold air made her breath appear as a cloud.

Edgar scampered about like a new colt, so eager to begin his training as a man. She remembered how she, too, had wanted so much to grow up fast. It seemed like everyone wanted to leave youth behind quickly, and when they realized their mistake, it was gone forever.

Elissa, Edgar, and their guards trooped across the castle grounds toward the main gate. The people in sight were busy with their daily duties, from caring for the horses to sharpening weapons to the laundry. Off to one side she spied Lord Geoffrey walking at an angle in order to intercept her and their escort.

"I thought I might accompany you," he said when he drew close. "If your majesties don't mind."

"Yes, yes," Edgar shouted. "Come see me with my sword."

Geoffrey smiled at him and took the small hand held up to him. They walked that way for a while, but the prince was too excited and he skipped ahead. The marshal dropped back to walk beside the queen.

"I decided no one would think it strange if I went along," he said. "At least for this first lesson."

"They may not," she said.

"I also thought you might have some difficulties convincing the guards not to go inside. They have been ordered to keep our soon-to-be king in sight at all times when he is out of the castle."

"That is true. So the plan is that you will go inside with us and they will guard the outer door?"

"Sounds good to me." He smiled, whether at Edgar's antics ahead of them or at his own cleverness she could not tell. Nor did it matter. She liked his smile.

It was still rather early, but there were people out in the lanes, about their business of the day. They stopped and bowed as the royal party passed, many smiling at their young prince. He had been taught the proper way to appear in public, however today was not the day to remind him of that. Such an enthusiasm should not be crushed so soon.

They arrived at Master Caedmon's academy and Geoffrey instructed the guards to take the two bundles inside. The door opened abruptly and the master himself invited them in. He showed the guards where to put the bundles, and then they took up their positions outside the door.

A young man who had been standing at the back of the room came forward and Caedmon introduced him as Boris, a young man from a country to the east.

"He is my best student at the moment," he said. "He will teach the prince the basics of sword fighting while we discuss other things."

She helped her son change from his good clothes into older ones, more suitable for the exertions he would be undergoing. His little face was flushed with excitement and she felt the first twinge of what it meant for a son to grow up and grow away. After today, he would cease to be her little boy in many ways, and she was sorely tempted to call it off, take him home, and protect him from the world awhile longer.

"Hurry up, Maman," Edgar said impatiently.

She looked down and smiled.

"Very well, my lord."

He grinned and impulsively put his arms around her neck and hugged her tightly. She sniffed back the tears that sprang to her eyes, and stood.

"There. You are finished."

He straightened, put hands on hips, and tried to look at her sternly. The pose dissolved into giggles and she stepped aside to let him approach his teacher.

"I am ready," he pronounced to Boris, who hid his own smile with a bow.

"We will begin with a light wooden sword, your majesty," he said and held it up. "You are a strong young man, but we must build up the right muscles gradually."

He handed the practice piece to the boy, who took it first with his right hand.

"You are right-handed, then," Boris said.

He showed Edgar the proper way to grip it and how to stand. He told him to swing the sword and corrected the swing. Elissa watched for a short while, almost sad that the childish awkwardness would vanish in the coming weeks and months.

Caedmon touched her arm and motioned for her to follow him. As she started out of the room, Geoffrey stopped her.

"Do you want me to come, too?" he asked.

"No. I will do this alone. For now."

He nodded, but stood watching as Caedmon led her up some stairs to the second floor. This practice hall was slightly smaller than the one on the first floor. A bank of windows in the far wall looked down on the street. On the wall to her left hung a rack with a dozen or more swords. Removing the swords, he handed her the bundle of clothes and pointed toward a large screen.

"That's your dressing area," the teacher said, pointing toward it. "Change in there and we will get started."

She nodded, grabbed up her bundle, and went behind the screen. There was just room enough to move around. She set the bundle on the chair, stripped down to her underwear, and hung everything on pegs set in the screen. The room was cool and she shivered.

Quickly, she pulled on Ethelred's clothes. She combed through her short hair with her fingers, as she recalled the startled look on Clara's face when she first saw the new hairdo. Hopefully, the need for her silence would not last much longer.

She walked back into the practice hall, feeling awkward and shy for the first time in years. Caedmon heard her and turned.

"I didn't believe you would do it," he said with a look of surprise on his face.

"Would you teach me if I hadn't?"

"No. Not only for the reasons I gave, but also because I did not believe you were serious."

"You see now that I am." She picked up the sword and drew it from the scabbard.

"Yes, your majesty. I see."

"Good. Now teach me."

He smiled and went to draw a sword from the wall rack at one side. She suspected he still did not believe that she would be much of a swordswoman. She started stretching arms and legs, trying to limber up.

"You said you had some training when you were younger." She nodded. "Let's see how much you remember." He moved toward her, flexing the blade with one hand on the tip and one hand on the handle. "Attack me."

With both hands, she held the sword to one side at a right angle to her body and smiled as they drew closer to each other. She swung the sword parallel to the ground, aiming for his waist. He parried easily. The vibration stung her hand. It was a familiar feeling.

Her blade bounced back slightly and she used that to curl her blade to the other side, coming around to strike his blade again. This time she raised the blade high, striking downward toward his shoulder. He simply stepped back and the tip of her blade nearly hit the wooden floor.

She was wide open to a thrust from him, and as soon as she regained her balance, she too stepped backward. He came at her then, swinging his sword in slow wide arcs. It was all she could do to ward off the blows and keep backing up at the same time.

Her arms were tired already and she wanted nothing more than to drop them to her sides. But he did not let up. Her hands were numb from the numerous impacts. He swung from her left and she raised her blade just in time. His slid down to the handguard on her sword, bounced off, and nicked her upper arm.

Startled, she yelped and dropped her sword. The tip of his blade pressed against the breast of her tunic.

"Don't ever drop your sword," he said tightly.

"But you cut me." She grabbed hold of the injured arm with her other hand.

"I could have killed you."

He backed away and leaned his sword against the near wall.

"Let me see it," he said.

She released her arm and held it out to him. He untied the wristband and pushed her sleeve up. A little blood had trickled down her arm. He pulled a bit of cloth from his pocket and pressed it against the cut.

"Hold it in place," he said, and disappeared into another room.

She did as he instructed, and he returned a moment later with a small box of salve. With a clean corner of the same cloth, he put salve on the cut.

"That will help stop the bleeding and keep it from getting infected," he said. "I use a lot of it here."

"I am sure you do."

He looked up at her, searching her eyes for any hidden meaning to her words. Apparently finding nothing, he gave her the cloth back and told her to keep pressure on the cut. Meanwhile, he returned the box of salve to its storage place, then retrieved his sword, cleaned the blade, and replaced it in the rack. He slid hers into its scabbard and laid it on the chair.

"You're better than I expected," he said. "But we have a lot of work to do. Your arms are weak. You are heavy on your feet. And I'm not sure if you have any killer instinct."

"Killer instinct?"

"Something you will need to fight well, not just to kill your opponent."

"Well, I know the ultimate goal of all this is to be able to kill an enemy."

"You know it. You don't feel it." He checked her wound, declared the bleeding stopped, and took the bit of cloth from her. "Feeling it will help you concentrate. It becomes a blood rage in battle. Nothing exists except you, your sword, your opponent, and his sword. There is as much instinct as there is skill in winning such a fight."

She went to the window and looked out on the street. People moved to and fro on their business of the day. Peasants, merchants, probably a tavern owner or two, maids, and wives. Surely their lives were simpler. But she would not trade with any one of them.

"Is this instinct something a person is born with?" she asked. "Or can it be learned?"

"A bit of both. I do believe you have potential as a swordswoman. I don't think you will ever be great."

"But you don't think any woman could ever be great," she interrupted.

He exhaled loudly and she turned to face him.

"Maybe," he said. "We will have to find out." He smiled at her. "Be here every day." He turned on his heel and started out of the room. "Change clothes."

"Is that all?"

The only answer was the sound of his footsteps as he descended to the first floor. She shrugged and did as he said. As she rewrapped the clothes bundle, she made a mental note to bring another shirt to replace the bloodied one. She made another to ask Caedmon if he would arrange to have the things laundered occasionally. Otherwise, they would soon reek.

Downstairs, she found Edgar and Geoffrey waiting for her. Her son's first lesson had also been a short one, which was a pity in a way: She would have liked to watch him if only for a moment. There would be other times, she consoled herself.

Edgar was clearly tired, but he was still too excited to walk normally on their way back to the castle. Again, people bowed and smiled at their prince and at her. The two guards kept an eye on everyone, but their somberness did not dim anyone else's spirits. It took a much larger presence to do that.

"Is that the patriarch's carriage?" Elissa asked as they entered the gate to the castle.

"Yes," Geoffrey said. Even in that one word she could hear his irritation. "He must have returned to find out what we are up to."

"Not good," she mumbled to herself.

"Send the boy to his room immediately," Geoffrey said. "Come downstairs when you are ready. Make it seem that you have been about your usual errands."

They did their best not to hurry in through the door. The lord marshal went to welcome the patriarch back while Elissa escorted her son to his room. She helped undress him then instructed Nurse to give him a hot bath. She left for her own rooms when she was no longer able to hide her agitation.

Calling for Clara, she began to undress herself. Hot water had already been delivered on news of her return. She stepped into the large metal tub and Clara scrubbed her with the sponge.

"Majesty, you have scratched yourself," she said, noticing the nick on her arm.

"It's all right," Elissa said, not wanting to make up some lie about how it had happened. There were more serious matters to consider.

Clara shrugged and began rubbing her briskly with a towel until her skin glowed, all the while chattering about how sad it was to see the young prince growing up so fast and how hard it must be on Elissa. The queen only half heard, her mind creating reasons for Dathan's unexpected return.

Unexpected only if she had been fooling herself. The news of Ethel's departure from the capital must have come as a surprise to Dathan. He would think he should have been consulted, and was probably quite sure there was a conspiracy against him. Well, there was one of sorts. And if it was in support of her, it had to be against him by default.

Clara began dressing her and she had to concentrate on selecting garments and making it easy to slip them on. At last, it was time to put on the hairpiece. Clara had styled it in a long braid during her absence.

The maid deftly pinned the piece on, blending in the short remaining hair. When she was finished, Elissa could not tell that it was a hairpiece.

She stood and hugged the maid. "Thank you, Clara. You have saved me much embarrassment."

Clara smiled and curtsied, and began clearing up the bath things

"I need to go down and check on the kitchen staff," Elissa said. "I understand that Patriarch Dathan has returned. I should pay my respects."

"Yes, ma'am. He arrived about an hour after you left."

Elissa checked herself one more time in the mirror then headed downstairs. She had just reached the great hall when one of Dathan's servants came rushing up.

"Your majesty," he said, bowing. "The patriarch asks if you would be kind enough to join him in his apartment."

"Of course," she answered. "I have one thing to check on and I will be right there." The man frowned. "Is anyone else with him?"

"The lord marshal was there when I left."

"Fine. I will be along in a moment."

She left him standing there and proceeded into the kitchen, where there was a great deal of bustling about. When asked what was going on, Opal said that the patriarch had ordered a meal for himself and his retinue. Everything was in order, and Elissa went in search of the chamberlain.

Job was in the dining hall, seeing to candles and firewood for the patriarch's apartment. Clearly, everything was under control and there was little reason to delay. Elissa set her steps toward the guest wing of the castle.

With so many gone, those halls were even quieter than the royal wing. The sound of her footsteps echoed back loudly. Perhaps it was her apprehension that made them seem so loud.

Although she had never visited him before, she knew the patriarch's apartment was midway down the main hall. A guard stood outside his door and he opened it as soon as Elissa neared him. Stepping inside, she immediately noted the blazing fire in the fireplace and how it had warmed the room already.

The great amount of furniture in the sitting room was sumptuous, mostly of darkly stained oak and red upholstery. An enormous desk sat near the left wall facing toward the center of the room. Behind it was a high-backed wooden chair; in front, two smaller chairs matching the one behind. Two red-upholstered settees faced each other in front of the fireplace, and four matching chairs sat against the walls. Other tables and smaller chairs were scattered about the room.

Geoffrey sat on one of the settees, staring into the fire. Had he not heard her enter?

"Lord Geoffrey," she said.

He turned, saw her, and jumped to his feet.

"Your majesty," he said with a bow. "I did not hear you come in."

"I guessed that," she said. "And where is the patriarch? He asked me to visit him, and I wanted to welcome him back to Winfield."

"He's in his bedroom changing from his travel clothes. He brought a sizable retinue with him." He said the latter with a raised eyebrow.

"So I guessed. The kitchen is very busy preparing a meal for them. Does he plan on their staying here in the castle?"

"No, he does not!" Dathan's voice boomed from the door-way to the bedroom.

Elissa turned and bowed her head slightly. His bow was deeper as was proper.

"I only wondered in case other preparations needed to be made," she said. "Job is preparing candles and having firewood gathered as we speak."

"Most of my people will stay at the monastery," Dathan said. "There is enough room for them there."

"Whatever is your pleasure, my lord," she said. "I did want to welcome you back. Your time away was very short."

"Hmph," he grumbled. "I left home the day after I got word you were sending the princess south. What in the world made you decide that? With whom did you consult?"

"Ethel is seven years old, my lord. It is time that she begin her training. She was also having some difficulty in adjusting to her father's absence. I thought it would be a good distraction for her to visit my family and see another part of the country. Lord Geoffrey and my uncle agreed."

"You did not make this decision on your own, then?"

"Why, of course not. I depend on the advice of our lord marshal. Just as my husband did."

Dathan gave her a sharp look, studying her face for a long moment, before looking toward Geoffrey lounging on the settee. He now knew one privy councilor she had aligned on her side. He was probably very sure most of the others would side with him.

He moved across the room and took the chair behind the desk. Elissa smiled inwardly. She knew that position made him feel that he dominated both the room and the conversation. Instead of taking one of the chairs in front of him, she sat in one of the upholstered chairs farther away, but facing him. He frowned but said nothing.

"How is the prince?" he asked.

"Quite well. He started his lessons in arms this morning."

"And whose idea was that?"

"Mine again. With the same approvals, of course. My Lord

Patriarch, I would have consulted with you on these decisions had you been here, but . . ." She left the thought hanging. "How was your trip and your visit home? I hope all is well with your lady wife."

"Yes, of course," he said dismissively. "There were several matters I needed to attend to. I am surprised you did not take the opportunity to return home, too, Lord Geoffrey."

"I did for a short while," Geoffrey said. He stood and walked to the fireplace. He placed a hand on the mantel and stared into the flames. "I did not want to leave the queen without any guidance at all, so I returned early." He and Elissa exchanged a meaningful look.

"We need to schedule the meeting to decide on a regent soon," Dathan said, oblivious to the exchange that had just taken place. "It will take some time to recall everyone."

"True," Geoffrey said. "We should probably send recall notices out in two weeks or so."

Dathan nodded. He even looked a bit smug, since he must feel certain that Quincy and Witram would side with him. That left Roric and Randall on one side, and Luther possibly undecided. He would probably work on gaining the old lord to his side and would possibly discuss the issue with Geoffrey to see how he actually felt. Dathan would hope that somehow he would be named regent himself. She shivered at the thought.

"What is it, your majesty?" Dathan asked, breaking off her reverie.

"Nothing, my lord. Just a chill."

She almost added, "As if someone had walked over my grave," but that would have been his cue to lecture her on proper beliefs. She hardly felt up to enduring that at the moment.

"Prince Edgar also needs to start lessons on religion," Dathan said. "Beliefs, ceremonies, all of the matters he will have to attend to as leader of his people."

"But he will not be crowned until his twelfth birthday," Elissa pointed out. "Surely there is plenty of time. It would be a shame to overwhelm him."

"He is to be king," Dathan said with mock patience. He leaned forward and placed his elbows on the top of the desk. "These matters are best left to us, your majesty."

A sharp retort rose to her tongue, but Geoffrey cut in.

"Hers is a mother's concern, my lord," he said. "Meanwhile, young Edgar's other studies progress well. Master Caedmon was most pleased with his first lesson in swordsmanship."

"Master Caedmon? He is teaching the prince?"

"Of course. He is the best there is. Would you have him learn from an inferior teacher?"

An argument ensued, the patriarch reminding the marshal of the falling-out between Ethelred and the arms instructor. From what he said, it was clear that he had no idea what the cause had been either. But whatever it was, in his mind it should preclude Edgar's being taught by a man his father would not approve of.

Geoffrey pointed out again that Caedmon was the best—look at how Ethelred had been skilled, both as a warrior and as a leader of armies. Surely even a king would set aside his own animosity to ensure that his son received the best training possible.

Dathan's arguments became weaker as he searched for something to bolster his opinion. At last he was forced to agree that the chosen course might be the best, but he would reserve judgement until results could be measured.

Elissa blessed the marshal not only for winning the argument, but also for sidetracking the argument that had nearly occurred between her and the patriarch. *A vital lesson in diplomacy learned,* she thought. Not that she had never learned any before—being a woman made that necessary. However, recent events had taxed her patience. She must continue to curb her tongue or her cause would be lost.

The two men began talking of other things relative to the government and selection of a regent. Every once in a while, Geoffrey would ask her opinion on something, making the patriarch frown slightly, although he said nothing. He must have decided that the marshal was simply being polite. For her own part, Elissa listened intently.

For the first time, she was privy to an official discussion relating to policy. There had been moments with Ethelred when he talked to her about something that had either upset or delighted him. Although she had always been interested, she had never had as much reason to listen so closely.

Suddenly, Geoffrey got to his feet.

"My lord," he said. "I beg your forgiveness. You must be tired after your long trip. I'm sure you need some rest."

"I am tiring," the patriarch said. "Thank you for your concern."

He stood in turn, but did not come around the desk.

"Your majesty," Geoffrey said, turning to her. "Shall we leave him to his rest?"

She nodded. "Thank you, my lord, for your advice," she said to Dathan. "Your wisdom is much needed in these matters."

He bowed his head, a pleased expression on his face. Geoffrey could hardly conceal his smile. The two men bowed to each other, Elissa bowed her head to the patriarch, and she and the marshal left the room.

As they neared the head of the stairs, Geoffrey said, "You did very well, your majesty."

"You, too, my lord. I have much to learn from you."

He smiled as they started down the stairs. "I am well practiced, not only in the art of government, but also in the art of handling Dathan. But don't be misled. No one wins with him all of the time. Even the king had to tread lightly. He has much power and prizes his position and authority."

"I know. Will he fall into step if he is not named regent?"

"If he has the right incentives. And they must be very good incentives, if he is to support you in that position."

"I doubt that he will ever support me."

"True." They had reached the first floor. Geoffrey stopped and he turned to her. "He will try to undermine your authority every step of the way before and after and during . . . You will have no peace. Consider this before you make the final commitment. If you do not feel that you can face that sort of pressure for years to come, back away.''

"My lord,'' she said, "this is for my children. There is no possibility of my backing away.''

She headed for the kitchen, intending to check on preparations once more. She watched Geoffrey walk away and fought back a tinge of anger. Everyone was telling her what to do. And it was so difficult to hold back her temper all of the time. So much was happening too quickly. She felt threatened at every turn. Felt that her children were threatened.

She missed Ethelred. More than anything, she missed the feeling of security he had given her. Why did he have to die in such a foolish accident?

Tears welled up in her eyes and flowed down her cheeks. She raced up the stairs and into her room. This time she did not try to stop the tears, and flung herself onto the bed, letting sobs shake her body for the first time.

10

Everyone had finally gathered in the dining hall, including the servants. It had been decided that Edgar would preside over the festivities. He sat at the head table, puffed up with pride. Elissa sat beside him, the first edges of concern for his attitude assailing her. The last thing she or Albor needed was a young prince who thought too much of himself.

However, now was not the time to deal with that. The kitchen staff was bringing out the dishes for the New Year's Eve celebration. There was roast pig, several guinea fowl, a lamb, stewed fruits, and peas; more than those at table could possibly eat. Most of the lords were still away, as was traditional, for this night was to show appreciation to the staff.

Also sitting at the head table were Dathan, Lord Geoffrey, and Lord Witram, recently returned from visiting Quincy. Everyone but Witram was in a gay mood, in spite of the so recent tragedy of their king's untimely death. This was a time to put the trials of the previous year behind them and move on to the new year. New hope. A new reign.

Except that Edgar looked so small in his father's grand chair, in spite of the boost from several pillows.

Elissa pushed that thought aside, determined to enjoy the

meal and the night's celebration. While they ate, musicians played in a far corner and jugglers amused the diners. After the meal, everyone except the royal family would open gifts. She had spent some time selecting gifts for the staff herself, but most had been purchased by the chamberlain. Job knew his staff well and always managed to select appropriate items. Also, they exchanged gifts among themselves, sometimes with great hilarity, as they shared inside jokes.

After that, the tables would be pushed to the sides, the musicians would mount the dais, and everyone would dance. It was her duty to be in attendance throughout the night, but she would see that Edgar went to bed, probably after he fell asleep in spite of himself.

She smiled over at him then checked the wine in his goblet to make sure it was watered enough. No need in his getting drunk along with everyone else.

She tasted her own mulled mead and considered getting a little drunk herself. She had not done so in a long time and had never done so in public. As a fairly new widow, would she be blamed? A widow of . . .

With a sharp intake of breath, she touched her hand to her breast. Tomorrow it would be a month since her husband had died. Did it seem longer? Too short a time? So much had happened and yet the effects of his death were still sharply felt. Her feelings had gone from certainty that her grief was for a man she had admired and cared for, but as a close friend, to knowing that she had truly loved him.

The evening progressed and she found herself caught up in the revelry. Between the antics of the jugglers and the guests at the table, Edgar laughed so hard that his sides hurt. Watching his pleasure was a balm for her battered spirit.

Nevertheless, her thoughts turned often to Ethel. Deward had planned to be in a large village by tonight where he had some friends. Messengers had been sent ahead asking if their party might stop and spend New Year's Eve and Day with them. She had made sure they took plenty of extra gifts and food for the celebration. She wondered if her daughter would persuade her great-uncle to let her open gifts tonight rather than in the morning. The seven-year-old was not only impatient about such things, but could also be quite persuasive, and Deward was so caring and thoughtful.

Yes, she would open them tonight. And probably wear the chatelaine to bed. Elissa smiled at the thought and caught Geoffrey looking at her. She nodded to him and concentrated on the food in front of her. As the meal wound down, gifts were exchanged and opened.

"Can't I open mine now?" Edgar asked.

"In the morning, dear," Elissa said. "We don't want to show everyone else up, do we?"

"No, Maman." He pouted for a short time, but eventually the continued antics of everyone around them had him laughing again.

It was nearly midnight when his chin touched his chest. Debris from the gift exchange lay scattered all around the hall. The musicians were playing and people danced. But when she rose to take her son to bed, everyone stopped. With smiles on their faces, they bowed and curtsied to her.

"Please, go on," she said. "Our prince is asleep and I will take him to bed. I will return momentarily."

With another bow and curtsey all around, the musicians resumed their play and the dancers resumed their antics. She bent to pick up her son, but Geoffrey intervened.

"I will carry him for you," he said.

"No need, my lord."

"I would like to."

She smiled and nodded her permission. She led the way out of the hall and up the stairs. Having seen them prepare to leave, Nurse had rushed ahead and had the bed ready to receive her charge. Geoffrey laid him on the bed and she began undressing him while Elissa watched.

"He ate a lot tonight," she said, remembering the sin-eating ceremony. "He may wake up with a bellyache."

Nurse nodded. "He probably will." She smiled down at him. "But he has a tough constitution."

"Yes, he does."

Once he was tucked in, she leaned down and kissed him on the forehead. "Good night, my prince," she said.

Geoffrey waited to escort her back to the dining hall. As they passed a window at the head of the stairs, she looked out.

"It's snowing."

He stepped closer to the window.

"Looks like quite a storm heading down from the north," he said.

"Tommy is out in that," she said.

They had both assumed that Geoffrey's agent in Ravelin had successfully gotten the messenger away from the castle two or three days ago. Elissa started down the stairs without another word.

Verald was throwing a royal fit. Trevor and Galen stood on either side of their father looking down at everyone else with expressions almost of glee. The lords and knights in the audience chamber tried to be as unobtrusive as possible, but the king knew whom to blame, even in his rage.

So far, only the guard outside the Alboran's room had been punished, as much for lying as for letting the prisoner escape. How did he expect anyone to believe that another person had sneaked up on him from behind in the night? Who would betray Verald?

No one, that was who.

The party of soldiers that was sent out to track down the fugitive had come back empty-handed after less than a day. Whatever tracks there had been disappeared under the new snowfall. He knew that was more than likely. Still it threw him into a renewed rage.

Then there was the theft of the prized horse, the one that once belonged to Lord Niall. Verald had prized him above all the others in his stable.

The king sat on his throne and shook his head. He had badly misjudged this messenger from Albor. Everyone had considered him something of a bumbler and a fool. However, what did his escape actually mean? Not much in the overall scheme of things.

He could not have had access to any sensitive information, nor could he have anything derogatory to say, except that he was locked in his room while the queen's message was deliberated. It was the priest messenger, who would return to Winfield when the roads were more passable, who carried damaging information.

What fools these Alborans were.

"Timothy, dismiss everyone," Verald ordered. "Niall, Tully, Aubrey, stay awhile."

Some of the councilors were home to celebrate New Year's. Among those remaining, questions had been raised again about young Niall's loyalty. Especially since the stolen horse had been taken from him by the king for a debt his father had owed. His was a very old noble family, although they had fallen on hard times in the past generation or two. Still, Verald trusted him as much as he trusted anyone. If only the younger generation had been raised with the same values his own generation had. He looked at his elder son, counting him and his brother among those and blamed their mother as he always did.

The room was cleared and Timothy bowed on his way out. The room fell silent except for the rustling of velvets as the three councilors moved up the steps of the dais.

"Has the copy of the queen's letter been made?" Verald asked.

"Yes, your majesty," Aubrey replied. "The priest will leave with it as soon as the roads are better."

"Good. Dathan can do with it what he will. Before that, we will send a reply to the queen ourselves, stating that we will send one of our sons to marry her. That should cover up the entry of the army into her lands."

"It will take all winter and spring to prepare for this invasion," Aubrey said.

"We can't move until late spring anyway," Niall reminded him. "The roads will only get worse once the thaw begins."

He knew his sons did not care about the marriage, except as a means of gaining power of their own. Verald did not worry much about his sons. Neither of them had the nerve to try to usurp their father without the help of their mother, who had encouraged them to rebel in the past. But as long as he kept them with him in the castle, there were no opportunities to plot against him.

ॐ 11 ॐ

Elissa supervised the preparations of the room, especially the fire in the fireplace. Not that the servants did not know what they were doing, but since word came back that Tommy had been found and that he was in a bad way, she had to keep herself busy doing something.

She was in the midst of refluffing the pillows on the bed when she heard voices in the hallway. She went to the door and looked out. Halfway down, two men carried a very limp Tommy between them. She bit her lower lip. She had sent him to his doom. A faithful servant. A good man. And if he lived, she would never hear the end of it.

Elissa pushed the door fully open and stepped back to give them room to enter. Behind her, the maids had started pouring warm water into the large tub. Job and the physician both had instructed that it be just warm to the touch. If the equerry's limbs were frozen, hot water or cold water would do more damage. She had to rely on their knowledge, never having faced such a problem herself.

The men placed him on the bed and the queen turned her back as servants undressed him. He moaned several times, the loudest being when they lowered him into the tub. The splash of water told Elissa it was safe for his modesty for her to turn around.

Tommy's face was so white. The tub was not overly deep and she saw for the first time how little hair he had on his chest. The men maneuvered him lower into the water until only his shoulders and head showed. After a moment his eyes flickered open, and he blinked.

"I told you not to wake me," he said in a strong voice.

"He's not so bad off," Job said with a smile in Elissa's direction.

She relaxed for the first time since she had received word that he was quite ill from being trapped in the snowstorm. She smiled down at him. He would be fine now, although it was still possible he would lose some toes. It was better than losing his life.

"Your majesty."

Elissa turned toward the serving girl who spoke. She had Tommy's clothes draped over one arm and held out a piece of paper in the other hand.

"This was in the inner pocket," the girl said.

Elissa thanked the girl and took the paper. On the outside, someone had penned "Geoffrey, Marshal, Albor." The wax seal bore no mark to indicate who might have sent it.

Should she resist the temptation to open it herself? The girl could not read and had no idea to whom it was addressed. No one had seen the exchange.

No, it was not a good idea. All of her efforts were aimed at winning the marshal's trust. Reading his letter was certainly no way to go about it.

But would he tell her what the letter said? The handwriting was not Tommy's—he was illiterate. She did not for a moment doubt that it must be from Geoffrey's spy in the court at Ravelin. Regardless of who wrote it, she should get it to the marshal as soon as possible.

She moved to the tub and knelt down. Tommy's eyes fluttered open again.

"Your majesty," he said and made as if to rise. "My horse . . ."

She put her hand on his shoulder.

"No, no, Tommy," she said. "Your horse will be taken care of. Rest and get well. I will leave you to their kind ministrations." She motioned around at the servants and physician. "I will come again tomorrow. Rest well. You are a good man."

He smiled and nodded, but the smile faded from his face quickly. His eyes closed and he would have slipped completely under the water if Job had not grabbed hold of his arm. The chamberlain started to apologize for having splashed water on her sleeve, but she told him not to worry about it. She stood and looked around at everyone. There were three serving girls, a physician, Job, and two manservants. Surely that was enough to pull Tommy through.

"I will be back tomorrow," Elissa repeated to them. "Do whatever it takes to make him well again."

"Yes, majesty," Job said. The rest bobbed curtsies and bowed.

With that, she turned and left the room, clutching the letter in her hand, and went in search of Geoffrey.

Not finding him in any of his usual haunts, she sent one of the servants to seek him out. As she waited in her sitting room, she turned the letter over and over in her hands. Finally, she propped it up on the mantel and picked up a piece of needlepoint she had been working on for nearly two years.

Although she enjoyed needlework when it went well, her tolerance for it when things did not was very low. Picking out mistakes was a mindless enough chore when she needed to wait. Very carefully, she undid a series of stitches with the needle. The repair was nearly finished when a knock came on the door. Clara appeared from her room to open it.

Geoffrey entered, his clothes a bit disheveled, a touch of dirt on his forehead and cheek.

"You wished to see me?" he said with a bow.

"Yes, Marshal." She started to retrieve the letter, but

stopped. With her hands on hips, she looked him up and down. "What in the world have you been doing?" she asked.

"I went to see what was going on when your Tommy was brought back," he said with a grin. "That horse he was riding was the largest I've ever seen, and I wanted to get a close look at him. Anyway, he was weak—seemed as if he could hardly walk. But when the lads tried to get him into a stall, he raised a terrible ruckus. It took me and six other men to control him. I suspect he was half mad from hunger, thirst, and the cold. He knocked me about pretty good and some of the others too."

"Well, you certainly look the worse for wear." She laughed. "Is the horse all right?"

"I think so. We tired him out finally."

"You suffered no broken bones, I hope."

"No, just a few scuffs and perhaps a bruise or two."

She reached up for the letter and brought it to him.

"Tommy had this in his pocket," she said, handing it over. "It's addressed to you."

Geoffrey's smile faded and he took the letter. He looked at his name written on the outside and the seal. Turning it over, he inspected the other side.

"I did not open it," she said.

"I didn't think you had."

"Don't think too well of me. I was sorely tempted."

"I would have been, too."

He smiled at her and she was glad that she had resisted the temptation. He looked down for another instant, hesitant to break the seal, perhaps fearing bad news. Elissa was not sure how it could be good news.

He broke the seal and unfolded the piece of paper. She returned to her seat while he read, picked up the tapestry, but then dropped it in her lap. Geoffrey was silent behind her and she wished heartily for a clue as to what the letter contained.

He sighed heavily and she heard the crackle of paper as he refolded the letter. Holding it in his hand, he sat in the other chair, his expression grave.

"It's from Niall. My contact in Verald's court. Your letter—the one you sent to Verald—has disappeared. No one in Verald's castle admits to knowing where it is."

"Who might have stolen it?" she asked in alarm.

He frowned at her.

"Yes, I know," she said, exasperated. "There must be a dozen or more who would have liked to get their hands on it."

She dropped the tapestry on top of the basket in which it was usually stored.

"Does your man say anything else?"

"He says that there is a real debate going on about what to do. Verald is of a mind to take you at your word and send one of his sons, or maybe even come himself. Others believe it's a trap. And still others think it's a wonderful time to think about a spring invasion."

Elissa jumped to her feet and began pacing. "What a fool I was to send that letter. It has started them thinking, and Albor could be in real danger. And now, the letter may be in anyone's hands."

"Even someone here," Geoffrey said.

"Here?"

"There are other spies in Ravelin. Probably others from Albor."

"Who else would send spies there?"

"Dathan for one. Roric for another. Maybe even Witram."

"Did Ethelred know about your spy?" she asked.

"Of course. He wasn't just my spy. I set it all up, but at the king's request. We have a whole spy network with agents in the capitals of every country that borders Albor and a few more distant."

"I never knew," she said. "Maybe I was a fool to think I could rule Albor until Edgar is of age."

"Don't start doubting yourself now. Ethelred believed in you."

"Did he? Or was it the fever and pain after all?"

She thought of his jest when Edgar was only two. Ethelred

must have remembered too. Why else would he have named her? Had it been another joke when he called her name on his deathbed? A joke being played on her and all of the nobles in his court, members of the Privy Council, even on Geoffrey, his best friend.

But she knew that he would not have intentionally put his country in danger by naming a weak or ineffective regent. Surely he had believed that she would make a good regent. Maybe even a wise ruler.

But by naming his queen, the patriarch, Roric, Randall, and all the others would rally behind Geoffrey, if they thought that the best way to unseat her.

"What are you thinking?" Geoffrey asked softly.

Elissa faced him, feeling almost guilty at the thoughts that had been roaming inside her head. She smiled. They were co-conspirators now, it would seem, so she might as well tell him her thoughts.

"If Ethelred believed in me, it was probably only that he felt I would be flattered at being named regent. He always saw me as a woman, my lord. And like the rest of you northerners, he viewed women as rather incapable creatures, no matter how much we might accomplish all around you."

"And that means . . . ?"

"That means he is still pulling our strings even though he is dead. He knew that, being flattered, I would accept the responsibility of regent. Perhaps I would even believe the privy councilors would not balk because it was his will. He knew how they would react, however."

She went on to tell him her thoughts of bringing the lords to work together behind the marshal in deposing her from the very position he had given her. Geoffrey listened thoughtfully.

"If he had named you outright, all of the others would have fought you, each in his own way," she continued. "But I am a threat of a different kind, a threat to their male egos. And to be rid of me, they would work together, which is exactly what he wanted them to do."

He remained thoughtful when she had finished. She resumed her seat, picked up the tapestry, and began working on the bad stitches again. If her powers included foretelling the future, she would . . .

Knowing would not matter. Nothing could change one's future as it was laid out by the Lady of the forest.

"So, how do we make his decision work for us instead?"

"You believe me?" she asked, surprised by that.

"It makes good sense. Especially knowing what I do about Ethelred. You are right. Although he loved you, even trusted you, would he have believed you could rule his country?"

He went to the table and poured himself some wine. She said yes when he asked if she would like some mead. He returned to his chair and handed her the goblet.

"I had thought of being regent," he resumed. "I still want to be regent. However, he named you on his deathbed and I will not have a mockery made of that. Not even by him."

"There may be little choice."

"We will work at it, you and I, and see if we can't find a way."

"Why?"

She took a drink of the mead, let it warm her throat as she swallowed. Once more she thought about getting drunk.

"Let's just say that it's a challenge and I never turn away from a challenge."

He smiled and winked. At that moment, she felt less alone and more hopeful than she had in some time.

Shouts came from behind the huge door. King Verald and his closest advisers, including his elder son, were arguing over the different plans for the spring. Niall paused in the corridor, wishing he could hear the words as well as the voices. But sometimes he was not admitted into the inner sanctums. His family had fallen into disfavor and near poverty. Once, they had been rich in lands and money, and had wielded power and influence. They had been close to the throne, although without any legitimate claim to it. Being close had been enough.

Niall had inherited a castle, a few acres of land surrounding it, and a place on the Council. The rest had been sold off bit by bit years before. When asked, Leonidas, the then king and Verald's grandfather, had refused to come to their aid, and the family had sunk lower, nearly losing its place on the Council and the respect of all others of the nobility.

Upon inheriting, Niall had dedicated himself to his own interests at the expense of the crown's. When the Alboran representative came to him with an offer, how could he refuse? The disloyalty of spying for another kingdom did not dissuade him. He was merely repaying disloyalty in like coin.

However, things had tightened in Ravelin these days. Some members of the Council were sometimes excluded from deliberations. Niall no longer believed in any kind of loyalty. Look at the Alboran queen, for instance. Ready to sell out her country just to hold on to what she had.

He would wager that even the lord marshal of Albor could be bought, in spite of his reputation as an honest man. Honest men in these times were fools, and Geoffrey was no fool. Niall could not help wondering how long he would be loyal to Ethelred's widow.

Here in Ravelin, Niall had made friends with Prince Galen, who also felt alienated. As the younger son, his future was not assured, and he had only recently been recalled to court.

The sound of footsteps coming up the corridor brought him out of his reverie and he resumed his way past the door. The ever-vigilant Timothy rounded the corner ahead.

"Lord Niall, what brings you to this part of the castle?" he asked as they came abreast.

"I was checking to see if the meeting was over. I wanted to speak to Verald for a moment."

"Oh? About something important?"

"I would not bother the king with something unimportant," he said.

"Perhaps you could tell me and I could bring it to the king for you."

"I'll wait. It may be important, but it isn't urgent."

Niall nodded to Timothy and went on his way. This was worrisome, but possibly no more than that. He had never given anyone reason to think that he was anything but loyal. He had been very careful.

Except for the horse on which Queen Elissa's agent had escaped. Arranging that was a touch of petty vengeance that was satisfying if dangerous. Also, there was the original of her letter that had disappeared. No one knew he had taken it, or even suspected him. Not even Geoffrey of Albor, to whom the news of its disappearance must have been disturbing.

Niall went into the great hall, where a roaring fire was kept going at all times in winter. Because the fireplace in his own room was small and wood was not plentiful, it was always chilly in his apartment. He stood with his back to the fire, absorbing as much warmth as he could stand.

He would have to be very careful from here on. No suspicion must fall on him. His only task in life was to make sure he got as much of this world for himself as he could, and to make others pay for it.

~ 12 ~

The worst storm of the winter raged outside. Snow fell thickly, and the wind moaned around corners of the castle. Inside, however, there was great activity. Nearly everyone had managed to return from the holidays before the storm hit and the rooms were full. Servants who had complained of nothing to do for weeks now complained of never getting any rest. At the moment, Elissa was checking on things in the kitchen.

Although she enjoyed the renewed activity, Elissa chafed at the need to be more careful in planning her own activities—especially her visits to Caedmon's academy. There was so much to oversee now and so many eyes watching her comings and goings that she had difficulty leaving the castle without comment.

So far, she had managed to get to the academy every day, although she could see disapproval in the councilors' eyes. They mumbled that she should leave overseeing such things to a man. When an argument ensued over who that man should be, she shrugged, and pointed out to them that they could not agree and that Edgar was her son, after all. Embarrassed by their own foolishness, they had given in.

Her biggest regret was the lack of sufficient time to practice her other skills. Elissa had reached the point where she could accomplish some of the things by voicing the correct words. However, while the spell worked, she was always under the impression that she floated above everything.

Something else had happened, too. Something that, like her magic, no one knew but herself. Something bewildering, even frightening.

Her womanly monthly cycle had ceased.

Her first thought was that Ethelred had left her with child, something that in itself was inconvenient at best. However, when she counted backward, the days did not add up. Like her mother, she had always been regular.

There was no one she could ask or talk to about it. She thought she remembered hearing that a tragedy or great emotional upset could interfere with a woman's cycle, and she had certainly suffered that. She could only hope that was the cause and everything would be right in time.

Millie entered the kitchen and approached Elissa. The girl had been stationed outside the Council chamber today to take the men's orders for food and drink. Although she was dull witted in some things, she was eager and willing to serve, and somehow always managed to execute her instructions correctly. She was one of those eternally pleasant people with whom the councilors could surely find no fault.

"What is it, Millie?"

"They're wanting lunch, majesty."

"Go tell Opal they are ready. She has everything prepared for them."

"Yes, majesty."

The girl curtsied and scurried off. The grin on her face was a clear indication that she enjoyed her responsibility. Elissa wished that she could say the same for herself, but being busy did keep her from worrying over what the councilors were saying. Or not saying.

No word had come out of their meetings for three days. She had not been sent for. And when they came out in the evenings, none of them said a thing that she had heard. She had caught Dathan looking at her oddly once or twice. And Roric and Randall always stared at her during dinner.

Eating together in the dining hall was a long tradition when the Privy Council was in session. She wondered if it was to let everyone keep an eye on each other. There was less chance of people talking too much about what went on behind closed doors when everyone was present to see and hear who said what to whom. It had also made it very difficult to speak alone with Geoffrey. Even when they had met—in a hall or moving through a room—he had shown no inclination to speak to her.

Seeing that everything was all right in the kitchen, Elissa started toward her own apartment. Perhaps she could concentrate on the words of magic for the rest of the day for a change. She had just passed through the doorway into the dining hall when one of Dathan's priests stopped her.

"They request your presence in the Council chamber after they have finished lunch," he informed her.

"I will be there," she responded. "Send someone to my apartments when they are ready."

"Yes, majesty."

He bowed and went back the way he had come.

She felt suddenly light-headed, and just managed to move to a chair and collapse into it. The moment had arrived when she must state her case. Those she could count on were Geoffrey, and Lord Witram. She hoped Lord Quincy had let himself be convinced by his friend, Witram. Roric, Randall, and Dathan would be against her. If all of this were true, Lord Luther's vote would be the deciding one. He was unpredictable, his behavior becoming more bizarre the older he got.

She stood on legs that were still shaky, but they got stronger as she walked. Her stomach growled. She needed something to eat. She had eaten only a little at breakfast, but her stomach did not feel as if it could handle food at the moment. She thought there was some dried fruit still in her sitting room, in case she felt the need when she got there.

She looked down at her skirts and quickened her pace. She must change out of the everyday work dress, and put on her best gown. No, maybe her second best. Oh, why hadn't she made that decision before?

Because part of her had never believed the Council would call her in. The possibility had seemed so remote, in spite of all her efforts, that it was a surprise. Now she must get ready.

She called for Clara the moment she entered her sitting room.

"Get my dark blue gown out," she instructed.

She was already undoing the dress she had on by the time Clara appeared. While she finished undressing, the maid opened the chest and got out the gown and the items that went with it.

"What is it, majesty," she asked as she searched for the shoes.

"I've been called to the Privy Council meeting. This is very important, Clara. They will be deciding whether I will be named regent or not. Everything must be just right."

Clara stared at her a moment and Elissa marked that in passing. The girl must think her mad to even consider such a thing. She recovered herself momentarily and helped her mistress to dress.

"Is the dried fruit still here from this morning?"

"Yes, majesty."

"Get it for me, please."

Elissa sat in the chair at her little table and Clara set the dish in front of her. She started redressing the queen's hair.

"Make sure the hairpiece is firmly attached. It would be too embarrassing if my hair fell off in the Council chamber."

Elissa smiled, but Clara said nothing. What in the world ailed the girl?

When the knock came on the door, Elissa had been ready for what seemed half an hour. Even in that length of time, however, she had been able to eat only a few bites of dried apple and peach. She had wanted to have some warm mead, but decided it would be best to remain as clearheaded as possible.

She managed to precede the priest who came to summon

her. It seemed important that it not appear that she was being led into the presence of the councilors. Led to her possible death was more like it.

Be positive, she told herself over and over as they made their way to the first-floor Council chamber. A guard outside opened the door and admitted her. Each councilor sat in his accustomed place—they were such creatures of habit.

Seeing that no other chair had been provided for her at the table, she hesitated only a moment before taking the chair that had been reserved for the king. Looks passed among the councilors. Even Geoffrey appeared nonplussed, but she was sure it was not because of her choice of seat. Things must not have been going well, and that meant something new may have been added to the pot.

"Your majesty," Dathan was the first to speak. "While discussing the possibility of your appointment as regent to guide the young prince through his minor years, some disturbing information has come to us."

"Disturbing, my lord patriarch?"

"Yes, indeed," he said. He put his fingertips together and looked at her over them. "It seems . . . Well, how can I put this delicately? We men are so unaccustomed to discussing such things."

"It seems," Randall piped up, "that you have dishonored the memory of your husband the king."

"And how have I done that, my lord?" she asked mildly. Her stomach rolled over and her heart pounded.

"It seems that you are with child, my dear," Dathan said in his most honeyed voice. "We have word that your monthly cycle has ceased."

How could they have found out? She had only realized it herself a few days before. And only one other person would have the slightest clue—Clara. But that she would have told anyone seemed not only remote but bizarre.

Geoffrey looked at her as if she had betrayed him, and she realized that he believed she had lain with another man. All of her hopes and plans were about to slip away.

"I assure you, my lords, that I am not with child. I have lain with no man since the death of my husband, the king. And the days are wrong for him to have fathered another child within me."

"Do you admit that your monthly cycle has ceased?"

"It is not unheard of for that to happen when a woman has undergone physical or emotional trauma."

Dathan laughed out loud.

"There can be no other explanation for such an occurrence. You are with child. As an adulteress, we could have you burned at the stake."

How could they even think of going that far?

"Have me examined by the physician," she said. "He can tell if there is a babe within me."

"There's no need—" Randall began.

"We owe her that much," Geoffrey said, cutting him off. "We must be absolutely sure before we take any final steps in this matter."

They argued further for a few minutes and it was finally decided to have Elissa examined by the physician the next day.

"Until he has done so," Dathan said, "a guard will be put on your rooms so that you have no opportunity to do harm to yourself or the life that you carry."

"As you wish, my lord," she said with a slight bow.

There was no use in arguing with him on anything at that moment. The man had his mind made up.

Two guards were summoned to escort her to her apartment. They stationed themselves in her sitting room at Dathan's orders, and she tried to act as if nothing untoward were happening. Instead of going to Edgar's room to say good night, he was brought to her.

"Why can't you come to tuck me in?" he asked petulantly. It was the first time she had not done so.

"Ah, my little man," she said and folded him in her arms. "Your maman has some things she just has to do tonight. I promise to give you double kisses tomorrow night."

"All right," he said. "But don't forget!"

"I won't. I promise."

A ewer of mulled mead was brought with supper and she made herself eat and drink. Before she finished, Geoffrey appeared at the door.

"Won't you join me for supper, my lord?" she invited.

"Thank you, your majesty. I would enjoy that."

He dismissed the guards, saying that his presence would prevent anything from happening. They should get some dinner while he was there, he said. They left quite willingly at that.

"Is it wise, Lord Geoffrey, for you to be alone with me?"

"I have to take that chance."

"They might think you are the one who fathered this imaginary child I'm carrying."

"No doubt the idea has already occurred to the patriarch."

He went to the sideboard and poured himself some mead. He was clearly restless and out of sorts, and she kept a surreptitious eye on him as she continued eating. She thought he would never say what was on his mind, but she waited.

Clara popped in every so often, asking if there was anything they needed. Finally, Elissa sent her for some wine for the lord marshal. For herself, she was tired of waiting for him to speak his mind.

"Now, sir. What is it you want to say?"

He looked her full in the face, his expression full of thunder.

"Is it true?"

The words came out between lips held so tightly she wondered that they could escape at all. It was not surprising that he wondered, in spite of everything she had done to earn his trust.

"You mean, am I with child?"

"Of course that is what I mean."

She put down the chicken leg she had been about to bite into, leaned back in her chair, and wiped her hands on the piece of cloth she used for a napkin.

"No, I am not with child."

"Then how could this . . . this woman-thing happen? How could Dathan have found out?"

"What I said about trauma is quite true, my lord. I have only missed a single cycle. As for how he found out, there is only one other person who is close enough to me to have any inkling about this. And I just sent her to find you some wine."

"Clara?"

"Of course, Clara."

"But I thought she was devoted to you. She has been your personal maid for . . . well, for years."

"I thought . . ."

Elissa stopped then and actually thought about her relationship with the girl. She had been appointed as her maid only five years earlier, after Megan died. Good old faithful Megan, who had come with her from the south, and who had been her maid ever since she was mature enough to have one. The last thing she had wanted was to spend her final days in the cold north, but she had come anyway.

Becoming her personal maid had been a definite improvement for Clara. The girl liked to talk and there had been times when Elissa was convinced the girl was ambitious. Now, she would have to be dismissed as soon as matters had settled down. She told Geoffrey that and he agreed.

"If she's the one who told Dathan, then you certainly do not want her in your household, much less as your personal maid. Will the physician be convinced that you are not pregnant?"

"If he does an honest examination and knows what he is doing, he will. I only hope Dathan has not been able to buy his honesty."

Geoffrey thought a moment.

"We will have to find a second physician then. One who has had no contact with anyone at court for some time."

The door opened and Clara returned with a pitcher of wine. She poured him a goblet full and set the pitcher on the sideboard.

"I won't be needing you for a while, Clara," Elissa said.

"Why don't you go downstairs and visit with the others?"

"Yes, majesty," she said with a curtsey, and left the apartment again.

"I suppose the guards will be back soon," Elissa said. She pushed the tray of food away and took a deep drink of the mead. "Somehow I don't think this is the only thing Dathan has up his sleeve."

"What else?"

The look of suspicion returned to Geoffrey's face.

"The encounter with Randall here in my sitting room that night you rescued me from him. He could easily tell everyone that I lured him in here, and when you appeared, I had to accuse him of accosting me."

"He could at that. Especially after this first accusation."

"And if they have learned about this 'woman thing,' who's to say they have not learned about the sword training? Everything together would be most damaging if it's revealed before I am ready."

Geoffrey put his booted feet up on the footstool, near the fire.

"If they are desperate enough to accuse me of adultery, they might even make accusations of witchcraft against me. Anything to degrade my reputation and perhaps to have my head."

"But as long as the accusations are not true, we can fight them. Prove they are lies made up by desperate men."

"Sometimes there needn't be proof, my lord. Sometimes the accusation itself is enough to destroy the person at whom it is aimed."

She went to the sideboard and poured herself more mead. The poker had been left to heat in the fire and she banged it against the stone of the fireplace to knock off the ashes. The mead sizzled when she put the hot metal in to warm it. Carefully, she replaced the poker with the end in the fire. She might want more mead before this night was done.

An examination like the one she would have to endure in the morning was one of the most unpleasant things she had ever experienced in the past. No doubt the technique had not improved any. And if Geoffrey could find a second physician in time, she would have to endure it twice. Better that than feeling the fire or a headsman's axe, though.

"Is there anything else they could find out?" he asked earnestly. "Anything they could use against you?"

"Not that I can think of, my lord."

He frowned.

"There is the matter of my hair," she said softly.

"Your hair? Oh, yes. It must still be very short. Does Clara know about this?"

"Yes. I could not pin it on and style it myself."

"Then it is very possible that Dathan knows . . . and the other Councilors."

"I'm afraid so."

"They will make use of this, make no mistake."

"I know."

She took a sip of mead. It had cooled and she wanted to warm it again, but did not have the energy to get up. Had she managed to give Dathan and the others all the ammunition they needed to destroy her hopes and the future of her children? Every time he surprised the other councilors with some new piece of information about her, they cooled toward her even more.

She needed the element of surprise. Somehow, she must . . .

"What if I'm the one who shows them tomorrow?" she asked.

"Shows them what? Your hair?"

"Yes."

"Why on earth would you do that?"

"To take the element of surprise away from Dathan and the others. Perhaps show them how serious I am about this. So serious that I sacrificed my beautiful hair so that I could learn to lead Albor's armies if need be. So serious that I take lessons to learn how to use a sword, not only to make myself a worthy warrior, but also as an example to Edgar."

"I doubt that the situation could be much worse than it is

right now," he said with a note of resignation in his voice. "Wait until the physicians have given their diagnosis."

He rose to leave.

"You can abandon me now, if you wish," she said, thinking the idea must have occurred to him.

"No, I cannot. I've made my choice and I will stand behind it."

"Well, there is one consolation."

"What?"

"If I am totally discredited by the time this is all over, they will not blame you. They will say I cast a spell on you, and you will be forgiven."

"I know," he said. "But I don't like to lose."

"Neither do I."

He smiled at her, bowed, and left the room. She stirred up the fire. A few minutes later, Clara reappeared. She must have been watching for Geoffrey to leave as her cue to return. Her manner was almost timid and Elissa suspected she might wonder if her duplicity had been discovered. For now, there would be no recriminations. When the right time came, however, there would be more than that.

Elissa let Clara undress her and help her into her nightdress. She was very tired, but knew sleep would be long in coming, if it came at all.

Tomorrow was going to be a very bad day. Anger at her predicament overwhelmed her as she lay in the dark watching the light from the fire play on the walls. Anger at herself, anger at the councilors, anger at men in general. But most of all, anger at Ethelred. Damn him for dying and leaving her with young children to raise and protect. Damn him for leaving her unprotected. Damn him for dying so suddenly that there was no time to prepare. And damn him for the emptiness of the bed beside her.

~ 13 ~

For once the day dawned sunny and bright. The storm must have passed during the night, leaving the world colder than Elissa ever remembered it.

Clara had brought her good news first thing: a letter had arrived from Ethel. Elissa could not imagine how a messenger could have gotten through that storm, but she was glad he had. She sat in bed propped up by pillows and read the letter.

It was short and the small, childish scrawl was sometimes difficult to read, but Elissa knew her daughter's hand. She was enjoying her newfound responsibilities and the tasks she'd been given. Even more, Ethel enjoyed being treated as a grown-up, although she complained about still having to wear her little girl's clothes and going to bed so early at night.

They don't understand that I am a big girl now, she wrote. *My maman said so. Didn't you, maman? Going to bed before nine is for little girls. And little boys, like Edgar. How is Edgar? Does he miss me? He's too mean to, I guess.*

Heaven forbid that she should admit she missed her little brother. However, at the end she included him in the hugs and kisses that followed her signature: *Ethel PR,* for "Princess Royal."

Elissa started to give the letter to Clara to take to Edgar, but decided to go by his room on her way downstairs. If the guards would allow her to, that is. Two new ones had replaced the night guards in the sitting room. Their noises had wakened her very early and for several minutes she could not imagine what the ruckus was. Then, in her sleepy stupor, the memories of yesterday were recalled in a rush.

Fear was the first emotion she felt. It washed over her in a flood and she thought of running away. It was so much more sensible than staying. The greatest fear she felt came when she remembered that Geoffrey had seemed to side with the other councilors for a time. His sense of self-preservation was eventually tempered by his sense of loyalty and fair play. Or she guessed that was what lay behind his refound confidence in her.

The seeds of that confidence had sprouted in rocky ground and were having a tough time finding the soil in which to grow. He and she were trying to accomplish something unheard of in generations. She knew the history and legends of more matriarchal societies, but they had all been overwhelmed by patriarchy, either by internal forces, or through invasion.

She rang for Clara again. "I will wear my red dress today," she instructed.

"Your breakfast is on the tray," the maid reminded her.

"I'll eat some while you fix my hair."

She threw the covers aside and shivered as Clara helped her into her warmed robe. She splashed water in her face, both to refresh herself and to wash sleep from her eyes. It was cooler than usual this morning. The cold of the night permeated the whole room. Or was it more the effect of possible doom hanging over her?

"When will the physicians arrive for the examination?" Clara asked.

"Sometime this morning. I will dress after they leave. But my hair must be done before they get here."

"Of course," Clara said.

She filled her mistress's cup as Elissa sat down at the dress-

ing table, then began pinning up the short hair in preparation
for setting the hairpiece in place. Elissa only ate a little of the
dried fruit, but the bread was fresh and still slightly warm. The
cheese tasted buttery, and combined with the bread, quickened
her appetite, something she would have said was impossible a
few moments earlier.

Clara finished pinning the hairpiece in place and they both
studied the result in the mirror. She had braided the long hair,
then woven the large end in with the other hair at the nape of
her neck. As usual, it looked completely natural and was a
style that would do well during the coming examinations.

"Thank you, Clara." Elissa stood, picked up the cup, and
sat in the chair in front of the fireplace. "Make sure the guards
have something to eat and drink, if they haven't broken their
fast already. Get the dress ready for me to put on later. I am
assuming the examination will take place on my own bed, so
I will wait here beside the fire. Once the physician arrives, I
want you to leave the room. When it's over, come back and
help me dress."

"Yes, majesty," Clara said and curtsied.

Elissa picked up a book and tried to read, but her mind
would not grasp the words her eyes had trouble seeing. When
the knock came on the outer door, she jumped, her heartbeat
quickening, and she nearly dropped the book.

She heard Clara open the door and greet the physician in
the sitting room. One of them told the guards they could go
until summoned. The door closed, and she assumed the maid
had left with them.

However, it was Clara who escorted two men into the bedroom. Geoffrey had been busy during the night.

Each wore a black cloak marked with the symbols of his
profession in gold thread, a sign they were on serious business.
One she did not recognize and she guessed he was sent by
Geoffrey. He was as old as Aldwin, the royal physician, whose
services she had rejected on more than one occasion, including
the births of her children. He had been in the room as a witness, but she preferred the midwife who was summoned from

back home. She was a woman and understood such things as childbirth.

The two men bowed to her. Their faces were solemn, but the stranger had a twinkle in his eye, as if he did not quite take this seriously. He introduced himself as Isak, and explained that it had been decided he would participate in the initial examination, rather than conduct a separate one.

"Would you not like to have your maid stay with you, your majesty?" he asked. "She may be of some comfort to you."

"No. I would prefer that no one else see my humiliation." And she no longer trusted the girl.

"Very well." He motioned for Clara to leave.

When the three of them were alone, Aldwin approached the queen.

"I would prefer this was not necessary," he said.

"Not as much as I, sir." She got to her feet. "I expect you want me on the bed."

"Yes, please. You may keep your clothes on. We will push them out of the way once you are comfortable."

Taking a deep breath, Elissa went to the bed and lay down.

An unusual quiet seemed to fill the castle. People she passed in the halls and on the stairs bowed or curtsied silently, as if afraid to speak to her until her innocence was proven. She did not doubt that everyone knew what had transpired in the morning. She could hardly walk.

When they were finished, she had stood arranging her nightclothes in a more decent way. The stranger winked at her and both left without a word. She had hoped they would tell her their findings before they left, but realized she would learn them from the councilors.

When Clara returned to help her dress, she also brought a message that the Council would reconvene at one in the afternoon. That gave her time to clean herself, for she had found that Aldwin's none-too-tender methods had made her bleed.

Damn him! Damn them all!

She was queen and should not be subjected to such handling.

Yet she could not refuse. Too much was at stake: her kingdom, her children, herself. And the reputation of the one man who believed in her.

She shook her head, then made as if she needed to straighten her collar when a courtier looked at her oddly as she passed.

She wanted to trust Geoffrey. She had to trust someone. Would that her uncle had some power in this court, but he was a southerner and none from that part of the country had much say. Once she was in charge, he would, by the Lady.

The two guards followed at a discreet distance as she turned down the hall toward the Council chamber. They had returned to her apartment about the same time as Clara, their expressions blank. She did wonder what they thought of all this. Would it be possible to win them to her side some way?

What was she going to do, win over the army two soldiers at a time? No, it would have to be all or nothing. The shame of it was, most of the councilors would never back her wholeheartedly. They would fight her every day. Excepting possibly Witram, but his gratitude at not being imprisoned would turn to bitterness one day. That she was sure of.

There was no way to replace them either. Their places on the Council were set by Alboran law: the richest and most powerful lords of the realm were to sit as advisors to the king.

A guard opened the door for her to enter, and she stepped inside. All of the councilors were present. Once more the chair at the head of the table was empty and she sat there.

No one spoke. She looked from one face to another. If they expected her to fear facing them, they had better guess again. Most of them looked tense. From that she guessed they had not had a report from the physicians yet.

A few minutes later, the door opened again and the physicians walked in. Aldwin looked unhappy and the stranger still had a twinkle in his eyes. He seemed amused by the whole proceeding.

"Well?" Randall said harshly.

"My lord," Aldwin said with a bow.

He swallowed twice, his large Adam's apple bobbing. She could almost see him sweat. Elissa realized he was afraid, which meant that he may have been ordered to reach a specific conclusion.

"My lord," he tried again. "My learned colleague and I have conducted the examination of our queen as requested. I am afraid . . ." He cast a glance at her and swallowed again. "That is, I must report that she is not with child. Nor has she been recently."

His learned colleague nodded in agreement with a smile. He winked at her again, standing slightly behind Aldwin so no one else could see. She fought back a smile, both of amusement and satisfaction.

Everyone was quiet for the space of several heartbeats. Disappointment, even anger, showed on several faces. Geoffrey, seated to her left, maintained a bland expression, except for the satisfaction in his eyes.

"Very well," Dathan said, breaking the silence. "We thank you both for your time and efforts. I am sure you did everything you could."

Aldwin bowed and the two left the chamber.

"Well, my lords," Elissa said. "Have you any more accusations to bring against me?"

"It isn't that we are harsh or unreasonable," Dathan said. "We are concerned for the realm left in our care by our king's death."

"Do you think I care less for this realm than you do?" she said harshly. "This realm is to be held in trust for my own son. I bore him as heir to his father, the king, whom I cared for a great deal. My loss is greater than yours, gentlemen. I have also lost a husband. My children's loss is greater than yours. They have lost a father."

"Caring for this country does not mean you are capable of acting as regent," Roric said.

"Not by itself . . ."

"We will not have a potential witch trying to lead us, either," Dathan said.

She exchanged a knowing glance with Geoffrey. When she looked down the table, she could see that the other councilors were surprised. Except for Randall and Roric, of course. Lord Witram had a look of hope at this turn of events.

"And what exactly does that mean, my lord patriarch?" she asked.

"There has been an accusation brought to me of your using a spell against one of our number."

"A spell? Surely you are joking."

"This is too serious for jokes," he said sternly.

"Of course it is. It is also too serious for lies."

"It is not a lie," Randall shouted as he jumped to his feet. "You burned me! Now, it's your turn to burn."

He pointed an accusing finger at her. His father put a hand on his arm and coaxed him back into his chair.

"Nothing has been proved yet," Dathan said. "But such an accusation requires a trial. If you confess to witchcraft, the trial could go quickly. If you contest the accusation, the trial would be a long, drawn-out affair. Don't you see the harm that would do our country? If you persist in this pursuit of the regency, we may never recover from the turmoil."

"There is an easier and quicker way," she said.

"And what is that?" Dathan asked.

"Trial by combat."

Even Geoffrey looked surprised at that. But she could no longer play these games.

"And whom would you choose for your champion? Surely you can see that no one would—"

"Myself."

"You would fight some warrior yourself?"

"No. I would fight Lord Randall myself."

"You can't!"

"Why not? Is he not the one who has accused me? Any man who would bring such an accusation against a woman because she rebuffed him must be a coward. But I would not have thought he would be too much of a coward to face me with a sword.''

Everyone spoke at once. Geoffrey leaned toward her.

"Is this your plan?" he whispered. "To get yourself killed?"

"No," was all the answer she would give.

"Quiet, please!" Dathan shouted above the others. Silence fell about them once more. "How can you possibly even think of such a thing? Randall is a trained warrior."

"As am I," she countered. "Do you think I am foolish enough not to know that only a warrior could be regent? That the regent would need to protect the kingdom and the prince? I have been training with a sword with one of the best masters in our realm. He says that I am nearly expert with a sword. I would not ask another to defend my name in a duel when I feel that I am perfectly capable of doing that myself."

"It's impossible," Roric said.

"You have no choice," she said, looking him straight in the eye. "A challenge for trial by combat has been made. You cannot ignore it or turn it down."

"Don't worry, Father," Randall spoke up. "I can handle the likes of her."

"You fool!" Roric said. "Don't you see what that could mean? If you kill the queen in combat . . ."

He left the thought hanging. She was not sure that Randall understood what his father was getting at, but she did. Great harm might be done to their family if he did kill her. Clearly, it would make everyone suspicious if they were named regent for her son, thus giving the others greater leverage for presenting themselves for the office. And if she killed him? The harm to their reputation would be nearly as great.

She sat back and folded her hands on top of the table. The challenge had been issued. They knew it would be difficult even to find someone to act as champion for her in a duel that could be to the death. But unless she withdrew her challenge, they would have to accept it. There was no other choice.

"Let us discuss this, your majesty," Dathan said. "This is unprecedented and we must—"

"Discuss it all you want," she said. She stood and looked at each of them in turn with a smile. "I will be in my apartment." She started toward the door. "Oh, Patriarch."

"Yes?"

"Please don't dismiss the two guards just yet. I feel I might need their presence over the next few days."

"Surely, you don't think . . . I mean . . ." he spluttered.

"Just a precaution," she said. "Just a precaution."

She left the chamber and was met by the two guards, who followed her to her rooms just as before. However, she insisted on stopping in her son's room.

Edgar was playing with his metal soldiers. The ones painted to resemble Alboran soldiers were all lined up on one side, the king figure at their head.

"Hello, Maman," he said, looking up from the floor.

"Hello, my little soldier. Who is winning today?"

She knelt down beside him and picked up the king. The face of the figure was cast and painted with very neutral features. Edgar could pretend it was himself or his father, whichever his pleasure was that day.

"We are, of course. We always do when Father is king."

Ah, then today the king was also Father.

"Maman?"

His expression had turned somber and he took the king from her outstretched hand.

"When will Father come home?"

He brushed at the figure's face with an index finger as if there were a speck of dust on it. Elissa put a hand on his little shoulder. No matter how she explained it, he was still too young to understand what death meant. Still too young to accept the loss of his father, who was king and hero in his little heart.

"He will not be coming home, Edgar," she said softly. "No matter how much we might wish it."

He looked up at her. Tears glistened in his blue eyes. His

reddish-blond hair, so like his father's, hung in his eyes.

"Never?" he asked.

His lower lip trembled.

"No, my son. Never. He lives in our hearts and in our memories, but we will never see him again."

A tear traced a line down his cheek and hung from his chin before it finally dropped to his lap. She sat back on her heels and held out her arms to him. Since he had started lessons in sword fighting, he had begun to think he was too big for hugs and kisses from his mother. Now, he leaned against her, and laid his head on her breast, his small body shaking with sobs.

They sat that way until she knew he must be uncomfortable. She shifted him to sit on her lap, and with his head still against her breast, she rocked him, humming a child's tune and stroking his hair. Nurse sat in her chair off to one side, her head down so that her chin touched her chest, asleep or hiding her own tears. Elissa fought back tears, knowing that if she started, she would not be able to stop them for some time. She was a widow, afraid and alone and, for the most part, friendless. However, this little boy in her arms needed her and she would die protecting him, if need be.

Gradually, his sobs slowed then ceased altogether. Shortly after, he sat up. She took the edge of her sleeve and wiped away his tears.

"You'll never leave me, will you, Maman?" he asked.

"Not for a very long time, my prince," she said and bowed her head.

That brought a smile to his face. Calling him that always cheered him up. No one but Nurse and she called him by that name.

"Are you going to be all right now?" she asked him.

"Yes, Maman."

"Good. Give the enemy a sound thrashing today."

"Of course," he said.

She started to rise, but instead picked up the king figure.

"This will be you very soon," she said. "You must grow up strong and wise, and ever so handsome."

"Like my father?"

"Yes, my prince. Like your father."

She kissed his forehead, rose, and went to the door. Before leaving, she turned around to watch him for a moment. The soldiers and their pretend war had his attention, and there would be no more tears for a while. Children were resilient and Edgar came from good stock.

She left for her own rooms. Clara appeared immediately, and suddenly Elissa could not stand the sight of her, but until her new haircut became general knowledge, she must tolerate her. She sent the maid for some mead, wrapped herself in a shawl, and sat down in front of the fire.

Just moments ago she had promised Edgar she would not leave him for a long time. Yet downstairs, the men in the Privy Council were debating whether to let her fight their champion in one more trial to prove herself worthy of becoming regent. The chances of her winning, should they choose a very good champion, were pretty bad in spite of her bold words. They were probably bad even against a fair champion.

She had voiced the challenge with such confidence. Even knowing there were many swordsmen much better, she had somehow felt sure that because she was right, she would win. Naive, of course. She had caught them all by surprise. Even Geoffrey. He probably thought she had lost her mind.

But she knew she was good with a sword. She had been practicing every day. Even Caedmon was beginning to believe she had a natural instinct for it.

Clara returned with the mead and announced that dinner would be served in the dining hall soon.

"Tell everyone I won't be down tonight," Elissa said. "Tell them I have a headache or something. Bring me a tray, quietly if you can. Then you may have the rest of the evening off. I'll need you back to undress me at the usual time."

"Yes, majesty." Clara curtsied and disappeared through the doorway again.

Elissa stared into the flames of the fire, letting her mind wander along many different paths to possible futures. When someone knocked on the door, she had drifted to sleep and awoke with a start. She placed her hand on her breast, wishing to stop the pounding of her heart. A knock came again.

"Who is it?" she called out.

"Lord Geoffrey."

Could he be bringing word of the Council's decision?

"Come in, my lord."

She had thought they might argue back and forth for days before reaching a decision. It would be out of character, but refreshing if this decision had been made quickly.

Geoffrey stepped through, bowed, and went to the sideboard for some wine. He carried the goblet to the other chair and sat down. He sighed deeply, a troubled expression on his face.

"Well, you have done it, your majesty," he said when she thought she could stand the suspense no longer.

"What exactly, my lord?"

"The councilors have accepted your challenge. They will allow you to fight their champion in a week's time. That should give them enough time to summon any other lords who are not presently at court. They seem to intend to make a spectacle of this."

"They think I will be beaten, I'm sure."

"How sure are you that you are ready for such a fight?"

Elissa shrugged. "I still have a lot to learn. But I am not defenseless either. I am prepared to do this."

"No matter who their champion is?"

"That, of course, will make all the difference in the world."

Suddenly, she felt very afraid. The names of the best-known swordsmen in the kingdom ran through her head. Which one would be most likely to represent them?

"Who is it?" she finally asked.

"Me," he said.

⚥ 14 ⚥

"They want you to fight against me?"

Elissa could scarcely believe what he had said. She suddenly found herself breathless, her hands gripped the chair arms, and she was about to leap to her feet.

"I hoped that I would fight Randall."

Dismay was clear in her voice. Her throat tightened and she swallowed. Everything was coming apart.

"His father has convinced him that it would not be in his best interests to kill the queen, his cousin's widow, in a duel. He wants to back out, and with the support of Dathan, his father, and Luther, they picked me to replace him."

"Well, don't they think you might feel it is not good for your future either?"

Her voice was shrill, a definite sign that she was becoming panic-stricken. Of course, she was. Fighting a duel to the death with her one ally on the Council was not designed to give her added confidence. Nor was the somber silence that seemed to grip Geoffrey.

"We will just have to find a way to convince Randall that he looks a perfect coward if he does not fight me," she said.

Geoffrey turned his back and stared into the fire. Was he

thinking of just the right way to dispatch her in the fight?

"Say something, Lord Marshal, or I will become convinced you are planning my death."

He smiled broadly. "Sorry," he said. "I have no intention of fighting you. And they know that."

Elissa let herself relax a bit. It was a dirty trick all around, especially for him to scare her like that.

"I am sorry," he said, when she told him so. "But you needed a lesson. You must think of all the possible reactions to your actions. You cannot expect everyone to react the way you want them to."

"Like chess?"

"Yes, like chess."

"Perhaps I should learn to play."

"Perhaps," he said with another smile. "Strategy can be learned in many different ways."

"Well, here is some strategy for you," she said, following a new line of thought. "The rules of the duel cannot be changed. It seems to me that Randall has two choices. He either fights me or he asks pardon for insulting me. He can't really name a champion, can he? I mean, he's known as a warrior and refusing to fight me—a woman and relatively untrained with a sword as far as he knows—would surely make him look bad."

"Killing you could only make him look worse. Perhaps that is the out for both of us, though. You are relatively unskilled. What if he named an unskilled youth in his household as his champion against you? For him, it would be a magnanimous gesture. For you, a way to possibly save your feminine neck."

"Is that not another insult to me? I mean, you know the rules that exist for warriors better than I, but it seems to me that if he refuses to fight me . . ."

"I think there are ways to get around that," he said thoughtfully. "Caedmon might be the one to consult on this."

"I must not lose face in this," she said. "The whole reason for my training with a sword is to prove that I am willing to sacrifice much for our country and prove myself worthy of leading our armies should the need arise. That means my opponent in this must be as good with a sword as I am. Maybe even better, if I am to impress the Council.''

Geoffrey nodded. ''We'll think of something. And it will have to be soon.''

Yes, Elissa thought. Soon, indeed. Her opposition would not let too much time pass before the challenge was answered.

Geoffrey went with her the next morning to talk to Caedmon before her lesson. Edgar skipped ahead and ran back to them more often than usual. He felt the tension in the adults with a child's bewilderment, and needed to expend his own tensions through physical activity.

Elissa had agonized over whether to tell him what was to happen. He was her son, after all, and prince of the realm, but he could not understand. Especially after she had promised she would not leave him.

The master was waiting in the doorway to the academy. The expression on his face was severe and possibly a little sad. Boris immediately took Edgar off to his lessons.

''You've heard?'' Geoffrey said as Caedmon led the way up the stairs.

He did not answer, keeping his own counsel until they reached the upstairs studio. As soon as they did, though, he turned on her.

''What were you thinking?'' he asked.

His voice was low, but intensity of feeling gave his words power. She was taken aback, unable to answer for several moments.

''You're referring to the duel,'' she started, anger making her voice dull, the words clipped.

''Of course I'm referring to the duel. Did you think word would not get around the village? Even worse, do you have a death wish? You are not yet a warrior. You cannot fight Randall with any hope of winning. You have been wasting my time all these weeks.''

''Is that what has made you so angry?'' She still managed to keep her tone dull. ''You think I have wasted your time?''

"Yes-s-s-s. You were becoming a good swordswoman. You could have become an excellent one."

"Well, if I am good, perhaps I have a chance of winning this fight."

"Not with Randall. But even if you win, you will never be any better with a sword than you are right now."

"Why?"

This surprised her. Surely, winning a fight would give her more confidence.

"If you win this fight, a part of you will believe that you know all you need to know. But in order to survive, you will do things the wrong way."

"I don't understand," she said, being drawn into the argument. "If they save my life, how can anything I do be wrong?"

"For that very reason. You must learn how to do things by the rules, before you can start breaking them. A fight to the death is never a pretty thing. For a novice, such a fight is clumsy and awkward."

Elissa moved to one of the chairs against the wall and sat down. Now she felt truly alarmed. She had not realized that a martial art could be like the magic she was also trying to learn. Fighting had always seemed more instinctive, and a matter of practice until movements became automatic.

"We are hoping she will not have to fight Randall," Geoffrey said softly.

"What other option is there?" Caedmon said roughly. "And you! How could you let her do this? Why didn't you offer to stand in for her?"

"She knows her own mind," Geoffrey said. "And you and I both know she's right about one thing. If she wins a trial by combat, her opponents will lose much of their credibility. As for me, I must maintain an appearance of neutrality. And that is becoming more difficult all the time."

"You're being naive, my lord. But back to this idea that she might not have to fight Randall. You have something in mind?"

Geoffrey briefly outlined his idea about Randall choosing a champion with as much experience with a sword as Elissa. It took only a moment, since it was an idea only, without detail as yet. Caedmon nodded and thought deeply for several moments.

"He would have to agree and there would have to be such a swordsman available," he said finally. "He would also have to find someone willing to fight a woman. I suspect at this stage Lord Randall would welcome a way out of this fight."

"Then the rules would permit that?" Elissa asked.

"Your majesty, this whole situation is without parallel. Never before, not even in the oldest myths and legends, has a queen ever challenged a man to a duel. For any reason. I think we will have to make up some rules as we go along."

"But—"

"Whatever we come up with must fit very nearly into those rules that do exist. Otherwise, your authority will still be open to challenge. My lord." He turned to Geoffrey. "I would suggest that Lord Randall be presented with this option as soon as possible. We must know who his champion is to be so that we will know how to train."

The marshal nodded.

"Your majesty."

"Yes."

"You will do nothing but train, eat, and sleep for the next week. A fight to the death is much different from what we've been practicing so far." He shook his head. "You will be ruined as a warrior in some ways. I hope you understand that."

"But I thought the whole purpose of training with a sword was to learn to fight."

"There is such a thing as learning just for the sake of learning. If we were able to progress in a more normal fashion, you would have become one with your sword. Every movement, every step, even every breath would have become so natural, so ingrained, that once you started actually fighting, you would be able to do it without thought. In the upcoming conflict, you will have to think out each move. Every counter. Every attack."

Elissa nodded, although she was beginning to think that much of what he said was foolishness. Fighting an enemy, thinking about what he would do and countering it, that was what it was all about.

"Did Ethelred learn to handle a sword in this way?" she asked, her curiosity piqued.

"He worked at it. He was a very good warrior, but he was impatient. Not everyone understands. I was sure it was within your grasp."

"Is that why you and the king had a falling out?" she asked.

Caedmon's face went blank and stiff. He turned his gaze away from both of them.

"We should begin practicing now, your majesty. And my lord, perhaps now would be a good time for you to talk with Lord Randall."

"Good idea," Geoffrey said. "I will be back to let you know how he responds."

He bowed to her and left, but she kept watching Caedmon. In the sudden quiet, the sounds of Edgar's lesson could be heard faintly from downstairs. The master walked over to the collection of swords.

She hoped the reasons for the split between the king and his teacher would not interfere with what she was trying to accomplish. But clearly they had been serious.

The week of grace went by quickly. Elissa went to Caedmon's school every morning and practiced with Geoffrey every afternoon. There was no time for anything else except to chatter with Edgar on the way to Caedmon's and tuck him in at night. As tired as she was every night, she wished for someone to tuck her in.

She gave up practicing her other skills. Time was too scarce and she was becoming uneasy about the feeling of floating every time she concentrated. Besides, she did not want to use any spells during the coming fight. It must be warrior against warrior, with no advantages outside of the ordinary. Of course, Garrick, Randall's champion, an eighteen-year-old squire who had been in his service for a year, had the advantage of size and strength.

Caedmon took this new development into consideration when he was told the young man's name. He was still concentrating on the basics. Now it was necessary that he teach her what her strengths were and how best to use them against this particular foe.

First, the master reminded her that she was taller than this young man, and her arms were slightly longer.

"Don't let Garrick get in close," Caedmon warned. "That's where his bulk will work very much against you. Don't let him push you around. Sidestep as much as you can. The duel will be in a very large and open area. Use all of it. Move. Being heavier, moving a lot should wear him out. Don't try to match him blow for blow. His arms will be stronger. Make him miss as much as you can. And use Ethelred's longest sword."

She went through the king's weapons and found the longest she had the strength to wield. Its blade was narrower than the others, but Geoffrey assured her the steel was strong enough to withstand any blow that Garrick could muster.

They assumed that Garrick would use his favorite sword, which was a short broadsword. He had never lost even a friendly contest when using it and he was known to be a man of habit.

After their evening practice, Geoffrey would often tell her the rumors he had heard from his people who wandered both the village and the castle. They ranged from the ridiculous to frightening half-truths. However, there was one that both took seriously.

"Some are saying that you are using witchcraft to turn yourself into a man," Geoffrey told her on the second night.

"Isn't that what Dathan was saying, too?" she asked.

"Close to it. But if others begin believing that, your task

will become much more difficult, I think. We must somehow convince everyone that you are still the same woman they have bowed to as queen in the past. The woman their late king loved and who bore his children."

"That will have to wait until after the duel, my lord. I have no energy to spare."

He had agreed that they must face one thing at a time, as long as they could. The duel was the first life-and-death situation they had faced in this adventure.

They had gotten into the habit of sending Clara away each afternoon and evening in order to have the rooms to themselves, chaperoned, of course, by the two guards who always waited in the hall outside the door, and Geoffrey's own equerry, Jason, so they did not worry too much about what people would say concerning what they were doing together.

On the third night, as they sat in front of the fire in her sitting room following practice, a knock came on the door. Josiah went to answer it and they were all surprised to find Tommy standing outside propped up on his crutches. He had not left his room since returning to Winfield. Within a few days of his return, two toes had been amputated due to frostbite. Elissa felt terribly guilty about having abandoned him.

"Your majesty," he said without preamble, "in spite of your abandoning me in my hour of need, I am here to offer my services. I have heard—by the grapevine, I might add—of the impending duel that is to take place between you and Lord Randall's champion. As your equerry, it is my duty to attend you in this."

"Tommy," she began. "It is good to see you and I do apologize for not visiting you in so long. However, I do not think this is a good idea."

"In spite of my physical tortures in the past few weeks—all suffered in your service—I must insist. I am quite well enough for this task. And frankly, after your lack of consideration for my welfare, I should think my wishes would be granted."

Geoffrey and Elissa looked at each other. Tommy had always been impertinent, but even for him, this was going too far. However, the lord marshal smiled.

"Such devotion should be rewarded," he said.

"Lord Geoffrey is right, Tommy," she said. "If that is your wish, then of course you will serve me in this."

"Thank you, your majesty."

Tommy bowed as much as he could with the crutches. Word came to her later that his recovery was hastened. Somehow the crutches disappeared and it became the practice that both he and Josiah would attend them when they were together on these nights. When she went to Caedmon's for lessons, he walked behind, carrying her sword and other equipment. He used his observations of the morning to remind her of things she did incorrectly in the evening. She thought he corrected her with an unseemly amount of glee, but she endured it because he was almost always right.

The worst thing was that somehow Edgar felt or suspected something was happening. At night when she tucked him in, he would hold on to her with his arms around her neck. When she asked Nurse if anyone had said anything to upset him, she was assured that had not happened. Children could have a sixth sense about their family members, Nurse said, looking worried herself. She undoubtedly thought it unbecoming for a young woman to indulge in such behavior.

Elissa agreed with that opinion each night when she pulled the covers over her aching body. She slept like a stone, only to wake up tired the next morning, trying to recall dreams that made her uneasy.

Another cause for uneasiness was the continued absence of her monthly cycle. She was not pregnant. The physicians had proved that, and none of the usual symptoms had occurred. The cause must simply be the physical and emotional stress under which she had been laboring for so long.

The night before the duel, she and Geoffrey refrained from physical practice. They went over strategy only briefly while they ate supper together in her sitting room.

"The whole castle buzzes with speculations about the duel

in the morning," Tommy told them as he poured wine and mead. "Some are even betting on the outcome, if you can believe that."

He snorted his disapproval.

"Probably few bet on me," Elissa said.

Tommy looked embarrassed.

"It does not matter, Tommy," she said. "I would not bet on myself either."

"Your majesty, you must have confidence," he scolded. "Remember what Caedmon said. 'Confidence can make up for other things as long as you don't become overconfident.' "

"Yes, I remember," she said. "I might feel more confident in the morning."

"Does it have to be so early?" Tommy asked.

The trial had been scheduled for six in the morning. She was rarely up and about at that hour herself.

"It is traditional," Geoffrey said, and Josiah nodded, looking at Tommy as if that knowledge made him slightly superior to the other. Tommy ignored him.

"Who will be there?" she asked.

"Everyone on the Privy Council and a few other witnesses," he said. "It will not be private."

"We can not have too many people see the queen make a fool of herself, I suppose," she said with irony.

Both of the attendants retired to a corner of the room, sitting to one side of the fireplace. Geoffrey reached over and took her hand in his.

"You will be fine," he said. "Believe in yourself and you will get through this."

She smiled at him. Her heart raced at his touch as feelings coursed through her body. She squeezed his hand in gratitude then pulled her own away.

"You can be sure Garrick believes in himself, too," she said.

As she lay in bed that night, it was not the coming fight that kept her awake. She remembered the warmth of Geoffrey's touch, his smile, his support over the past weeks. There was as much danger in that as in Garrick's sword.

∽ 15 ∾

The atmosphere in the tavern was gay. The fire burned brightly, warming everyone against the cold that pressed against the outside of the door. All manner of people enjoyed the ale and the warmth, although most of them were men. Farmers from surrounding villages were there to enjoy camaraderie with servants from the castle, merchants, even some members of the religious orders.

Everyone hooted and hollered at the tunes a one-eyed man played on a small wooden flute. In a corner farthest from both the door and the fireplace sat the only person not having a good time. He glared at the assembled crowd, as if daring them to bring their revelries closer to him. A bare space surrounding his table said that everyone had taken that dare seriously, but were too busy to bother taking him up on it.

Add to his look the fact that everyone knew who he was, and they were wise to stay clear. However, a man entered the tavern and, after looking around, spotted the dour face and made his way through the crowd toward him. He ordered some ale as he passed the serving maid, then sat down right next to the man.

"Well, your highness," the newcomer said with a slight

smile. "It would seem that you are not happy with the day's events."

"Be careful, Niall," Prince Galen growled. "I am in no mood for your bantering tonight."

"I am sorry to hear that. Perhaps I should leave you to your gloomy thoughts then."

He made as if to rise, but the prince stopped him with a hand on his arm.

"Stay," he said. "I am in need of distraction."

Niall settled back into the chair. The maid brought his ale, sloshing some of the foam when she set the tankard down. He tossed two copper coins on the table and she scooped them up and was gone.

"I suppose you heard what my father and the Council decided this afternoon."

"No, I have not. Everyone is being unusually close-mouthed right now, and I am not as near the inner circle as you are."

Galen sighed and leaned his chair back so that it stood on the back legs. He put his feet up on the table. His expensive boots were scuffed and scarred, just the way he liked them. His older brother always kept his shined. He was quite a dandy.

He downed the last of his ale and banged the wooden cup on the table. The maid appeared almost instantly with a fresh one.

"They have decided to send my brother to Albor after all," he said when she had gone. "He is to try to woo this widowed queen while my father prepares an army to back him up. Everyone believes that Albor must be in a state of terrible disarray right now, and they want the army just in case force is needed."

"There's a good chance. Most of the Alboran nobles would certainly not welcome Trevor as their regent."

"Nor as their king."

Niall looked sharply at the prince. "And there is no role for you in all of this?" he asked, knowing too well what the

answer was. Verald doted on his older son, his heir. He showed
little kindness for the younger, sometimes not even acknowl-
edging his presence for days. There were some who said it
was because the young man favored his mother so strongly.
The king had never loved the queen, in spite of her great
beauty. He married her only because his own father insisted
on the match. Once he had done his duty by siring two sons,
he banished her from the capital, sending her to live in a small
village on Ravelin's northern border.

Her own father, Lord Harmon, had quietly sworn vengeance over the slight to his name, but never backed his
daughter and grandson. Instead, he had remained neutral,
which did not endear him to either side. Some said he was
simply biding his time.

Before anything was resolved, the old king died and Verald
had himself crowned as soon as possible. He ordered the
priests of the Davidian order to grant him a divorce, which
they felt obliged to do. Everyone thought he would remarry
soon, but he never did. Instead, he preferred to amuse himself
with whatever women he could lure into his bed. Surprisingly,
he never took a woman by force. It would have been fitting
to his personality if he had.

Released from her marriage vows, the queen had plotted
with young lovers several times to take the crown for Galen,
twice directly involving him in the intrigues. The people of
the northlands were known for long memories.

In the meantime, not even his grandfather cared about what
happened to Galen. When he reached manhood, his father did
acknowledge him as his son, something everyone assumed he
would never do. He had invested a lot of time and energy in
the older son, who resembled the king so much that it was
uncanny. Trevor never acknowledged he had a brother and
looked through him when they met by chance.

Niall remembered how shocked people were when Verald
invited Galen to that first Council meeting just over two years
ago. Trevor had thrown a tantrum. Galen was so dazed that
he could hardly answer the summons. Ever since then, he had

been included in many meetings when he was in the capital. His life got better overall. Courtiers, nobles, servants, nearly everyone speculated at some kind of falling out between the older son and father, but nothing was ever confirmed. Galen was clearly still the second son.

After being given a better position within the castle, Galen smothered his resentment of the old slights. It was during the early days that friendship first developed between Galen and the older Niall. Both had been denied an inheritance, leaving them bitter and cunning, each in his own way.

Galen sat forward, bringing all four legs of the chair to the floor. He leaned closer to Niall and began talking rapidly.

"I had a vision this afternoon, you know," he said. "It was very revealing."

Niall feigned interest. The prince often had what he referred to as visions, which were more like daydreams.

"In this vision, Trevor died on his way to Albor and I was sent in his place. Isn't that marvelous?"

"And if you went to Albor, highness, whom would you court? The queen or the princess?"

"Oh, the queen is older than me. Would you not think the princess more suitable?"

"She is less than a third your age."

"True. Perhaps I could have both. Marry the queen until her daughter comes to marriageable age and then marry the daughter."

"Of course, you would become king rather than regent."

Although the idea seemed somewhat preposterous, it was something Niall had considered before. Possibilities and plans had whirled in his mind.

"Of course. And I would name you as my lord marshal. You have been the only true friend in my whole life and I would shower you with titles and gifts. I'm sure Albor could afford them."

"Make me a present of the current marshal's domains and you have yourself a deal."

"Really? You think we could pull it off?"

"It's worth consideration, your highness."

Niall bowed his head. When he raised it, the wide grin on his face delighted Galen, who grinned in return and clapped his hands together like a child. Perhaps with each other's help, they could both have what they wanted after all.

To avoid any uninvited onlookers, the duel was moved to a private tournament practice arena. The men who cleared the ground of snow must have wondered what their masters could possibly be planning. They had been ordered to spread a thick layer of straw over a layer of sand, and erect two large tents, one at each end. Other preparations were similar to those made for actual tournaments, but such were never held in winter.

Several huge bonfires had been laid the night before and were set ablaze before dawn. By the time everyone began arriving, they provided warmth for a good part of the sidelines.

Most of the men who took care of the preparations were sent away. Only a few remained to tend the fires and take care of other needs.

Elissa arrived in a closed carriage with Geoffrey and Caedmon just as the eastern horizon was lightening. She hurried into her tent at one end of the arena. The tent was warmed by a small fire in the center. Tommy and Josiah had brought everything and set up tables, chairs, swords, even a cot in case she needed it later. Peering through the slit in the tent wall, she studied the ground on which she would soon fight for her life.

"Could we not have found a large hall or something for this?" she asked. "It is cold out there and the ground will surely be slippery."

"The choice was theirs," Geoffrey reminded her. "You made the challenge and they had choice of either weapons or venue. It was lucky for you they chose venue, since at the moment, the only weapon you have any skill with is a sword."

"There was little likelihood any other weapon would have been chosen, and you know it," she said irritably.

The stress of preparing for this day and the fear that threatened to consume her had made her snap at everyone for the past two days. Getting no sleep the night before had not helped her mood either.

"It is time to get ready," Tommy said.

She jerked around to look at him, sharp words on the tip of her tongue. He stood solidly on both legs without his crutches, but he was still a reminder of how self-centered she had been. This time she swallowed the words.

She sighed. No one deserved her wrath except herself. She was the one who had gotten herself into this position, and now she felt too cowardly to go through with it.

She had seen her opponent only once. He was a stocky man, who very much resembled his master, Lord Randall. From what they could learn of him, he had also trained with the sword in very much the same way as his master. From then on, her training was based on that knowledge.

The tent at the other end was busy with men coming and going. A small group started her way and she stepped back from the flap.

"Some men are coming this way," she said.

Tommy went to the opening and looked out.

"It's Lords Cannody and Alfred with some of their retainers."

"They're coming to pay their respects," Geoffrey said.

"Caedmon told me," Elissa said. "All of the lords are supposed to do that."

Geoffrey nodded. He was watching her closely, and trying to be nonchalant about it. But she knew her voice and her actions gave away how nervous she was.

"How do you wish to receive them?" Geoffrey asked.

"What do you mean?"

"They will all see you in your male attire and short hair. Do you want to do that now or when you enter the arena?"

"When I enter. There will be nothing anyone can say or do about it then."

Tommy nodded to her from the entrance and she quickly sat in the chair provided for her, wrapping her cloak around her and pulling the braided fall of hair over her shoulder where it would be visible. Her equerry pulled the flap back and the five men entered. Their expressions were bland except for a hint of laughter in their eyes. They considered this a joke, she thought as they approached her. They would learn soon enough that it was not!

They bowed in unison, mumbling good wishes. She thanked them and they left.

For the next half an hour the scene was repeated several times. Even Dathan came with some of his priests to wish her well. However, when he left her tent, he went inside the other and stayed. It was nearly time to begin when Witram arrived. Fear shone from his eyes. His position was different, but he showed his courage by staying with her to show his support. Luther and Quincy showed no partiality, milling around with the other onlookers instead.

"It must be near the time," she said unnecessarily.

Caedmon knelt in front of her. For a moment, she expected him to repeat the words and actions of the lords who had visited. Instead, she realized that he had just come down to a level where he could look her straight in the eyes.

"You have worked hard to become a good swordswoman," he said. "Your instincts are good. Your technique is smooth and natural. Concentrate only on what the two of you are doing."

She nodded and held out her hand. Instead of shaking it as she expected, he took her hand in his own, bent over it, and kissed it. Her other supporters came to her and took turns doing the same thing. She smiled at them, rose to her feet, and unpinned the braid. The horn sounded again, the signal for the combatants to present themselves.

Elissa took a deep breath, nodded to Geoffrey, and turned to Tommy. He handed her the wool gloves with leather palms that she had chosen to wear. Then he presented the sword which she took and raised in front of her, studying the shining steel of the blade. In order to win, that blade must become stained with blood. It would be cleaned afterwards and its shine would return. But her opponent would not return to his former condition.

Nor would she after today. No matter who was victor.

She took a deep breath and handed the weapon back to him. Tommy raised the tent flap and she stepped through into the cold morning. Garrick already stood before his tent, flanked by Roric, Randall, and Dathan, among others. She stood outside her tent with her supporters until the horn sounded again. Both parties moved to the center of the arena, straw crackling under their feet.

Garrick did not look quite as short as she remembered. He walked without grace but with a confident stride. He looked surprised, as did all of those around him. Her costume had immediately caught their attention. Wait until they realized how short her hair was.

Normally, the king would have presided, or in his absence, the lord marshal. In this case Lord Cannody had been asked since he had no known prejudices in this particular contest. When everyone reached the center, he welcomed them, reminded them of the rules, and asked if they still intended to go through with the duel. Both having answered yes, he asked who their seconds were.

"Garrick fights as my champion," Randall answered. "Therefore, I act as his second."

"I act as second for her majesty," Geoffrey said.

"Very well," Cannody said. "Both of you realize that this is trial by combat." The two nodded. "That means this is a fight to the death." They nodded again.

The horn sounded the third time. Dathan stepped forward and bid the combatants to pray for guidance in the coming struggle. It was the gods who would decide the issue which had brought them to this morning, this field, this fight.

Elissa closed her eyes and thought of her son lying asleep back in the castle. She asked his forgiveness for what she must do and the chance she must take of making him an orphan, in spite of her promise to always be with him. She thought of her daughter, happily learning the ways of being a woman. For them, she must win here today. Doubt tried to creep into her mind and she crushed it with the words "I must."

The horn sounded, but this time differently, as if somewhere in those notes had been written the knowledge of violence and death. Elissa reached up and took off the fur hat that concealed her short hair. She shrugged off the cloak and Geoffrey's man caught it. A shocked murmur rose from those lined up opposite. Garrick took a step backward.

"Blasphemy!" Dathan shouted. "Witchcraft!"

She smiled at him and ran her gloved fingers through her short hair.

"We shall see, will we not?" she said directly to the patriarch. "That's what we are here for, after all."

She took her sword from Tommy. Anger that had been building for weeks surged to the surface, and suddenly, she wanted to fight the young man. Him or anyone, for thinking that he had the right to judge her or keep her from doing what she should and wanted to do. She would kill him for that and to protect her children from others like him.

"We cannot let this continue," Dathan spluttered. "No man of honor should have to face such a foe."

"We will see about that, too," Geoffrey intervened. "Everyone agreed that these issues would be decided here, this morning, in this arena."

"But her hair," the patriarch said. "And those clothes. She is becoming a man. I can take no part in such witchcraft."

"Then leave, sir," Elissa said. "We will carry on without you."

He glared at her but stood his ground. He had sanctioned this combat along with everyone else. The dawn's silence surrounded them. The glow from the east had spread to the whole sky and the sun would soon rise above the horizon. It was to be a clear morning.

The horn would blow one more time to signal the beginning of combat. She strode to the nearest bonfire and held her hands and the sword over the flames to warm both. She closed her eyes, feeling the warmth, letting it move up her arms, excite the nerves and muscles. When she turned back, no one had moved, not even her opponent. Obviously, the cold did not bother him very much.

She moved to face him and the horn sounded the last time. Both groups of supporters moved out of the arena. Elissa fixed her gaze on Garrick's eyes. His look was one of confidence, even cockiness. What did he see in her eyes? There was no fear there, she knew.

She stepped forward quickly, swinging the sword high. His sword took the blow. She swung low, but he blocked again. The sound of steel striking steel rang in the air and suddenly the sun was above the horizon. It shone from their blades as they struck out at each other. Always blocked. The light from her own blade blinded her once and she leapt back and to one side. His blade did not come very close, but the exchange had caused her breathing to come faster. The cold air made her lungs and her head hurt.

They exchanged blows, neither getting past the other's defense. His expression had turned grim and determined. That probably meant that she was better with a sword than he had expected. If only he was worse than she had hoped.

He stood his ground as if he were anchored, making her come to him. He attacked only after countering her. She charged with a rapid flurry of blows, dropping to one knee for the last, making a sweeping swing at his ankles. That forced him to jump back. He stumbled slightly, but regained his balance quickly.

With a roar, he charged, forcing her backward as he swung hard and fast. No finesse in this attack. Just brute strength. One of his blows slipped down her blade. The tip of his sword caught her left forearm. A burning pain raced up her arm, taking her breath away. She backed even faster, desperate to find a moment to deal with the pain.

He pressed harder, the blows against her blade coming faster and faster. Her arms were becoming numb from the impact. Would he never take a breath?

He stumbled again and she raced around behind him. He whirled quickly, not letting her attack him from the rear, but she had a moment—just a moment—in which to press her hand against the wounded arm. The sleeve was sticky with blood, but it was already freezing, the wool turning stiff. She had to put an end to this.

Garrick lunged at her and she stepped aside. She noticed that when he made that particular move, the point of his blade was down. She let him take the offensive, noting that he attacked in a precise pattern. And when she countered his horizontal swing from her right, he came back with the lunge.

When next he lunged, she stepped aside as before. As he moved past, she pushed the tip of his sword down with her own. She slid her sword down the edge of his, toward the ground, whirled around, and arced her own blade in a circle. The sharp edge caught him in the shoulder, biting deeply. Blood stained the blade when she pulled it free.

The tip of his blade grabbed at the ground, throwing him off balance. He stumbled, nearly losing hold of the handle of his weapon. Now, he looked surprised.

In two paces, she reached him. With a sweep of her leg, he was flat on the ground. His sword lay within reach of his hand. Elissa kicked it away, then stood with a foot on either side of him. She turned the sword and gripped the handle with both hands, prepared to plunge the tip into his heart.

He closed his eyes tightly prepared for the final blow. He was not helpless, in spite of being flat on his back with his blood staining the straw. Given a moment to recover, he could be back on his feet and fighting her again. But in that moment, her anger was gone. He was too helpless for her to kill there at her feet.

His eyes opened slowly. Of course, he was wondering why the blow had not fallen. He looked at her, still poised for the coup de grace. Suddenly he smiled.

"I knew you hadn't the stomach for it, witch!"

Everything she had been fighting against was there in that one sentence. Rage boiled inside her. She screamed as if the sound was meant to tear him apart. And drove the sword into his breast.

✺ 16 ✺

Clouds darkened the morning sky, making it difficult to tell when the sun actually rose. Perhaps it would stay down just because she wished it to.

Elissa turned over on her side, away from the window, so she would no longer have to look out. The world was not as it should be, or as it had been. She was not as she should be and wished to stay in bed all day, all week—maybe never rising again. Never facing those around her, most of whom had praised her the day before, albeit reluctantly.

Sleep had not come all night, just little snippets of blackness. But even then, the visions of her victory had come unbidden to mind.

In all the weeks of practice and training, she had taken pride in her growing skill with the sword. Being able to meet the demands on her body filled her with satisfaction. Learning grace in her movements, building strength in her arms and legs, had given her more pleasure than she had known for some time.

Not once had the reality of the purpose hit her. To show their lordships how serious she was, and how she could learn the skills a monarch must know, had been *her* purpose. But *its* purpose . . . ah, that was different. Death was its purpose. Had always been its purpose.

How it would feel to kill another human being she had not known. Was that what Caedmon had wanted to steel her against? He said always that a truly skilled swordsman was a beautiful thing to behold. How could anyone be so remote from the cruelty of it?

That cruelty had held her motionless in the arena the morning before. The look in Garrick's eyes, the cry of pain, the twitch of his body, as life abandoned him. She had seen men die before, but never at her own hand. How could she live with this?

And all of the others who came to congratulate her. They would not have believed that she could win against a more powerful opponent. That she was a woman who could actually fight with a sword was not conceivable. But they had to accept not only that she had done exactly that, but she had also proved herself innocent of their charges of witchcraft. This victory would make having herself named regent easier. But there were still obstacles to overcome.

Those obstacles were far from her mind when her opponent's body was lifted up and carried away.

"It was a good fight," Witram had said with admiration.

He had stood with her more comfortably when those on the other side approached to offer their congratulations. Their expressions showed they were stunned by what had happened.

"You fought well," Roric said grudgingly. "We drop the accusations we have made against you."

Randall looked at his father, resignation showing on his face for the moment.

"This trial is over," Dathan said.

The cold had made his nose very red. That and his shifting eyes made him look rather foolish. Elissa was just as glad that he could not look her in the eye. She knew her misery must show in her face.

"I'm going home," she said into the silence.

She turned on her heel and walked stiffly to the tent.

Tommy wanted to tend her wounded arm immediately, but she could not stay in the tent any longer. She started out the back. Geoffrey grabbed hold of her, making her stop. That was when her legs almost gave way. He steadied her, helping her to the chair.

"It's a normal reaction after a first kill," he said.

She glared at him. *"First* kill? I will never take another person's life."

Her teeth were chattering now and Tommy wrapped her in her cloak.

"Get me out of here," she pleaded.

"In a moment," Geoffrey said. He took a goblet from Josiah and held it for her. "Drink this."

She twisted away.

"Drink it!"

Without the strength to stand on her own, she certainly did not have the strength to resist him. Perhaps if she drank, he would at last let her get to the carriage.

She took a deep drink. It was mulled mead, and as always, the first swallow burned and took her breath away. But the sweetness was good and she began to relax a bit. Taking another drink, she sat back in the chair. She was relaxing too much. Tears threatened to come to her eyes and she could not cry. Not in front of everyone. But women cry when they are hurting or upset or lonely, and the tears escaped.

Geoffrey gripped her wrist for a moment, and in that moment, she knew that he had experienced the same regret under similar circumstances. She looked up at him. He turned away, not wanting her to see too much in his face.

Tommy looked concerned. Josiah's face was immobile. Caedmon showed both understanding and pride. And Witram looked relieved. Behind him stood Quincy, whom she had not seen following them. It would seem he had made his choice.

All of these men stood around her in a half-circle except for Geoffrey, who knelt in front of her. It would seem they were committed to her cause, and all because she had managed to kill that young man out there in the arena.

She shook her head. The path she had started along was a foreign one to her, but she was now even more locked into it than before.

"I am all right now," she had said. "We will return to the castle."

They nodded, both in relief and agreement. She got to her feet and Tommy helped her remove the gloves, then set the cloak properly on her shoulders. He handed her the dressier gloves and the warm hat. In the background, Josiah was cleaning her sword. She did not recall seeing anyone remove it from the body or bring it into the tent. She turned away from the sight of blood on its blade and moved toward the back flap.

Caedmon had ridden in the carriage with her while the others followed on horseback. The voices of those outside came to her, but she could not make out the words. The master had said nothing. What was there to say? She had no words to describe how she felt and was not sure he could understand.

Alighting from the carriage, she had thanked the men for their support and made her way to her apartments. Clara had food and mead waiting in the sitting room. Elissa had dismissed the maid, telling her not to return until she was summoned. She had spent the rest of the day alone, neither eating nor drinking.

Her common sense said she should keep herself busy, occupy her mind, and that she had slipped into a state of shock. The longer she brooded about what happened, the more difficult it would be to get herself on an even keel again. But she knew it had been ages since she was on an even keel.

She went to bed late and without Clara's assistance, but sleep was impossible. Remembering the fight and its end mixed in with speculations on the motives of the men now bound to her side. She tossed and turned until at last it seemed the sun might rise.

A noise came from the other room. She sat up and listened intently. It had sounded like the outer door opening. Then she heard the sound of its closing. Was it one of the guards from the hall come to check on her? Perhaps Clara had gone out

for breakfast. But the faint sound of footsteps came from beyond the door to her bedroom. It could be her imagination
playing tricks on her. The click of the latch on the door being
lifted sounded harshly, louder in the silence to her over-
sensitive hearing.

Her sword . . . it was probably with Tommy. Her mind
raced to identify some kind of weapon in the room and suddenly stopped. She lay back on the pillow, fear fleeing before
knowledge. The door opened and a dark figure entered. Quietly it started toward the bed.

"Good morning, niece," it said.

"Good morning, Uncle. Welcome back."

In another part of the castle, another meeting was being organized. Word had been sent the night before, and Roric and
Randall had agreed to come. Dathan waited in his own sitting
room, watching servants lay out breakfast on the large table
standing against one wall. He had risen at his regular time, but
this morning it had been more difficult than usual to drag himself out of the warm bed.

Sleep had eluded him most of the night because of his
realization that things were collapsing around him. Plans created to stem the collapse were immediately discarded. With
the lord marshal supporting the queen, and now Lord Witram
joining him in that support, her position was stronger. Witram
had already brought Quincy to her side as far as he could tell.

Luther was as undecided as ever, but he seemed to lean to
her side also, citing the king's deathbed declaration. How
could he go against that? he had asked. Dathan had cited many
traditions and the Salic Law that prohibited a woman from
ascending the throne of Albor. However, Luther pointed out
that she was not asking to rule as queen. She was simply asking to be allowed to guide her son until he could rule on his
own.

"Besides, it has always been the king's right to name both
his successor and the regent. That Ethelred chose to name his

queen in this instance does not go against any law that I am aware of."

Dathan had been surprised by the lucidity of the old man's argument. He seemed to choose the worst times to have his wits about him. Even his son, Lord Gilbert, who at the age of sixty-three was his oldest surviving child, shook his head at his father's stubbornness. Dathan could only take comfort in knowing that the old man was not yet completely committed to supporting the queen. And there was always the chance he would die at any time.

Dathan threw off these musings when Roric and Randall arrived. They were all soon seated at the table, helping themselves to food and wine. It was time to make use of the information that had come to him some time before. It might be grasping at straws, but he must use any chink in the wall Elissa was building around her.

"Your invitation mentioned a possible basis for declaring the queen unfit," Roric said around a mouthful of cheese and bread. He took a long drink of wine to wash it all down.

"Information came to me a few weeks ago," Dathan said. "If it is true, she would be condemned by her own hand."

"If?"

Randall looked from one to the other. He ate little this morning, although his appetite was usually as large as his father's.

"I had reports that our queen sent a letter to King Verald of Ravelin. In it she asked him to send one of his sons for her to marry. She offered to make him co-regent with her."

Roric hit the table with his fist. "That's treason, by the gods!"

"Of course it is."

"Why have you told no one before?"

"Because I have no proof. The letter disappeared and there is not even a single clue as to who took it."

"We could simply spread word around that she did this,"

Roric said. "Perhaps just the possibility of such treason would be enough to ruin her aspirations."

"That is possible, but we must make our next move more certain. We all thought this duel would be certain. If only your son had fought her—"

"He could be dead now, too."

"Surely he is a better swordsman than that man of yours."

"Much better," Roric said, frowning as if even the hint of such a slur on Randall's reputation was not to be allowed. "But she was better than anyone thought, too. More of her witchcraft, I'll wager."

"You cannot say that to very many people, my lord," Dathan said smoothly. "She proved her innocence in trial by combat. Such proof is sanctioned by the gods. To say otherwise would be blasphemous."

"Fah on you and your gods," Randall said. He spoke quietly but his eyes shone with rage. "If the gods were on our side, or had a hand in any of this at all, she would be dead now."

"Do not curse the gods, you foolish pup!" Dathan let his voice grow loud. "Even they can do only so much against witchcraft. It is up to us to bring it into the daylight. We did not do our best in this."

Randall collapsed into a sulk. His father patted his shoulder absentmindedly.

"That is not the important thing at the moment," he said. "You didn't bring up this letter without having some sort of plan on how to use its existence against the queen."

Dathan put down his fork and leaned back in his chair. He smiled at his guests, but Randall just sat scowling. Roric, however, was quite prepared to listen.

"First, we must join forces," Dathan said. "Combined, our strengths will be difficult to thwart. We will decide which of us will be regent to the young king and what the roles of the other two will be. Second, we will find someone who can state that he knows of the letter Elissa sent to Verald. Someone whose good reputation and honesty cannot be doubted. So, even though no one can produce the actual letter, such testimony as to its existence, and its delivery, will be accepted by nearly everyone."

"Such a thing might even bring Lord Geoffrey to our side," Roric said.

"Unless he knows of it already," Dathan said.

"Surely he does not. How could he support her if he knew?"

"She has bewitched him? I cannot say why he follows her," Dathan added hastily. "I only know that he does, but you are right. If he knew the truth, he would certainly abandon such a traitor."

"Who do you think knows and would tell of the letter?"

"The very person she would send on such an errand."

Roric thought a moment, then smiled. "Tommy, of course. Her little lapdog."

Dathan nodded. "I'm sure there is some way to persuade him to tell us. The first task will be to get him away from the capital."

Roric nodded. "But he can't read. How would he know what was in the letter?"

"The important thing is that he delivered it. Everyone will recall his nearly freezing to death and having to be brought home. Where else would he have been? That absence will support the allegation that he took a letter from our queen to King Verald. Such a secret communication is bad enough. As to its contents, Tommy would have heard something about that."

It was midmorning when father and son left the patriarch's apartments. Roric was well satisfied with the morning's work.

"She will be ruined, Randall. And we will be in control of the young king."

"So you believe Dathan will support you as regent in the end?"

"It really doesn't matter, does it? By the time all of this comes to a conclusion, he will have no choice."

"And what will become of Elissa when it's all over?"

"She will disappear, perhaps while journeying back to her home in the south."

"We camped not far from here last night. I wanted to see you first thing this morning," Deward said when Elissa asked how he could be there so early.

He stood up from the bed and took off his cloak. Elissa grabbed up her robe, put it on, and stepped into her slippers. He poked at the fire until the embers flamed up then added more logs. He dropped into the large, comfortable chair beside the fireplace and regarded her as she stood before the fire, warming herself.

"Now, what is it that has you so upset?" he asked.

"You knew I was upset?"

"Of course. I am not sensitive to your every mood, but when your emotions are so strong, I can feel them."

She pushed the footstool near his chair with her foot and sat on it. She put her head on his knee and he caressed her hair. It was just as it used to be when she was a child and troubled in her mind about something.

"I killed a man," she said.

"Was it a fair fight?"

"Yes, it was."

He considered that as he continued stroking her hair. "Tell me," he said.

Elissa sat up and started at the beginning with the challenge. As the tale spun out, she was surprised that she could remember so many details. As it wound down toward the end, she hesitated. Contemplating the conclusion made her ashamed and she was afraid that Deward would also be ashamed of her. He sat silently waiting for a while, then reached out and stroked the back of her hair.

"You said earlier that you killed him," he prompted quietly.

He would hear the details eventually, Elissa reasoned. They might as well come from her.

She told how Garrick lay on the ground, how he could have

reached out and grabbed her ankle, done something to defend himself. She repeated his exact words and felt the same rage that had seized her in the arena. She raised her arms and thrust downward in imitation of the killing blow.

"He looked so surprised." She turned to face Deward. "He didn't even try to defend himself. He was so sure I would not make that final blow."

"His last words make it seem he was fighting in a rage," her uncle said. "He saw you only as a foolish woman without the killer instinct. He forgot how the she-wolf will fight to protect her cubs."

Elissa jumped to her feet and began pacing.

"I was the one who killed in a rage," she said. "There was nothing so noble about it. I wasn't thinking of my children or their futures. I was angry at him, at Randall and his father, at all of the men who had made fun of me and tried to deny me this one thing."

"It is not a small thing you want," he pointed out. "I realize there is a certain amount of ego and lust for power in what you're trying to do. No, no. Don't deny it," he said, forestalling her retort. "Power is addictive. And although you never had a great deal as queen, the possibility of having it now is so very tempting. And the possibility of losing what you did have is very frightening. I don't blame you, Elissa. It is only human. And in this case, I believe it is necessary. Nothing can guarantee your children's safety, but having you as regent will come closest."

She had stopped pacing to stand in front of him. She started to thank him, but he cut her off again.

"I am very pleased that your lessons with Caedmon have gone so well. However, in spite of this trial by combat, your enemies will keep trying to bring you down. We must strengthen your position gradually but leave them with no doubts of your intentions. Is Witram still firmly behind you?"

"So far, yes. And he has more or less convinced Quincy to back me also."

"Good. So long as we don't give them any ammunition to use against you, we just might succeed."

"Well, there is one thing."

He looked up sharply. "Oh?" was all he said.

"There is a letter."

"To whom?"

"King Verald."

"From you?"

She nodded and sat back down on the stool.

"I sent it when I thought no one here would support me."

"What did it say?"

She told him. As she did, the frown that wrinkled his forehead grew deeper.

"And no one has any idea where it is?"

"No."

"Unless the informer had lied."

"That is always possible," she admitted. "But Geoffrey thinks not."

"How did he take this bit of news?"

"He was furious. I think he was ready to give up on me right then and there. Only his sense of honor prevented him from doing that. But I cannot make any more mistakes, even small ones. I don't think he would forgive much more."

"I should hope not. Even I find it difficult to overlook this one." He considered a moment and she lay her head back on his knee. He stroked her hair again.

"We will have to assume that no less than one of your enemies knows about the letter," he said. "But without the actual letter in hand, they will have difficulty in proving it was ever written. Has there been no official word from Ravelin?"

"None."

"I would think they would say something. Anyway," he said eagerly. "Get yourself dressed. We will have breakfast and talk with Geoffrey. I want him to know that I intend to be involved in this as much as possible. As an uncle should be."

He kissed her forehead and she stood. Deward left the bedroom and she called for Clara.

17

The lords of the High Council arrived one by one. Verald had summoned them to advise him on the possible marriage of his son, Prince Trevor, to her majesty, Queen Elissa of Albor. This was the first full meeting of the Council called to discuss the subject. It had taken nearly a week for the heralds to reach the outlying regions and for their lordships to make the reverse trek to the capital.

The winter was usually a quiet season, of course, since travel was so difficult. Many welcomed the opportunity to get home for a while, and be with their wives and families, who nearly all stayed behind. Someone had to look after things back home, after all.

One of those returning was Lord Harmon, the king's father-in-law. It was his dour countenance that Niall watched for day after day. He did not have the power to implement the plan that had come to him. But Harmon could. And once he had heard the plan, he would welcome his chance for revenge for the slight done his family by Verald when he rejected Harmon's daughter as queen.

When the entourage was at last sighted in the courtyard, Niall set his plan in motion. The first was to have Galen invite his grandfather for an intimate dinner in his newly acquired apartments. That had been Niall's doing also. With the chamberlain's help, he had arranged to give up his own small room and Galen's small room in exchange for an apartment for the two of them. The bribe had been a large one, but pooling their resources, they had managed it. After all, the prize would be very large if they won, and the small rooms just would not do for entertaining the powerful duke.

It had taken most of the days of waiting to compose the invitation in such a way as to intrigue Harmon, arouse his curiosity, and tweak his need for revenge. However, it must also be done in such a way that no one else would read any plotting into the message. Niall was certain that he had accomplished all of that, yet he paced the sitting room nearly the full day before the answer was delivered.

Lord Harmon would be delighted to have dinner with his grandson. He was also glad to see that his circumstances had improved.

Niall and Galen looked at each other and smiled when they read the last part. Improved? Not yet. But they were about to.

They arranged with the chief cook to send up a separate dinner and ferreted out a special wine to serve. They borrowed table linens and settings from a merchant in the town who thought he had made a large sale to the castle.

Everything was ready when the knock came at the door. Niall answered it himself, opening the door to admit the grandfather. One of his guards entered with him to stand unobtrusively in a corner, while the other took his place outside the door. Prince Galen looked quite handsome in his borrowed finery. His accomplice had made do with some things he had stored away against just such a need.

"Grandfather," Galen said. "Thank you for coming."

"You are looking especially handsome tonight," the older man said.

Galen grinned widely, pleased that his new clothes were noticed.

"I purchased them just for this occasion," he said. Which

was sadly true. "Would you care for some wine?"

"Of course. Wine is one of the reasons for living."

Niall poured out three goblets. Once everyone had one in hand, Harmon raised his. "To the king," he said. A traditional toast, but it seemed full of portent on this night.

"The king," the other two echoed and they touched their goblets together.

"Let us eat," Niall said.

The table was round so that there was neither head nor foot. They contrived to get his lordship between them but with space enough that he would not feel crowded. Niall asked how his journey had been and the two of them listened to the travails of traveling for three days in snow and icy cold. It was good fortune—or good planning—that inns were built just the right distance apart for a day's journey, he said.

As they ate, his lordship talked of family, describing members in a way that showed he realized that his daughter's son did not know many of these people. Gradually, Niall realized that he might even regret having neglected his grandson and saw this as an opportunity to make up for those lean years. Their plan could be even easier to achieve than he had hoped.

"I would like to visit your lands this summer," the prince said. "Would that be possible?"

"Of course, my boy."

His lordship leaned back in his chair and looked from side to side, giving each of them a sharp scrutiny.

"Now, tell me the real reason you invited me for dinner."

Galen looked surprised, but Niall laughed out loud.

"You are as sharp as everyone says, my lord. We do have a reason, of course." He looked to the prince, who shook his head.

"You tell him."

Niall nodded and with a smile turned back to the older man.

"You know, of course, that Verald plans to send Trevor to Albor to marry their queen," he said. "Either that or take the country by force if he has to."

Harmon nodded.

"We think it's a bad idea," Niall continued. "It will mean exposing the eldest son to dangers that he should avoid. He is the heir to our throne, after all."

"I suppose you think Galen should be the one to go."

"Yes, we do."

"As a way of protecting his brother."

"Not entirely."

"Oh?"

Niall looked at his friend, whose eyes shone with hope and excitement. The next words would either start both of them on a totally new and better path, or send them spiraling down into the oblivion they had already tasted.

"Obviously, we cannot achieve much by ourselves," Niall said. "Your son-in-law has allowed Galen to live here in the castle again, and to attend some meetings. However, his position within the court is still as an outsider for the most part. He needs your help as a member of the high council as well as his grandfather."

The old man turned to his grandson.

"You want me to intercede for you? He asked. "You want me to present a different plan to the king?"

"Yes. Not only to better myself, but also to . . ."

This was the tricky part and they both knew it. Helping his grandson gain power within the court would never have been reason enough for Harmon to act in their behalf. However, revenge might be. It was not only their trump card, but also the one thing that might destroy any chance they had.

"It may also be the first real opportunity you've had to avenge the insult to your family," Niall said. He spoke low so that he was sure the guard in the corner would not overhear.

Harmon looked from one to the other. His face did not betray what he might be thinking at that moment.

"If you can convince the others on the Council that it is not wise to expose Trevor to the possible dangers of this journey, and further convince them that his brother should be sent instead, the king would have little choice. Yes, we know that he could ignore the advice of the Council and do whatever he chooses, but if a large majority of his advisors are against him, he will have to think twice.''

''What do we gain if Galen goes to Albor and the queen rejects him?''

''He is a handsome young man,'' Niall said. ''Any woman would be proud to have him fall in love with her.''

''But women are unpredictable. And since no word has been sent to her so far, she may have given up and either married someone else or abandoned her hopes of being regent to her son.''

''I . . . we . . . have the means of making her want to marry him,'' Niall said. ''I doubt that she will refuse him.''

''And what might that be?''

''I would prefer not to say at this time. I will say that it is an object and that it is not here in the castle.''

''By the gods! You have the letter!''

Galen looked at him sharply, but Niall kept his eyes on his lordship.

''What letter is that, sir?'' he asked with complete calmness.

His lordship laughed. ''Well done, sir,'' he said. ''My grandson has an able companion it seems.'' He looked Niall up and down. ''And what is your reward to be in all this?''

''I am to be master of my own lands and advisor to my master, Prince Galen,'' he answered.

''I see. And will your lands be in Ravelin or in Albor?''

''Perhaps both. They say that the armies of Albor are among the best in the known world.''

''That's what I have heard also.''

Niall took up his goblet and raised it toward the older man. ''Can we drink to a spirit of cooperation among us?'' he asked.

''Not just yet. I need more information about your plans.''

''We thought we would sit down with you and formulate such plans,'' Niall said. ''After all, you have much more wisdom and experience than we do.''

''That is true, sir. But don't spread the praise too thickly. You may find the bread upside down on the floor.''

Niall smiled again. "I take your meaning, sir, and will try less."

"Good. But first, let us finish this fine meal before it gets much colder."

"You see!"

The whole village may not have seen, but some of its inhabitants must have heard. No sound came from the floor below. Edgar and his teacher must be listening, wondering what the deuce was going on above stairs.

Elissa very deliberately relaxed her grip on the sword handle, trying to let her own rage race through her and exit somewhere. She and Caedmon had already had words earlier in the week and she wanted to avoid a full confrontation this time if possible.

The master threw down his sword. It was all she could do not to follow suit. How dare he! He had promised before the lessons began that he would never, never holler at her.

But since the fight with Garrick, it seemed that she never did anything right. And she was totally unsure whether it was because she had picked up a bad habit or two, or if he resented her not following his advice.

One thing for sure: She had a clearer idea of why he and Ethelred eventually stopped practicing together. This attitude was unbearable even for her, and with his royal pride, the king must have found it to be even worse than she did.

As calmly as possible, Elissa moved to one of the chairs under a window and sat down, resting the sword across her knees. She stared into the reflections in the flat of the blade, finding herself wondering about the work that went into making such a weapon.

Caedmon took a few random steps in the center of the room, bringing her attention back to the problem at hand. He stood with his back to her, arms folded across his chest. With a sharp exhalation, he placed his hands on his hips and moved his weight more to his left leg. He had said something once about the right leg having suffered a serious wound years ago and not being as strong as the other. Usually there was no sign of that weakness.

She leaned forward with her forearms on her thighs and sighed. Such confrontations must stop or she would never get any better with a sword.

"Master," she said.

He stayed with his back to her and did not answer.

"Caedmon, this cannot go on."

His shoulders rose and fell, whether a shrug or another exhalation she could not tell.

"I understand that I have erred in regards to my training here . . . ."

"Do you really?" he said and turned to face her. "It is nearly impossible for anyone to unlearn—"

"I know, sir!"

She lifted the sword from her lap, and leaned on it with the tip pressing into the wooden floor.

"You keep telling me that. Over and over you say that what I learned in that fight for my life is now ingrained in every muscle in my body. That those muscles will not listen to reason now and learn the correct way to counter that blow or this thrust."

Her voice was rising along with her anger, and for once, she did not care to hold it in check.

"What's done is done. We cannot go back. We can only go forward. Take what is here, in this body, in this head, and make of it what we can. And we don't have months or years in which to do it. These arguments and temper tantrums keep me from learning."

She was nearly shouting by now. Although they had argued before, this was the first time she had let her own anger show so fully. She got to her feet, raising her sword at the same time.

"I told you in the beginning, I would not be a good student if you shouted at me, or bullied me in any way. If you cannot keep your promise not to do so, then perhaps . . ."

She had worked herself into a near frenzy. Frantically, she

held on to some semblance of control. She could not—would not—say the rest of the words and cause that breach she feared so much. With a scream, she whirled around, swinging the sword horizontally. The blade caught the back of the wooden chair, slicing through the splats. Part of the chair went flying across the room, hit the floor, and bounced against the wall. The remainder of the chair clattered to the floor where it sat. Her own feeling of surprise equaled the look on his face.

"Now!" she said, taking a deep breath. "Do you want to continue teaching me or not?"

She realized the tip of her sword pointed directly at his chest and she lowered the blade to rest the tip on the floor.

"We've come this far," he said. "Might as well see it through."

He turned away too quickly for her to be sure that the corners of his mouth had turned upward a bit.

It was her turn to exhale loudly. As she glanced away from her teacher, she saw Geoffrey standing just outside the doorway and guessed that he had seen everything. She could not see the expression on his face, but she sensed that he, too, was more than a little surprised by her outburst.

He turned and disappeared down the stairs. In another moment, the sounds of swordplay came from below. Elissa took a deep breath and flexed her arms and legs. Her muscles had cooled down, practice would have to restart slowly to avoid cramps.

Caedmon worked her hard, but did not raise his voice again. When she would counter or thrust in a way that he had not taught her, they stopped and compared the movement to the "proper" way. Sometimes they discovered a way to blend the two, other times they found a way to break her of the improvised method. However, there was one counter that Caedmon grudgingly accepted as an effective one that would have to be refined, of course. She even remembered having used it in the duel.

As he moved past, she caught his blade with her own and pushed it down. Whirling, she slid her sword down the edge of his, toward the ground, then arced it in a circle. The sharp edge caught him in the shoulder, biting deeply.

"I must stop now," she said.

The memory of the blade cutting through flesh and bone was too strong. For a moment she saw blood on the blade of her sword.

Caedmon looked at her curiously a moment then nodded. "The morning is nearly gone," he said. "You had best return to the castle." He smiled. "I'm sure Edgar has had his fill for the day."

She smiled back. "He told me the other day that if he didn't get so tired, he could practice all day."

The master laughed aloud, the first time she had heard him do so. The sound of it, and the banter that had produced it, had banished the disturbing memory. It had also reminded her how little laughter there was in her life these days.

Caedmon disappeared downstairs with a wave over his shoulder. She changed clothes quickly behind the screen, leaving the male garb to be collected by the washer woman who washed his things, too. The sword she placed in the rack on the wall, and went downstairs. Everyone gathered together for the walk back to the castle.

Edgar was too tired to run ahead as he had on the earlier trek. He began complaining before they had gone fifty feet. Elissa motioned to one of the guards and he picked up the young prince, who immediately rested his head on the man's shoulder. In moments he was asleep.

"He did well again today," Geoffrey said. "He has a ways to go before he will ever be as good as his father, though."

"My Lord Geoffrey, he is only five years old. He still has the awkwardness of a child. How good can a child of that age be, after all?"

"You're right, of course," he said.

"I wonder if we are pushing him too hard?" she thought out loud.

"He pushes himself, I think."

"Perhaps because he senses our feelings on the matter. I don't want him ruined by this."

"He won't be. He is his father's son, after all."

"Yes, he is. He grows more like Ethelred every day. Or perhaps that's what I want to see."

Geoffrey did not respond and her thoughts remained on her son. The last thing she wanted to do was make the son into the image of his father. Edgar had his own personality, his own dreams and hopes. He must be molded into a king—a good king—but without sacrificing too much of himself.

Once I am named regent, she thought, *I will host a masquerade.* A night of gaiety. That would bring smiles to a lot of people. Oh, it would be good to hear music again, and see women in their best gowns and the gallant men dressed in their own finery. And to see Edgar being just a little boy.

At the castle, she ordered Edgar to bed for a good long nap and went to her own rooms. She wanted to start on the plans for the masquerade. Even if she was not named regent, the party would still be a good idea. But she would not accept that she would not be regent. Not after everything she had gone through thus far.

Before she could start on planning, however, Deward appeared at her door. After the usual greetings, he quickly got to the reason for his visit.

"How are your other skills coming, niece?" he asked. "I hope you have not been neglecting those."

Elissa looked around apprehensively. Clara had not appeared since her return and she suspected the girl was downstairs or in the village somewhere. However, she could just as easily be in her own room at the moment.

"Uncle, do be careful!" she said. "I don't know where Clara might be."

"I saw her going to the kitchen just before I came up," he said. "I may be old, but I'm no fool."

"Of course you aren't. I apologize."

"And don't think you have distracted me. I would like to know how your other practice is progressing."

Shaking her head, Elissa sat down in her favorite chair. He stood to one side, watching her.

"I don't seem to have the knack for it anymore," she said. "It seemed easier when I was a child. Sometimes the voice works, sometimes it doesn't. I have made a few small things move. That is about all."

He sighed. "Niece, it takes constant practice to find one's talent. It does not come with a few days or weeks of practice."

"I know. But there are so many other things going on right now. I am so tired."

"Do you intend to give up on this, then?"

He stirred the coals in the fireplace and put logs on the fire. It blazed up anew and he sat down in the other chair, staring into the flames.

"I don't want to, but how much more can I do? There are the lessons with Caedmon. Working with Geoffrey on getting the Council to accept me as regent. The duel. The castle."

"Do you think anything will be easier if you become regent?"

"Of course not."

"You want to be more than queen and mother to the heir to the throne?" She nodded. "Then get help with the things you would not do if you were king. Managing the castle, for instance."

"But—"

"You cannot do it all. I'm sure that Job could do quite well overseeing the general operation of the castle. Set up others as heads of different areas. For instance, someone to oversee all kitchen operations, cleaning operations, special events, and all reporting to Job. He reports only to you."

"But even that will take time."

"At first, it will seem to take more time than if you did it yourself. But gradually, the tasks will be taken care of and you will not know exactly how or when."

"Um . . . maybe you could *oversee* that for me?" she suggested with a grin.

"I don't think so. If I were you, I would ask one of the

other wives who has a castle of her own to manage. Someone whose household is known for its efficiency. She will know better how to organize things.''

"I know just the woman. She will be joining her husband soon.''

"Who?''

"The Lady Margaret. Roric's wife.''

Deward laughed out loud. "That could be interesting,'' he said when he caught his breath. "And politically sound perhaps.''

"We will see.''

Clara arrived with two ewers, one containing wine, the other mead. Both were mulled with spices and the fragrance was wonderful. After she poured each of them a drink, she played with the fire a moment, but it blazed happily without her assistance.

"Would you like lunch, your majesty?'' she asked.

"Yes, I believe I would,'' Elissa said. "Some stew and black bread would be nice and warming. Uncle, what would you like?''

"The same.''

The girl nodded and left. She would be gone for a time, giving Deward an opportunity to raise his question once more. Which was exactly what he did as soon as they were sure the maid was gone.

"You yourself said that, as a woman, you need an edge,'' he reminded her. "Magic is the one thing you can have that they do not.''

"I'm not so sure. It just doesn't seem to be working for me.''

"We know you have the gift. We just have to rediscover the key to unlock it.''

"Why are you so sure? The Lady gives me protection when I ask. And I have moved small objects with a word, but I can't do it anytime I want. Oh, I know that I burned Randall that one time, but I was enraged. I cannot let rage be the catalyst.

That means a lack of control and we both know how dangerous that can be."

"You cannot stop now," he said, leaning toward her, looking as serious as she had ever seen him. "The bottle has been reopened."

"That same bottle was opened when I was a girl," she reminded him. "And nothing bad ever happened when I quit practicing."

"You were . . . different then."

"Different? In what way."

"You were a virgin."

"Of course I was."

"Not only are you no longer a virgin, but you are a mother yourself. That changes things."

"Would these changes have also happened had I kept practicing?"

"Your soul and your body would have been better in tune with each other and the magical power."

His words and tone indicated how serious he considered this to be. In the past few weeks, she had simply shrugged off that training, promising to get back to it one day. Just not right now

"My child, you were born with the caul over your head," Deward went on. "That is a sign of a great gift. You still have it, don't you?"

The tissue that had wrapped her head at birth had been dried and kept for her. All of her young life, she was told what a strong portent it was. When she left home, her mother gave it to her, wrapped in silk and placed in a velvet bag, in spite of her giving up magic once it was known she would become queen in the north. It was part of her inheritance, part of who she was as a woman of the south lands.

"It is safe, Uncle," she said. "Even though I still don't know what good it is. Maybe it was not meant for me. Maybe it was a power that I would pass on to my daughter."

"The power is in you. It must be that we have been going

about this all wrong. Maybe your power lies in an area outside the normal magic.''

"What would that be? I have never seen anything beyond the normal.''

"There have been women throughout our history with unusual powers. Unusual, but not necessarily better or worse than the normal ones. I don't remember if they were born with cauls or not.'' He shook his head. "But those born with cauls are often different, and stronger.''

He stood and paced. "I still don't know what it means or how to go about discovering what it could be. I will meditate on it. Meanwhile, you do the same. You must not give up on the one thing that could give you the edge.''

She agreed to do so, set the goblet on the table beside her, and scrunched down in the chair. She was tired and hated the thought that Geoffrey would arrive after lunch to start her lessons in government and diplomacy. She cursed herself often these days for not having been more observant when Ethelred was alive. He probably would have been amused had she shown interest and indulged her.

She sat up, irritably pushing away such thoughts. Where was that girl with lunch? She should have been here already.

The door opened and Clara came in, with two other servants in tow. They carried trays of food and two more ewers of drink. The table was soon set and she dismissed Clara to her own meal in the kitchen.

"One of the first things I will set Roric's wife to doing is finding someone to replace Clara,'' Elissa said when she and Deward were alone again.

"Why? She seems competent enough.''

"She has betrayed me. She must have been the one who told Dathan about my monthly cycle. No one else knew.''

"But from what you said, she did not tell anyone about your cutting your hair.''

"That's true. Everyone was surprised at the duel.'' She dipped her bread in the stew and took a bite. "I wonder why she told no one about that.''

"Perhaps she was playing both sides against each other. Keeping some information from them gave you a small element of surprise in that whole affair."

They concentrated on the food. The stew was particularly good with lots of meat chunks. The hunting must have gone well in the past few days. When they had finished eating, they piled the trays of dishes onto the sideboard and returned to the chairs before the fireplace, drinking, while Deward told her about his visit in the south. Everyone was well, except for Elissa's aunt Stella, who was old and failing.

Geoffrey appeared right at the appointed time and Deward took his leave. She settled at the table again, prepared to listen and learn from the lord high marshal.

He was explaining the duties of the Privy Council when a knock came on the door. Job apologized for the interruption, but wondered if either of them had perhaps sent Tommy on some errand. They had planned to work together that afternoon on a couple of projects, but the equerry was nowhere to be found.

"I haven't seen him since this morning when he got everything together for my trek into the village," Elissa said.

"Maybe he stayed in the village," Geoffrey said.

"I've checked there, my lord," Job said. "But I will check again. Thank you for your help and my apologies again."

He retreated through the doorway and the two of them returned to work. However, Elissa had difficulty concentrating. A sense of foreboding settled over her and she wondered if there would ever come a time when every occurrence did not seem fraught with danger.

∽ 18 ∾

It took a full day to realize that something had indeed happened to Tommy. A search had been organized the morning after Job reported he had not shown up as expected. He was nowhere to be found when Elissa was ready to leave for the academy. Not quite ready to panic, she had named a search party and sent them looking. But they had found nothing when she returned to the castle just before noon.

Geoffrey set out with some of his retainers to search the nearby countryside just in case he had ventured out and gotten lost. As soon as he had left, Elissa asked Deward to join her in her sitting room. As usual, she had dismissed Clara. Instead of waiting in her rooms, she checked on Edgar, uneasy now that another possible kidnapping had occurred. She warned the guard outside his room to be on the alert or his life was in peril.

Back in her rooms, she paced, but did not have long to wait. Deward knocked on the door, but entered before she acknowledged.

"What has happened?" he asked anxiously. "It isn't Edgar, is it?"

"No, Edgar is fine, Uncle. It's Tommy. He's disappeared."

"Disappeared?"

"Yes. No one has seen him since we returned from the academy yesterday. He was supposed to work with Job on some project and never showed up. I am afraid for him."

"He carried your message to Ravelin, did he not?"

"Yes."

Deward sighed. "This could be very bad."

"I know." She sat in the chair and pulled her legs up, hugging her knees to her chest. "We must find him, but there is no clue," she said.

"Not to mention what he could tell given the right incentives."

"He would never willingly betray me."

"Willingly or no, he could be convinced to tell everything he knows."

She felt all color drain from her face. "Surely, no one would torture him."

"Of course they would. The stakes are very high."

"There must be some way to find him. Is there no spell you know or could teach me quickly that would tell us where he is being held?"

"None that I can perform. I am the proverbial teacher. I know how things can and should be done, but..." He shrugged expressively.

Among her people, it was the women who held the greater power in the magical arts. But the greatest teachers were men. It was as if by not practicing the arts themselves, they had a better understanding of them.

"Locating people at a distance is a difficult feat," he went on. "I know ways it can be done, but usually there was a strong bond between the two people."

"Can I do it someway?"

"I don't know. It is such a special skill." He shook his head. "I am not even sure I remember how."

"Remember," Elissa commanded. "Or find it in one of your books. We must rescue Tommy." Deward bristled slightly at the commanding tone in her voice. "Please?" she added, and he calmed down.

"I will try. I will come back tonight with whatever I may have found."

"Thank you, Uncle."

Meanwhile, Geoffrey returned and reported finding no sign of Tommy or anything amiss. He had set some of his men to inquiring about who had left the castle and who remained. Word came later that none of the Privy Councilors had gone out in days, although three of them had sent their carriages home, all for different reasons. Roric had sent his to fetch his wife, Margaret, who was to reorganize the castle. Witram had sent his to bring more of his clothes, citing his old bones and the continuing cold. Dathan had sent his carriage, but not home. He had sent Cardinal Ensley on a short inspection tour of the monasteries west of Winfield.

The timing for the latter seemed rather odd, but even in that event, there was nothing on which to hang suspicions. Then there were merchants, other nobles, and retainers coming and going every day. There was no way to justify searching any homes, stores, or farms. And they would have to search them all in order to search those Elissa suspected most. By the time they found Tommy, it would be too late. Her enemies would either know everything he knew, or he would be dead.

The only way in which to find him in time was to use magic. But she had failed to master even the simplest technique. Did that indicate a lack of skill or possibly a lack of interest? Maybe she did not have the powers of concentration necessary. She must find them, for she would not have Tommy die for her.

She clung to that reasoning. Even to herself she could not admit that her fear was for herself as much as for him. If they made him tell about his trip to Ravelin, Randall and the rest would have another bit of information with which to block her ambitions. Especially if Tommy had overheard anything about the letter's contents.

"Is that your journal?" she asked Deward when he returned. "The one you have carried for years?"

"One of them," he said. "I have kept a journal most of my life. This one I carry with me always. The basics and the details of most of what I learned are in here."

He waved it at her then set it on the table. He stood with his hand on it for a long moment. Elissa had been standing with her back to the fire. Now, she moved toward him.

"Did you find what we need in there?"

"Most of it."

"Well? Can you teach me the technique?"

"I can teach you as much as I found. I don't know if you can learn it. And I don't know if you will want to."

"Why not? If it will help us rescue Tommy . . ."

"For all magic, there is a price to pay."

"I know that."

He took her hands in his and led her to a chair. She sat down and he pulled the other chair near and sat down beside her.

"Sometimes the price can be very high. Or potentially high."

"Why would this one cost more than any other?"

"It is called shadow turning. It is a matter of extending yourself out from your body. There is a danger of losing yourself."

"Will I fly where I want to go?" she asked.

"No," he said. "You fold the shadows against one another. You turn them as if they are doors into the other place. They connect, but there is a route. You cannot just go from here to there. The journey is made in steps or stages."

"How will I know which shadow to turn?"

"If you are a true shadow turner, you will know. I'm not sure how," he said quickly, to forestall her protest. "As I said, there isn't much literature on this. But what little there is says you will know."

"What if I am not a true shadow turner?"

"You could become lost when you turn the first shadow."

"Lost? And not find my way back?"

"Yes," he said after a long pause. "I have no other details. You will just have to try and see what works. However, make certain that you are specific as to what you want."

"You mean I can go outside of my body and I might not be able to come back?"

Deward nodded.

"You might become lost. And there is the danger of someone harming your body if it is left unprotected."

Elissa disliked the idea now. But what else was there to do? Of course, even this might not be enough if she could not learn quickly.

"It is dangerous and difficult and I do not believe you can learn it in time and be safe too. It will be even more dangerous than your duel with Garrick."

She thought for a while, weighing the different dangers and needs against one another. When she made her decision, it was not without a great deal of trepidation.

"I will try it." Deward started to say something, but she went on quickly, "We agree that magic is a must if I am to prevail in this enterprise. And I have not had much success with any other form of magic. The need is great right now, but if I cannot do this, then I should give up magic altogether."

"What will you do if you give it up?"

"I had thought to bring someone up from the south. Someone who is experienced and is loyal to me."

He nodded. "Now?" he asked, meaning the shadow turning. She nodded in turn. He told her what he had found in the book and described what he remembered being told. He had never seen anyone try this particular feat, he reminded her, and would have little or no idea if things were going wrong.

He fetched a footstool from a corner and set it in front of her chair. Elissa put her feet up and settled down as comfortably as possible. She took a deep breath and told him she was ready.

"First seek the Goddess and ask for her protection," he instructed.

She closed her eyes and pictured the Lady of the forest in

her mind's eye. For several moments the image would not come. Then she understood the reason: She was afraid.

I will protect you, the Lady said. Elissa opened her eyes and saw the Lady standing before her.

She held out both hands and the white light sprang from them in long ribbons. The ribbons floated toward Elissa and began wrapping around her. Very quickly she was wrapped in them from head to foot. She could see through them and move her arms freely, yet the glow of protection gave her confidence and strength.

However, when she tried to leave the spot where she stood, her legs would not move. She tried to remember the instructions Deward had given her. But panic suddenly took over her mind.

In that moment, the ribbons of light peeled away and her eyes opened slowly on the reality of her sitting room.

"What happened?" Deward asked.

"I had it, but I couldn't hold on to it."

Tears sprang to her eyes again. The close contact with the Lady was lost. Her body trembled without the warmth of the light. Deward got her shawl from the bedroom and wrapped it around her. When she stopped trembling, Elissa spoke again.

"Now I know another reason this isn't often tried. The sadness is overwhelming."

"The temptation is to dive into that world and never come back. Most of that will pass."

She slid down in the chair, coaxing warmth back into her body. "We'll try again in a little while."

"You are too tired."

"There isn't enough time to do this cautiously," she said. "Tommy could die any moment."

"He could already be dead."

"If he is, I need to know that," she snapped. She did not want to hear that.

"And you need to know what he may have told his kidnappers, don't you?" he persisted.

"Yes. Lady help me, I do."

•   •   •

The light ribbons surrounded Elissa for the third time. On the second attempt, she had not gotten this far.

She reveled in the feeling of peace and safety. She had lost those feelings after Ethelred died and they were like food to a starving person. This would be the real danger. Reluctantly, she reached her hand out toward the nearest shadow in the corner of the room, saying, "Courtyard of this castle," at the same time. With some difficulty at first, she turned the shadow and walked through an opening. Deward had warned her to take small steps at first. If, that is, she was ever able to go anywhere at all.

She walked a short distance; something solid lay under her feet, but she could see nothing. It was as if both time and space waited for her to pass through to the other side.

The next moment she stood in the courtyard. A man swept away the skiff of snow that had fallen on the bricks during the afternoon. A woman crossed the courtyard with a bundle of dirty linens, heading for the laundry. A few children played and other adults moved about on one errand or another.

She stood there, the solid bricks pressing against the soles of her boots, the cold air touching her skin, the world around her as real as it ever was. But no one saw or sensed her presence.

Tentatively, she took a few steps, following the woman headed toward the laundry. She was far enough behind that the door closed before she got to it. She had passed through walls getting to the courtyard. Could she walk through the door? She held out both hands and walked into the door, scraping the palm of one hand on the grey-weathered wood. Crying out, she grasped the wounded hand with the other, standing a moment until the pain subsided.

With her uninjured hand, she reached down and lifted the latch. The door swung inward and she stepped inside. The air was hot and humid from the water boiling over fires in the huge fireplaces and in the large tubs.

"Marta, go and close that door," the woman at the far side ordered.

The woman Elissa had followed looked around.

"I did close it."

"So now you're telling me there are ghosts in the laundry room?" The older woman laughed derisively.

"Well, I did close it," Marta said as she dropped her bundle and moved back toward the doorway.

Elissa jumped out of her way. If the world felt solid to her, she might feel solid to the world, even if they could not see her. She stood and watched the women working for a moment, but after the cold outside, the damp heat was suffocating, even in the large space. She turned to leave. What would they think if the door opened on its own again?

She opened the door and the women began fussing. Elissa smiled to herself, enjoying the joke as if she were a little girl. This could be a lot of fun, she decided. But the need to continue was urgent. In the courtyard, she walked to the shadow against the castle wall, reached out, and turned it.

"Return," she said aloud.

And found herself back in the laundry. Not exactly where she wanted to be. Marta looked up from the tub of laundry she had been stirring. She looked more than a little nervous.

Elissa was more concerned that the command Deward had remembered did not mean what he thought. Would she have to retrace her steps to the sitting room one place at a time? She grasped the corner behind her.

"Return."

That placed her back in the courtyard. Nothing in that to frighten the washerwomen.

Finding the same shadow, she turned it and said, "Return to my sitting room."

First she was in the place of light. "Thank you, Lady," she said and the ribbons of light uncoiled from around her. She felt bereft.

"No! Give it back. Please."

She was alone and only silence answered. But no. In the

distance someone called her name. Whoever it was wanted her to come back.

When her vision cleared, she saw her uncle kneeling before her, a look of deep concern on his face. The room seemed very dark after the place of light.

"You cried out," he said. "I thought I would lose you."

"Oh, Uncle," she said, as tears streamed down her cheeks. "I felt so safe there. I did not want to come back."

"We had best forget this," he said sternly.

"I have no choice but to go on," she pleaded. "It will work. I can find Tommy this way, and quickly."

"What good is it if you find him, but don't return yourself?"

"I will return. I promise."

She reminded herself of her promise to her son that she would not leave him. That was the promise she must keep.

～ 19 ～

Early morning came and went. She should feel tired, but she did not. Each moment in the light seemed to give her renewed energy. Several times she had started there, then stepped out to another place, into what Deward called the real world. That place of light was becoming just as real, maybe more so. Every time she returned to him, he reminded her of her children and her quest.

At sunup, she sent word to Caedmon that she would not be able to get to the academy this morning. She could almost hear him fussing about that, but this was more important. She sent apologies to Geoffrey, but would he please accompany Edgar alone today?

So far, she had made it to the three nearest castles, including Roric's. Each venture took time—more in this real world than in the one beyond. Because of that, she had decided to skip the castles between the last one she visited and Randall's. She was convinced he, Roric, and the patriarch were the ones involved in this kidnapping. Therefore, his or Dathan's was the most logical place for them to hold Tommy.

Deward insisted she eat something before this next venture and she had agreed only to please him. In the end, she ate

ravenously, but refused any mead. Somehow she knew that
the strong beverage would impede her control. Instead she
drank warm water with a piece of dried lemon.

Sated, she stood and stretched the many kinks out of her
body. She had sat in the chair for hours and was rather stiff,
but still neither tired nor sleepy. Instead, she felt so very alive.

When she had finished stretching, she found Deward was
watching her.

"Don't look so concerned, Uncle. I am quite fine."

He shrugged.

"Randall's castle is a pretty good distance. Do you feel
sure about the stages?" he asked.

"Yes. I wish I knew how, but the route does seem clear.
It will take a while, so you are not to worry."

He frowned, but said nothing. They moved back to the
chairs in front of the fireplace.

"Promise you will return," Deward said to her in an
agreed-upon formula they had begun using sometime during
the night.

"I promise."

Elissa closed her eyes and prepared to go. Once wrapped
in the ribbons of light, she spoke the name of a nearby castle
and turned the shadow. She walked through the dark zone
between shadows and in moments was there. It felt safer to
appear first in the courtyard where there was plenty of space.
She had wondered what would happen if she somehow imagined herself in a room and ended up in the wall instead.

At last there was only one jump left. And if Tommy was
not there? The last choice would be Dathan's castle.

Elissa shook off the dark thoughts, and made the last jump
to Morrow Castle on the edge of Elder Forest. Once in the
courtyard, she studied the building, reacquainting herself with
its layout. She had visited there only once many years ago,
when Randall married Rowena, daughter of a nobleman poor
in social stature, but rich in treasures. The new bride had conducted a tour for the queen and other ladies, describing what
she and Randall hoped to do with this room and that.

Randall's castle was one of the oldest in the kingdom. Strewn about was evidence of rebuilding and refurbishing. He apparently intended to honor his wife's wishes. But the extensive shoring up of the foundations, and the holes in the stone walls, made Elissa wonder if anyone was actually living there at the moment. If they were not, then Tommy might not be here either.

Time was running out. All she could do was search as she had in the other castles.

She sped up the stairs. The upper floors would be the best starting place. As she had suspected, the rooms were dark and deserted. The air felt even colder than that outside. What pieces of furniture remained were covered with sheets and tarps. The majority must be stored somewhere other than the castle.

Quickly, she moved from room to room and found not one sign of Tommy. A few workmen worked on projects in the public rooms on the first floor where fires burned in the fireplaces.

She stood among them, listening, but there was precious little talk. What there was, dealt with the technical aspects of what the men worked on, or the tools with which they worked.

Suddenly, however, one of Dathan's priests appeared in the dining hall from the kitchen. The cowl of his cloak hid his face and he carried bundles which might contain food. The workmen ignored him as he walked among them, heading for the main doorway. Elissa decided to follow.

Leaving the castle, he passed through the main courtyard, and across the large open field between the castle and the edge of the forest. He whistled as he walked among the trees, clearly familiar with his route.

Elissa stayed close to him as he moved quickly yet without haste. It was cold enough among the shadows to encourage haste. Following behind, she caught an occasional whiff of the food he carried.

At last, they reached the entrance to a cave opening into a low hill. He bent down to enter. The floor was very steep at first and he slid in loose rock and dirt. She followed with little difficulty. Where there was still light from outside, he stopped and lit a small oil lamp with a steel and flint, both left waiting for him on a small shelf of rock. Then he retrieved the food bundle and followed the narrow tunnel farther in.

More light ahead indicated his destination. A large chamber opened up with several lamps and even a small fire for warmth. The manner in which the smoke wafted upward indicated an opening to the outside somewhere that acted as a natural chimney.

"It's about time you got back," one of the men said to the priest.

"It's a long walk from the castle," the priest replied. "Next time you get the food." She recognized his voice and it made her sure she had come to the right place.

The first man growled something and took the bundle and placed it on the rough table set to one side. He untied the cloth and began setting out loaves and jugs, some of which held soup or stew. A third man took a chair at the table and watched as everything was divided up.

"Should we save some for the prisoner?" the priest asked. He pushed the cowl back, exposing Gerrold's face.

"Not much need. He won't last the night out, I expect."

Elissa stifled a cry by biting on the heel of her hand.

"Did he say anything yet?"

"Nothing useful. Never thought a prissy pants like him would have the guts to keep from telling everything he knows. And I used every type of persuasion I know."

Gerrold and the man took their seats and all three began eating. There were two tunnels leading out of the chamber other than the one by which she had entered. Nothing told her which was the way to Tommy, for she had no doubt that was who they were talking about.

"You are sure he is dying?" the priest asked with his mouth full.

"Go check for yourself," the gruff man said, jerking a

thumb toward one of the tunnels. "I'm sure he would love the company."

The priest looked in the direction the man indicated. "Maybe later," he said. "I'm too hungry right now."

Elissa left the group and entered the tunnel to which the man had pointed. It was not long before total darkness surrounded her. She moved to the right so that her hand touched the wall and stepped carefully along the rock floor. A little farther and there was no sound at all, not even the scraping of her boots on the floor. Then a soft noise came from ahead. The most forlorn sound she had ever heard.

The chamber was very dark and she could just make out his form lying on a low cot. She sensed immediately that he was dying. He cried out again and she moved closer.

Suddenly, he smiled in her direction.

"You're here," he said softly. "I'm so sorry. I never meant to tell them anything. Say you forgive me."

"You said nothing, my dear friend," Elissa said as she sat on the edge of the cot. "You were as true to me as any man could be, and brave, and strong. Carry that knowledge with you to the grave. And my eternal gratitude and love."

"Oh, my dear lady, thank you. I have loved you above all others."

"I know. Rest now. Sleep."

"Help me, my lady. Hold me."

She wrapped her arms around the shattered body of this, her greatest friend. He had asked for her help and some instinct guided her. His energy flowed from him, and she absorbed it as a succubus would feed from its lover in the night. She knew the moment when all life passed from him and she laid him back down on the cot.

Tears flowed down her cheeks and she sat with him, holding his hand, not wanting to leave him all alone in this darkness. But she must. She had to return to Winfield and have Geoffrey lead a party here. This was what she needed to make the others fall in line. By the Lady, she would make them pay for this.

⌒ 20 ⌒

A table had been set up in the center of the chamber. Several lamps and candles burned, enough of them to brighten nearly every corner.

It was her first time in the dungeon and Elissa hated it. The place reeked of cruelty and pain, and in spite of what they had done to Tommy, she almost pitied the two men sitting side by side at one end of the table.

She had only contempt for the other two men sitting opposite her and Geoffrey. It was their doing that Tommy was dead, their orders that had actually done the deed. And now Roric and Randall were caught.

Under more normal circumstances, they might expect to be tried, convicted, and hanged. But now, they were more good to her alive than dead. Their own signed confessions lay on the table in front of them, matching the ones in front of her.

"You do understand that I will not press charges against either of you, so long as you support me and my children as rulers of Albor?"

"I do," Roric said.

He was experienced enough to know that for the moment he was beaten in this particular game. Maybe he would have another chance in the years left to him. But it was a game to him, she realized. A game in which he had still enough power and authority to make his remaining a player of benefit to her.

Randall, however, was another player entirely. He was ambitious and did not like being beaten. The possibility of having another chance in the future meant nothing to him. He silently refused to agree.

"Lord Randall, I need your verbal agreement in front of these witnesses," Elissa said.

He looked at those witnesses, standing against the wall behind the queen and lord marshal: Deward, the queen's uncle. Lord Witram. Job, chamberlain of the castle. Jason, Geoffrey's equerry. Phillip, the new chaplain of the castle, and one of Dathan's priests.

Elissa leaned toward Randall. Their gazes locked.

"My lord," she said. "In essence this changes nothing. You lose nothing. In fact, by agreeing, you save everything. If things were different, you could face death for this attack so close to my person. Be grateful that the kingdom still needs you and your father."

There was so much more she could say, so much hate she could express, but Elissa held back. Venting her anger would only make things more difficult in the weeks and months to come.

"For pity's sake, Randall, agree!" Roric said. "Get it over with."

The son lowered his gaze and nodded. "I agree," he said.

He looked back up into her eyes and seemed about to add some caveat, but he said nothing more. Elissa leaned back in her chair, keeping her gaze level until Randall looked away once more. In that last look, however, she knew he was not giving up. Not by any means.

"What about those two?" Roric asked, indicating the ones who had actually carried out Tommy's torture.

They were broken men, both in spirit and in body. After what they had just gone through, would they be any further threat to her?

"Discuss that with Lord Geoffrey," she said. "Decide between you what would be best." She rose from her chair and everyone followed suit, even Randall. "For now, I am glad this affair is over. If anyone needs me, I will be in my apartment."

She walked away with Deward behind her. Everyone in the chamber remained standing until she was out of sight.

Why did she not feel victorious? In part, it was because nothing would bring Tommy back. Also, Dathan had managed to escape. The first day in the dungeon, Gerrold had hung himself with his own sash. Either he had feared his master would kill him, or guilt had overwhelmed him.

Unfortunately, the other two conspirators knew nothing directly of the patriarch's involvement since they had neither seen nor spoken to him. So, he was still a danger, but one without co-conspirators for now.

Once in her sitting room, she and Deward worked on the plans for changing responsibilities within the castle, as they had discussed once before. Roric's wife would arrive within the next few days, and she would take over the arrangements. Her loyalty had more or less been proven when she refused to come to her husband's aid. Job and Opal were thrilled with the possibility of more responsibility.

Tomorrow, Elissa intended resuming her lessons with Caedmon, something she found she missed when she was unable to get to the academy. The meetings with Geoffrey had been ongoing most of the time. There was so much to learn about neighboring countries, other lords with lands throughout Albor, the port authority that oversaw the shipping and access, and another dozen or more things she would have to oversee as regent. In just a few years it would all have to be taught to Edgar, too, although he would soon be introduced to some of his future responsibilities.

She and Deward went to work and Clara appeared, bearing a tray with lunch, followed by another servant with the mead and wine ewers. Without a word, she served them, then disappeared into her own room. They ate as they worked. In the back of her mind, Elissa felt relief that the maid would be gone soon.

The work for the day was nearly finished when Geoffrey arrived.

"What was decided about the two men?" she asked, unable to wait for him to open the subject.

"They are being sent to work on one of the ships sailing out of Sutton. There are a few of the king's ships on which prisoners spend their final days."

"Are they sent on dangerous voyages or something?"

"Yes. Voyages for which it is difficult to get regular sailors to serve."

She nodded her satisfaction. Hopefully these two would never return. That left only Dathan to deal with and that might prove an impossibility.

Geoffrey finished his wine and went on his way, promising to return later in the day. She and Deward moved to the more comfortable chairs in front of the fire and she closed her eyes. The past few days had been hectic and exhausting in so many ways. All she wanted now was to sleep for hours. But Deward was not going to let that happen just yet.

"We have not talked about your little escapade," he said.

"I do not want to discuss it. Not yet."

"You are dwelling on it. I can tell. And that is a bad sign. I told you that this could be a very dangerous skill to attempt. Frankly, I am surprised you accomplished it so easily."

Elissa looked over at him and sighed.

"It was not the first time," she said.

"Not the first?" His voice had risen in both volume and pitch. "Why did you never tell me?"

"I didn't understand what happened before. But several times when I tried to concentrate on saying the words, I seemed to drift away. I thought it was just that my attention was drifting. It wasn't until you taught me how to search for Tommy that I realized what had been happening."

"You moved in the shadows?"

"Not exactly. Several times I felt like I was floating above the very thing I was trying to move. As if I had left my body."

"You were very lucky."

"I know. But I made no effort to leave this room. And the Lady was watching over me."

"We will have to work very carefully on this. It will take some time to find out everything you can do in the shadows. I have never known anyone—"

"I will not do it again," she said.

"It's a rare and wonderful gift."

"It is very frightening and there is so much I don't understand. What did I do to Tommy and how did I know how to do it?"

Deward looked at her curiously. "Tommy? Did he know you were there?"

"Yes. Or he seemed to. He was in terrible pain and hallucinating."

"But he died from his wounds shortly after you found him."

"Yes. No. He was in so much pain."

She stood and moved toward the fireplace; placing a hand on the mantel, she leaned against it, wanting the heat to drive away the new cold inside her. She could feel her uncle's eyes on her, knew the questions that must be rolling around in his mind, but he said nothing.

"It was so dark in that chamber. No one else had been able to see me, no matter how bright the sun or the light. Maybe he hallucinated or maybe he really saw me. I don't know. But he spoke to me. Oh, he was in so much pain. I could almost feel it myself. And he was dying. We both knew that."

The feelings returned, the sorrow and helplessness. Elissa shook her head, trying to make them go away. Tears rolled down her cheeks, the tears she could not shed there in the cave. She turned to face Deward.

"At first he apologized for having told what he knew, but I assured him that he had not. I overheard those terrible men say so. Then, he told me how much he loved me. That he always had. And finally, he asked me to help him. I could not refuse him."

Deward inhaled sharply.

"What did you do?"

"I put my arms around him and held him."

"Is that all?"

"No."

The memory of the rush of Tommy's life essence into her body made her shiver. Often, it felt like his spirit was still inside her.

She described that to Deward. He frowned and said nothing. Clearly, he was disturbed by this and had no idea whether it was good or bad.

"A succubus," he murmured.

"Me?" she asked sharply. "They are the evil spirits that take advantage of men while they sleep, aren't they?"

"They do many things," he said. "I will send for more books, I guess. I don't know what else to do." He stood and took her hands in his. "Don't worry, Elissa. The Lady was protecting you. Nothing bad could happen."

She nodded, and hoped he was right.

He left soon after that, and she lay down for a while. She was tired, and dozed until a knock came to the door. Clara answered it and Elissa heard Geoffrey's voice. She waited for the maid to come into the bedroom.

"The lord marshal is here," Clara announced.

"Thank you. Tell him I will be there in a moment."

When Elissa came into the sitting room, she knew immediately something was seriously wrong. Geoffrey paced up and down. She had never seen him so distracted.

"What is the matter, my lord?"

"It would seem the man is full of surprises."

"Who?"

"Lord Niall."

"A letter came. He demands that you spurn Prince Josiah in favor of Prince Galen."

"The younger one?"

He nodded.

"And what makes him think we would accede to such a demand?"

"He has your letter."

Elissa sat down, trying to think. This was worse than she had imagined.

"If you do not agree, the letter will be made public knowledge," Geoffrey continued.

"And you believe he is serious about this?"

"Yes, he is. Very serious."

"With things the way they are right now, do we need to worry about that letter any longer?" she asked. Geoffrey looked puzzled. "I mean, everyone on the Privy Council must side with us. Even this letter would not be enough for them to abandon me and my children right now. Would it?"

"Every little thing they can dig up they will use against you. Any excuse. And if they find enough, they just might succeed in denying you what you want most."

Still, she could not panic. There was a way to get past this new problem. She just did not know what it was yet.

"I will send for my uncle and the three of us will work on this. I would think some solution should be found as soon as possible."

Geoffrey nodded agreement. She called for Clara and sent her to find Deward. Once she had seen him, she was to have a dinner brought to the apartment, then she was to take the night off. No one was to disturb them until Elissa sent word. Clara rushed off on her errands.

The queen and the lord marshal sat very quietly for a while. The crackling of the fire was the only sound.

"I thought you were going to get rid of her," Geoffrey said suddenly, making Elissa jump.

"Who? Oh, Clara. I am. Or Lady Margaret is once she arrives."

Deward arrived at that moment, out of breath from rushing. He was very anxious to know what had happened, and Elissa asked Geoffrey to tell him. He had finished by the time dinner arrived and any discussion waited until the table was laid and all the servants had left. The two guards who now followed Elissa everywhere were still on duty outside the door. That should keep anyone from eavesdropping. Not that much could be heard through the heavy wooden door. But Elissa was learning well the need for security.

"Well, I am out of suggestions," Deward said, leaning back in his chair.

As they ate, they had suggested one thing after another as a way of handling the threat from Niall, each more ridiculous than the last. One of them had been that they would sit down and write fifty or more similar letters and circulate them everywhere. Maybe it would make people believe the whole thing was a stupid plot to discredit Elissa, Geoffrey had said. Or whoever had said it in the first place.

By the end of the meal, they were full and comfortable and were on the second ewers of wine and mead. Deward drank some of both beverages, occasionally extolling the advantages of one over the other, giving precedence to the one he was drinking at the time.

Elissa realized they were getting drunk—a first for her—and it was all right. As long as no new crisis arose this night. Tomorrow they would all three be very sick and penitent, but it was good to laugh and not worry so much for a while.

And to make silly suggestions for ridding themselves of Lord Niall and his prince.

"We could always agree," Geoffrey said. "Invite the prince to come, marry Elissa . . ." She started to protest. "No, no, wait," he said holding up a hand. "When he crosses our border, we attack him with our larger army. Kill him and Niall. And everything is over."

"But what about the letter?" Elissa asked.

"He will have to bring it with him. That will be one of the conditions to your agreeing to marry the prince."

He chuckled to himself and Deward sat grinning broadly.

His eyes were so vacant, it was impossible to tell if he had actually heard a word Geoffrey said.

But Elissa had heard and she was not so drunk that she could not appreciate that this might very well be the suggestion they needed. She got up from the table and started toward her desk.

"Where are you going?" Geoffrey asked.

"To write that down," she said.

"Write what down?"

"What you just said."

"What'd I say?" His words were becoming more and more slurred.

She turned to look at him and burst out laughing. He stood facing her, one hand holding his goblet, the other on his hip. His feet were apart and askew so that his legs seemed impossibly twisted. His hair fell over his forehead like bangs and his smile was not only crooked, but silly, too. And somehow his jacket sleeves seemed to have shrunk so that they were too short for him.

"What?" he demanded.

"You look foolish," she said, hoping that her tone was kind.

"I am foolish."

"Why? Because you are an honest man doing what he believes in?"

"Am I?"

"You know you are." She moved back toward the table, trying to remember what she had wanted to do.

"Maybe I am. But no, that's not what makes me foolish." In spite of being drunk and slurring his words, he had suddenly become serious.

"What then?"

"A beautiful woman makes me foolish. Love makes me foolish. Like all the other men in the world."

He swung his arm wide, slopping some of the wine on the floor. She had moved just out of arm's reach. They looked at

each other and she saw the things about him that she always
tried to ignore: His blond hair that she would love to run her
fingers through. The hands whose touch thrilled her even when
they just brushed against her arm or shoulder. The lips that
seemed so inviting. She wanted to lay her cheek against his
chest and feel those arms around her.

Along that path lay danger.

But the warmth of the mead held her there, made her want
to face that danger, court it even. Oh, the warmth of the drink
inside and the warmth of a man's naked body pressed against
her own. She could almost smell him, feel the texture of his
skin. She shivered at the thought of his fingers on her body.
Now there was madness.

She turned away abruptly. There was something she had
intended doing. She must . . .

"I had better go," Geoffrey said behind her.

She almost cried, "No! Take me in your arms and make
love to me. It has been so long."

"Good night, your majesty."

"Good night, my lord," she said without turning to face
him. "We will finish this tomorrow."

"Finish?"

"Discussing the problem of Lord Niall."

"Oh. Of course."

His footsteps crossed the room, the door opened and closed,
and he was gone. She could feel that he was gone. She put a
hand to her forehead. It was time to sleep. Tomorrow she
would not remember any of this.

A sound startled her and she turned toward the table. Deward sat in his chair with his head cradled on his arm on the
tabletop. He was snoring. She smiled, then went to the door
and motioned for the guards stationed in the hall to come in.
She pointed at her uncle.

"Get him to his room, please," she said. "It has been a
long night."

Although one of them reminded her that they were not supposed to leave her alone, she insisted that they take care of Deward.

"Get him there and let his own man get him to bed. Then hurry back here."

They had no choice but to obey.

Except for the crackling of the fire, the night was very quiet. Roric and Randall were both in the castle. She was alone with enemies surrounding her in the dark.

She wrapped a shawl around herself and peered up and down the hallway. Empty and silent. She slipped out, closing the door as quietly as she could, and stole silently to the door of her son's room. The guards there saluted as she approached. She told one of them to stand outside her apartment and fetch her when her guards returned. He hurried off with a befuddled look, probably wondering where her own guards were.

She stole into Edgar's room. A single lamp was left lighted in case he had to get up during the night. Her eyes first glanced to the far side of the room where Ethel's empty bed was a reminder of her missing child. To drive those thoughts away, she moved to stand beside the other bed and looked down on the sleeping child.

Nurse appeared from her own bedchamber.

"Your majesty? What is wrong?"

"Nothing. I could not sleep and I don't get to spend much time with my son these days."

Nurse nodded and seemed about to take her place in the rocking chair in the corner.

"Go back to bed," Elissa said. "I will only stay a short while, then I must try to get some sleep. You must sleep, too."

"Are you sure?"

"Yes. I will just watch him sleep for a while."

The old woman nodded knowingly and shuffled back into her room. However, she left the door partly open just in case. The lamplight sputtered in the wake of her leaving, throwing dancing shadows on the walls, floor, and ceiling. Elissa pulled a chair up near the bed and sat down. Leaning over, she brushed a stray lock of hair from Edgar's forehead, then sat back.

At times like this, her heart became so full of love that it must surely burst. It was an ache in her breast that choked off her breath. It was a hole in her stomach that almost made her ill. And she knew she would die if anything happened to either of her children.

She also knew at these times that everything she did was for them, to ensure their futures and try to make them worthy of this kingdom their father had left for them. They represented the final melding of the two peoples from north and south and would be claimed by each as their own.

She snuggled into the chair with the shawl warm around her, tucked her feet up under her, and drifted off to sleep. Sometime later, she awakened to the sound of loud voices in the hall. Then someone pounded on the door. Edgar sat up in his bed, eyes wide with fear just as Nurse reappeared. She looked as frightened as the young prince.

"Who is there?" Elissa called out.

She grabbed up her son, who began to struggle in her arms.

"Let me get my sword!"

"Wait, Edgar," she said. "It may be nothing."

He quieted, but she still felt a thrill of pride in his eagerness.

The pounding on the door continued and Elissa swore under her breath. The door was unlocked for goodness' sake. She handed Edgar to Nurse and went to the door.

"No, your majesty!" Nurse said.

"They can get in anytime they want to," Elissa said. "Besides, I think I recognize one of the voices."

When she opened the door, she came face to face with Geoffrey. The startled look on his face was almost laughable.

"You're here!"

"Obviously," she said.

"Your guards say they returned to your door and you were gone. Thank goodness you're safe."

She feared he was about to put his arms around her while several men surrounded them, noisily expressing their relief. She held up a hand to stop them all.

"I sent one of Edgar's guards to tell my guards where I was when they returned."

"He was not there, majesty," one of her own guards said.

"He was supposed to be. Was he new? Did he know where my apartment is?"

Everyone exchanged looks until the second guard outside her son's room spoke up.

"He was new, majesty, but I'm sure he knew   he musta known where your rooms are."

"Then all of this is my fault," she said. "I assumed he would know where to go. I suppose your next task is to find him."

There was a general agreement within the small crowd.

"I will say good night to my son, then you two"—she pointed at her guards—"may escort me back to my apartment." She turned to Geoffrey, who looked angry and relieved and confused all at the same time. "And you, sir, may escort me too, if you wish."

He laughed at that, and she smiled. She turned back into the room.

"Good night, to the rest of you." She looked back over her shoulder. "Except the ones who will be looking for our young guardsman."

With a smile she closed the door on them. Laughing, she scooped Edgar into her arms and whirled around.

"My protector," she said. "Remember this night when I

am old and frail. Remember the feelings of manhood that coursed through your body, and know that someday I may need you to protect me.''

''Yes, Maman,'' he said and hugged her neck tightly.

His little arms were stronger than she remembered. Must be from the sword training, she thought. She laid him on the bed, covered him and kissed his cheek.

''Good night, my prince,'' she said.

''Good night, Maman.''

She straightened up and went to Nurse, kissing her on the forehead.

''Thank you for taking care of my son,'' she said softly.

''Yes, majesty. And maybe one day he will protect these old bones, too.''

Nurse smiled. Elissa gave her a quick hug.

''He just might,'' she said. ''Good night, Nurse.''

She stepped away and Nurse dropped a short curtsey.

''Sleep well, my child,'' she said.

The queen turned and left, feeling odd. It was not the first time that Nurse had curtsied to her. This night, however, it seemed like a reminder—or a confirmation—of who she had become.

Once in the hall, she found her two guards and the lord marshal waiting for her. Edgar's guard had resumed his post beside the door.

''When are you relieved?'' she asked him.

''In just under two hours, majesty.''

''I suppose one guard will be sufficient for that short a time,'' she said. ''Lord Geoffrey?''

''Yes, your majesty. But if you would feel better, I can have another man sent up while the search for the lost guardsman goes on.''

She started down the hall toward her own door.

''Yes, I think I would feel better if that were done.''

He gave the order to one of her guards, who hurried off to the guardroom on the ground floor.

"I will stay with you until your full complement of guards is on post outside your door," he said.

"I thought you might," she said.

The night's adventure, or threat of adventure, had made her giddy and a bit reckless. That and all of the mead she had drunk earlier. She was warm and felt desirable and desirous. If the latter were the right word.

She wanted to be held. To feel the warmth of a man's body pressed against hers. The thrill of his hands caressing her body.

You cannot do this, she told herself. But she wanted to.

You cannot risk losing everything you have won thus far. She could not wait any longer.

Think of the dangers. Think of the pleasure, the thrill.

He has a wife. Yes, he does.

And she is sickly and delicate. But that is no excuse.

They walked into her sitting room, which was cooler than it should have been. The guard insisted on checking out the rooms to ensure there was no one lurking about. She sat in her favorite chair and the lord marshal stirred up the fire. The spell was still on them, so clearly understood when their eyes met.

Except he could not be her husband. Not now. And damned if she was going to wish the woman dead. She was queen and must behave more circumspectly.

The guard pronounced the rooms safe. As he left, Geoffrey thanked him and asked that he let them know when the second guard returned.

The door closed and they were alone. If they waited, the moment would pass. But they did not wait. Elissa rose to her feet. Geoffrey was three steps away. He crossed that distance instantly, took her in his arms, and kissed her. She leaned against him, accepting the kiss and responding. Oh, it had been so long.

Their bodies pressed together, not urgently, but gently. They were tentative yet sure. Such an odd combination of sensations and attitudes. Yet, it felt right.

A knock on the door parted them. She bid them enter and

the guard stepped just inside to announce the return of his companion.

"Thank you," Elissa said.

"It is time for me to go, then," Geoffrey said. The guard backed out and closed the door.

"Yes, I know."

He sighed and his hand lifted as if to touch her one more time. Their eyes met. She stepped close and reached up to kiss him on the cheek.

"Good night, my lord," she said.

"Good night, your majesty."

He took her hand and kissed it. Then he left, leaving behind regret in his wake.

Breakfast had been laid by one of the serving girls, and Deward sat enjoying it with her. Elissa had once more sent word to Caedmon that she would not be there this morning. But she had seen Edgar off for lessons. He had left even more eagerly than ever, after the night's alarm. Elissa thought she was beginning to detect a slight swagger in his walk, which made him even more endearing than before.

Geoffrey was due to join them anytime so they could discuss the problem presented by his ex-spy. It was hoped that they would make better progress this morning than they had at dinner the night before.

Although she had a headache, Elissa regretted nothing that had occurred during the night. She understood that Geoffrey had felt compelled to leave as much for her sake as his, and in spite of his desires otherwise. And she was grateful for his levelheadedness, something she had not felt.

Besides, they had too much to do these days. Everything could still come apart, and the date for naming the regent had been reset for three days hence. Everything was now in her favor except for that damnable letter she had written in despair. If only she had waited, but she had felt there was too little time.

It is done, she reminded herself. All that could be done

now was neutralize its effects somehow. At least with Tommy gone, no one could testify to the delivery of the letter.

She sighed.

"What is it, niece?" Deward asked.

They had been sitting quietly eating for a few moments.

"A bad thought."

Her uncle smiled. "You should be having lots of those at the moment."

"True. But for a moment I was glad that Tommy was dead. That is unforgivable."

"Don't be so hard on yourself. There is a practical side and an emotional side at work. Both are honed to a new sharpness these days. You meant no disrespect to his memory nor do you miss him any less."

"No, I do not."

"Then accept the practical side, and be grateful for the sacrifice he made. He held out, giving your enemies nothing they could use against you."

She nodded just as a knock came on the door. Geoffrey entered at her summons, looking agitated.

"What is it?" Elissa asked.

"The guard you sent from outside Edgar's last night?"

"Yes?"

"He has been found dead."

"Where?"

"On the third floor landing of the back stairs."

"Did he fall?"

"No. He was killed. With a knife."

A shiver ran through her. She looked at Deward, who placed a hand over hers clutching the arm of the chair.

"Is there any clue as to whom or why?" she asked, her voice dull and distant.

"None."

"When was he found?"

"Not long after I left you last night."

"Then you've had little sleep."

Geoffrey nodded. She motioned for him to sit, which he did.

"Now, tell me everything."

"When I got back to my rooms last night, I couldn't sleep. All the excitement, you know." Their eyes met for an instant and she lowered her gaze. Everyone else would think he meant the excitement caused by her seeming disappearance, when she knew it was that and more. "Less than half an hour after I got there, one of the guardsmen I had sent to search for their lost comrade reported having found him."

He poured himself some of the honeyed wine and took a deep drink before continuing his story. Only taking time to grab his sword, he had bid the guard to lead the way. They wound up on the back landing where the young man lay in a pool of his own blood. A knife protruded from just below his sternum, a fatal thrust, to be sure, but not one that would immediately incapacitate a strong, young man. His killer must have held him there as his life ebbed away.

Elissa shivered again. The value of a quick death had been shown to her too often in the past few months.

"The only thing the scoundrel left behind was the knife."

He hesitated then looked at Deward, who raised an eyebrow. Her uncle nodded, indicating that Geoffrey should tell it all, whatever the rest might be.

"The knife that killed him. Is there anything distinctive about it?" she asked.

"It . . . it belonged to Lord Randall."

"Lord Randall? No, he wouldn't be foolish enough to kill one of my guards. He wouldn't even be in this part of the castle. He knows better."

"We both know that he never meant to support you as regent," Geoffrey said.

"But to make a move so soon! He isn't that stupid. What would he have been after? Me? Edgar?"

"Either or both? Meaning to kidnap or murder? Who knows? I do know that he has left the castle."

"Strange," she said. "Clara has disappeared too."

• • •

Edgar returned from his lessons at the academy and Nurse brought him to the queen's apartment so they could have lunch together. Deward excused himself right after lunch to take care of some matters of his own, leaving the two of them to talk. Elissa wanted to be sure that Edgar was not adversely affected by the events of the night before.

To the contrary, he had thought it a great adventure and glowed when she praised him again for his courage. Nurse reappeared to take him for his nap and lessons after that.

"Come to say good night, Maman?" he asked from the doorway.

"Of course," she replied. "Sweet dreams."

He grinned and let himself be led away. Alone, she thought of her son with a smile. He would make a good king, given the right guidance. But she was still concerned that he was without a playmate. When everything had settled somewhat, she would have to readdress the problem of finding some boys to live in the castle and be his companions. His cousin, Randall's son, would be a good choice, she thought. He was nearly a year younger than Edgar, which would make the prince the natural leader. He must learn about comradeship, but in a way that he understood that he was in command. Graciously, of course.

Thoughts of Randall's son brought her to thoughts of Randall himself. He had sworn to support her and the king's family in the years to come, but only at his father's insistence. Now, a party had been sent out to find him and bring him back.

She shook her head, praying that what they suspected of Randall was not true. She went into the bedchamber and got her sword. For a while she practiced, finding it a bit awkward in her gown, but not wanting to take the time to change. She only had a short while before Deward returned. This afternoon, they were to work on the plans for the new household setup. The problem of replacing Clara might have been solved by the girl's disappearance.

They were in the midst of that discussion in the late afternoon when Geoffrey returned. He looked better rested but still agitated.

"No word of Randall?" she asked.

"None."

"Where could he go?"

"Not to his own castle, nor to the cave on that land," Geoffrey said. "I suppose he could go to Ravelin."

"I don't think so," she mused. "He wants the throne. He certainly would not help King Verald or his sons to become rulers in Albor."

"Indeed," Geoffrey agreed. "Then he would have nothing."

They speculated further on possible whereabouts of the man. Even the possibility that they could be wrong about him. But it became harder to believe. Elissa was quite convinced that he was irrational and capable of anything.

This thought tortured her after her two mentors had left. She tried to lie down and rest until Deward returned to dine with her. Before that she would see Edgar to bed. No matter how busy she became, she must not neglect to spend time with her son, over and above that time they would soon spend in his other lessons. And in many ways, once she was named regent, they would spend even more time together. Perhaps until they were tired of one another.

She smiled at that. Most sons did not spend so much time with their mothers. Nor their fathers for that matter. Usually it was companions their own age, tutors, and nannies, with whom they spent their time. Tomorrow she would speak with Roric about having Randall's son come to court. That should surprise him greatly, if he knew where his own son was and what he had done. Somehow she suspected Roric had no part in that, but she could be wrong. Just as she had been wrong about Randall's oath.

She drifted off to sleep, awakening when one of the downstairs maids appeared to tell her dinner was on its way up to Edgar's room. Deward would come soon after.

Elissa rose, washed the sleep from her face in cold water,

and let the maid help her dress again. Deward arrived just as Elissa entered the sitting room. Their own dinner came shortly after and the girl made herself scarce again, promising to return in time to help the queen get ready for bed. They ate in comfortable silence. She felt a little woozy from her nap and the effects of the drinking the night before, so she drank the mead sparingly.

Their hunger sated, they sat back in their chairs at table and drank their drinks in comfort. Conversation remained sparse for some time. At last, Elissa tried to shake off her lethargy.

"Do you believe it really is necessary that we find Randall?" she asked. "It has occurred to me that, with the selection of regent being made very soon, there is no time for him to actually cause any trouble. Especially with him hiding out now."

He shook his head.

"He could reappear at any time," he said, "and cause no end of problems if he wanted to."

"Then we continue to search for him."

"*You* might find him faster."

"No, Uncle. I cannot . . ."

The memory of the search for Tommy was too clear, the threat to herself too undefined. She did not know how to control it enough nor what all of the dangers might be. If she ever tried shadow turning again, it must be on a smaller scale and with less importance attached to it.

When she told Deward that, he nodded again. "You must be the judge of that. If you are too frightened or unsure, that in itself could place you in danger. All magic must be performed with a sure hand and heart."

Elissa could not tell by his tone or his words whether he was disappointed in her or not. She knew he meant what he said, and she knew that danger did exist in what he described. And she needed more practice in a less threatening way.

She rose from her chair. "I must put Edgar to bed," she said. "Do you want to wait here for me?"

"No. I think I will be off to bed myself. I need the rest after last night." He smiled at her and stood to kiss her on the cheek. "You get some sleep, too," he said.

They walked into the hall together and the two guards assigned to her for the night prepared to fall in step behind her.

"It has occurred to me," she said, "that you might also need some guards. Just because of your relationship to me."

"That might be true," he said. "But I do not think that is a good idea."

"We will talk about it tomorrow," she said, and turned toward her son's room. "Good night, Uncle."

"Sleep well, niece."

∽ 22 ∽

Elissa had always thought that, when great and momentous things happened, one was supposed to feel different. The sun changed colors. Two moons suddenly appeared in the night sky. The world simply should not look the same. But it did.

Elissa looked around the Privy Council chamber, empty except for herself, the old immense table, the chairs, and the usual decorations. In the end, she was confirmed as regent with little pomp and ceremony. Only Dathan had voted against her. Even if she could, she would not seek revenge against him. He might be needed one day.

The meeting was held in the early afternoon as planned, in spite of Randall's continued absence. No word had been heard of him in the castle, with the probable exception of Roric. But he would hardly tell her or anyone else if he had heard from his son. She had wanted to believe in Roric's pledge to support her as regent, but his vote in her favor meant very little. Randall's disappearance meant much more. And the father must resent her role in this possible loss of his only son, a resentment that would grow over time.

She moved around the table, standing behind each of the chairs in turn. Back to her chair—Ethelred's chair. And his father's before him. And back into the mists of history.

With all her might, she tried to recapture the elation she had felt earlier in the day. To find within herself the excitement she had felt at the mere possibility of achieving this goal. But all she felt was a letdown, as if the struggle was the exciting part, not reaching the end of the struggle and facing all that meant. If she could hold on to it for the foreseeable future, she had taken on a burden that would prove heavier than she had imagined. Even now, the enormity of it lay on her shoulders and at the pit of her stomach like lead.

With growing dread, she wished that this task had been given to Geoffrey. She still suspected that was what Ethelred had intended all along. However, his method had not proved equal to the task. And even he had not understood the loyalty and honesty of the lord marshal.

Elissa went to the door and took a last look around the chamber. This would become her second home in the days and years to come. Plans would be made. Policy would be set. And some of the others would fight her all the way.

She was up at dawn, having managed only short catnaps for the rest of the night. First she reviewed some documents that she needed to go over with Geoffrey and later the Council. Breakfast appeared at the usual time and the maid came back to help her dress. Elissa toyed with the idea of going to the academy in her practice clothes, but decided against it. Her position was not that secure yet.

When it was time, she got Edgar and they left the castle together with their coterie of guards. Just outside the gates of the castle, they found Geoffrey waiting for them. They walked together, talking and laughing in the crisp morning air. For that short time, she felt young and free, even frivolous. However, Caedmon brought her back to earth.

He seemed unusually critical of her efforts this morning, no matter how hard she tried. Granted, she had missed her lessons several days in a row, but surely she was not that bad. Well, it wasn't just that, she finally admitted to herself. She was distracted and unable to concentrate fully on what he said and give correct instructions to her muscles, which in turn seemed to have forgotten much. This time, she took his scolding without a word, admitting to herself that she deserved it. By the end of the session, however, she had become more in tune with what she must do.

The lesson ended finally, and she stood looking out one of the high windows at the street below as she wiped the sweat from her face with a cloth. The village was alive with activity. Seeing that gave her a good feeling, but she reminded herself that it was not exactly her doing. Not yet. She could only hope to do her best to bring prosperity to her kingdom. Only then would it continue through her time and into the next several generations.

Caedmon cleared his throat behind her. She turned to find him studying her.

"I was hard on you today, I know," he said. "But you needed it."

"I know. And I accept it. This time."

She smiled and he smiled back. The thought that he would make an excellent privy councilor crossed her mind, but the others would object. Most strenuously. He was not of noble birth and his falling-out with the king probably would add to their objections.

She went behind the screen and changed clothes. The sun coming in through the windows was warm on her skin as she stripped down. She stood for a long moment with eyes closed, letting the bright warmth bathe her skin.

Caedmon shuffled his feet somewhere near the door and she grinned. He was getting restless waiting for her to leave. Would more students arrive after lunch? The academy was in excellent repair, so he must be doing very well with fees for classes. She certainly was paying him well. But it was worth it and she was positive that he would never charge her more than anyone else.

Well, she thought. *There is one other man I can trust in this world.*

And that was not a bad feeling.

Caedmon accompanied her downstairs where Edgar and Geoffrey waited. They said goodbye and started back to the castle. Geoffrey told her of Edgar's excellent progress and the prince beamed with pleasure. When the lord marshall had finished, Edgar supplied more details, adding a bit of demonstration now and then.

As they neared the castle gate, a horseman, dressed in the livery of the northern marches, galloped through, his mount lathered and breathing hard. The poor animal had been ridden hard over a long distance, and no matter how Elissa tried to convince herself otherwise, that had to mean bad news.

They rushed into the castle. She sent Edgar to his rooms with his guards, and she and Geoffrey made their way into the great hall. Job was talking with the horseman there. When the chamberlain spied Elissa, he turned the man toward her.

"There is your queen, Sergeant," he said. "Tell her your news. And be quick!"

The man saluted Job and stepped toward the queen. Geoffrey took her elbow to slow her down so that he could take a position slightly between her and the man. The two guards flanked them, their spears held ready for quick defense.

"Where have you come from?" Elissa asked.

"The northern border, majesty."

"Who is your commander there," Geoffrey demanded.

"Captain Bergerson."

"How is his rheumatism in that cold?"

"He doesn't have rheumatism, sir. He has bursitis."

Geoffrey nodded, mostly satisfied that the man came from where he said.

"What is your news?" the queen asked.

"Word has come that King Verald is gathering an army at his capital."

"How many?"

"Let's go up to your sitting room," Geoffrey interrupted. "You can warm yourself by the fire and tell us everything."

Elissa looked at him sharply, her irritation about to boil over. He spread his arms wide, indicating the rather public place in which they stood and she nodded understanding.

As they turned to leave, she told Job to have food and drink brought up and to send someone to fetch her uncle.

She bade the sergeant to sit with her at the table. It was cool in the room, and she kept her cloak on while the first guard rebuilt the fire. The second guardsman returned from searching the other rooms, then took his place just inside the door. Once the fire was going well again, both guards retreated to the hallway.

"Do you need to warm yourself at the fire, Sergeant?" Elissa asked.

"No, majesty. I'm quite warm."

She nodded. "Tell us your news, then."

"There really isn't much else. We got word from some friendly locals that a large party was gathering in King Verald's capital. No one has any idea why."

"Is it military or something else?" Geoffrey asked.

"You mean like the king or someone going for a visit somewhere?" The marshal nodded. "Didn't get no word on that, sir."

"But it is unusual for such a large group to prepare for a trip at this time of year?"

"Well, yes. Although right now isn't so bad. You see, the snow has stopped falling like it always does around now. And the roads are still frozen so there isn't any mud to get bogged down in. In about a month, with the spring thaws starting, the roads will be damnable. Begging your pardon, majesty."

She nodded forgiveness.

"Is that all the information you have?" she asked.

"For the moment, yes, majesty. The captain thought you here in Winfield should be told just in case."

"He was right," Geoffrey said.

The food arrived, and the table was set. Hunger had left Elissa and she picked at some bread, cheese, and cold meat, and watched the two men eat their fill. While they ate, the lord marshal plied the sergeant with questions about conditions on the border. She laughed with them when he told of how everyone had grown weary of snowball fights.

They had finished lunch by the time Deward appeared, and were bidding the sergeant a good trip back to his post in the morning. Once he had left, they told Deward what they had learned.

"There is nothing to tell us where this group might be going?" he asked.

"Not so far," Elissa replied. "It seems a bit too soon for Verald to be sending them to force me to marry the prince."

"Just because this second son wants to better himself with such a match doesn't mean his father agrees with that," her uncle said.

"I do not know," she said. "It certainly would help us if any confrontation could be delayed as long as possible."

"To the contrary," Deward said. "It might be best to get it over so you can go on with what you must do."

"How bad do you think this will make the relationship between our two kingdoms?" Elissa asked Geoffrey.

"We have never been the best of friends," he said. "Although it has been years since there were any open hostilities." He thought for a long moment. "I doubt that we could ever trust them fully regardless of this situation," he said at last.

"Do you think Randall might have made it into Ravelin?"

The two men sat quietly thinking that over.

"He might," Geoffrey said.

"What about Verald's queen?"

"Niall said she has not been seen at court for some time. Not since the last time she incited her sons against him."

"All right," she said. "If there should be a war, will the councilors rally behind me . . . us . . . or will they use it as a means of discrediting me as regent? With or without the letter?"

Geoffrey shook his head. "They surely are looking for some good excuse to rid themselves of you. Don't doubt that for a moment. But none of them can act overtly, except

Dathan. You have won them to your side with threats and that is not a good basis for loyalty.''

"I know." She rose from the table. "I expect it is time we found out. They must be waiting for us right now."

Geoffrey nodded. Deward took her hand and squeezed it.

"Remember always, that you are queen," he said.

She leaned down and kissed his forehead. He stood and walked out with them, turning for his own rooms as they headed downstairs.

"I think you should tell the others," Elissa said. "It is important that they believe you are advising me in all things for now."

"I am," he said flatly.

"Yes."

A flash of fear raced through her mind, but she did not try to hold on to it. She had to trust someone completely and this man was the only powerful candidate for that trust. If he turned against her, she was doomed.

They arrived at the door to the Council chamber. The guard opened the door and the one who had accompanied them joined him in the hall. One of the guards was to remain outside her apartment at all times now.

The lords looked up. Dathan looked irritated at having been kept waiting. Roric looked weary. The others appeared wary. They stood until she had taken the chair at the head of the table.

"My lords," she began. "We have received serious word from the northern border. Lord Geoffrey will tell you in de- tail."

They listened quietly as he relayed the message from Cap- tain Bergerson. Their expressions had changed from curiosity to chagrin, except for Dathan, whose face reflected only anger. The silence remained for several moments after the lord mar shal finished.

"I warned you," Dathan growled. "King Verald has just been waiting for an excuse to invade Albor. He has always wanted our southern ports. Now, with this . . . woman . . . as regent, he thinks we are too weak to defend ourselves."

"Be careful, Patriarch," Geoffrey said. "Elissa is our queen and should be shown the respect she is due."

"She should first earn that respect."

Geoffrey started to rise, but Elissa spoke up.

"Gentlemen, this is not the time to air personal grievances. Or to debate what has already been done."

Witram spoke for the first time. "She is right. We have confirmed the queen as regent. It would be unseemly to try to change that when our kingdom may be threatened. Our task now is to decide if this is a real threat, and if it is, how we will answer it."

The others nodded agreement. She breathed a soft sigh of relief. They were willing to give her a chance to prove herself. And this possible crisis was enough to make or break her.

"Let us discuss our options, then," Geoffrey said.

Dathan watched as everyone nodded agreement and with a shrug he accepted their decision.

The debate was lively, each councilor having a strong opinion. Quincy, who had the northernmost lands of them all, urged that they immediately gather the army together and put it in the field. Even if Verald never crossed the border, their presence would remind him that Albor was still capable of defending herself. However, he was reminded that it would take several days since the various units were scattered around the country. Then he argued that they should send as large a force as they could muster within a few days.

Although everyone agreed that steps should be taken to alert the army, no one else thought the threat was that immediate. It was decided to send another company to reinforce the one stationed along the border just in case, and to gather several companies between them and the capital.

It was late by then, and Elissa knew they were expecting to return to their rooms. It was time to bring up the other issue she wanted to discuss. She was only slightly encouraged by the fact that Geoffrey had raised no objections when she mentioned the subject earlier.

"My lords, there is one more matter we should discuss," she said.

For the most part they looked surprised.

"One of the places at this table has been vacated and I believe we should fill it."

"What?" Roric almost shouted.

"Lord Randall seems to have abandoned his seat, my lord. I believe it best that we bring in another to replace him."

"This is unconscionable," Roric said. "You've no idea where he is or why he left."

"I agree," Dathan added. "He may have been kidnapped, for all we know."

Quincy looked like thunder and Witram had crossed his arms over his large belly.

"That is true," Luther said. "However, he has been gone for some time. The replacement need not be permanent. Is that not right, your majesty?"

After the reactions and strong objections of the other two, it seemed politic to accept his suggestion.

"Of course, Lord Luther," she said. "Do you know of a possible candidate?"

"The rules give us two possibilities as I recall. But we should check that out before we talk with any of the other lords."

"Will you do that for us, then?" she asked.

"Of course. First thing in the morning."

"Good. Then we can leave this until tomorrow afternoon?"

Roric still looked like thunder, and when everyone was leaving the chamber, she almost dismissed her next task. However, it was too important for Edgar and she hoped it might smooth some feathers. Unless her request only increased his consternation. It was quite possible, after all, that some might mistake her intentions.

～ 23 ～

Clara woke when Randall got up. It was still very dark, the fire had nearly gone out, and she shivered without the warmth of his body pressed against hers. She heard him stir the fire and add more wood. When he did not return, she finally sat up to see where he was.

He stood at the fireplace gazing into the flames. His expression was as serious as she had ever seen it.

"What troubles my lord?" she asked.

He turned his head and looked at her. A smile touched the corners of his mouth for a moment but died.

"I did not mean to wake you. The fire was going out."

She got up and went to him, pressing against his side as he put an arm around her.

"I heard you moan before," she said. "More bad dreams?"

"Yes. They sap my endurance and make me believe I will fail. I cannot fail."

"I know. And you will not. The dreams are not real. They cannot harm you." She pressed her cheek against his chest. "When they come, hold on to me ever tighter and I will chase them away."

Randall laughed softly and pressed her tighter against him.

"Ah, my Clara," he said. "You make it all possible some-how. The way you believe in me makes me think I can do anything."

She did not remind him of their failure to kidnap the young prince nor the murder of the guard when he caught them in the royal wing. Those things could have happened to anyone.

He stiffened, suddenly alert.

"What is it, my lord?"

"Shhh. Listen."

A moment passed.

"I hear nothing."

Then she did. A familiar sound of crunching snow. It sounded very near the door. Randall pushed her aside and leapt for his sword standing in its scabbard against the wall near their pallet. The door crashed open and three men rushed in. One reached Randall before he could grab hold of his sword.

"I would not, my lord," the intruder said.

Clara cried out and ran to stand between the man she loved and the sword that pointed too near his breast.

"How dare you threaten his lordship!" she cried.

"I have my orders, ma'am."

More soldiers came inside, but Clara was only conscious of them as background noise. She did not mind her hands being bound, but that they should lay their common hands on a nobleman was unbearable. She struggled to get free so that she could help Randall until the soldier tying her was forced to hit her, knocking her unconscious.

When she woke, she was on the horse once more. The cold penetrated more deeply than ever. Ahead of her rode Randall, his shoulders slumped, his proud head bowed.

It was all the queen's fault. Elissa would be made to pay for shaming him so, if it was the last thing she did.

The new meeting room was slightly smaller than Elissa's sitting room and was on the first floor. It had occurred to her when the messenger came from the northern border that, although it was all right for a king to meet with his advisors and others in his own apartment on a regular basis, it might not be seemly for a queen to do so.

After discussing it with Deward and Geoffrey, she had ordered this room furnished so they could meet and receive visitors there. She actually found that she preferred it since it made her apartment a retreat once more.

Another room had also been cleaned out and prepared for occupancy. This one was on the second floor not too far from Edgar's. Just yesterday Fergus, Randall's son, had moved in. So far the introductions of the two boys had gone well, and they had already found mutual interests.

Now, Elissa was trying to understand a bit more about finances. She was amazed that there was no single person who oversaw such matters, and she suggested that someone should be given the responsibility. Geoffrey agreed to discuss it, but seemed not to favor the idea.

A knock came on the door and the marshal bade them enter. Job opened the door and stepped in, closing it behind him.

"Your majesty," he said, "there is a messenger."

"About Lord Randall?" she asked.

"Yes, majesty."

"Send him in."

In a moment, the soldier was escorted in. He looked more excited than weary, although his journey must have taken him no less than three days.

"What news have you?" Geoffrey asked the man.

He bowed to the queen.

"I was sent ahead, majesty, to tell you. Lord Randall and his companions have been found. They will be here within the next day or so."

"At last," Geoffrey said beside her.

"What companion?" Elissa asked.

"A woman named Clara."

"Of course," she said.

• • •

Voices were subdued in the audience chamber. It was the first ceremony to be held since Elissa had been installed as regent. The second since Ethelred died. As king-to-be, Edgar sat on the throne, his eyes bright with excitement. The queen-mother sat on his left, ready to preside over her first official function outside of the Council chamber. Everyone still in Winfield was present—even Job, who acted as doorman and chamberlain.

At some cue from outside, he pulled the wooden doors open. The prisoners stood just outside the threshold. He stepped to one side.

"Lord Randall of Albor and Mistress Clara Bowden of Lochnere."

They entered the chamber, unbound, led by the captain of the royal guard and flanked by the soldiers who had brought them back. The whispering had stopped and now the only sound was that of the footsteps of the prisoners and escort. Clara walked beside Randall, casting occasional adoring glances his way.

They all stopped at the foot of the low dais upon which the thrones sat. Randall looked up at Elissa haughtily then turned and bowed to Edgar. A murmur went up from the crowd. Elissa glanced at Roric, who looked pained.

"Your majesty," Randall said. "May I ask why I have been brought here as a prisoner?"

Edgar frowned down at his cousin, but kept silent as he had been instructed.

"My Lord Randall," Geoffrey said. He stood on Edgar's right, his place as lord marshal. "You have only been brought for questioning about your disappearance immediately following the murder of a royal guardsman."

"You suspect me of such a crime?"

"Suspect? No, my lord," Geoffrey said. "We merely thought you might have seen someone in the halls that night. It was very late and few were wandering about."

"I—"

"You will be held under house arrest until called before the Privy Council for questioning," Elissa said, managing to keep her voice impersonal.

Randall's jaw muscles twitched and he could not help but turn his head to look at her. There was such loathing in his expression that she blinked.

"Until that time," she continued, "only your father and your wife will be allowed to visit you. Besides your jailers, of course."

Clara flinched.

"As for you, Mistress Clara, you will be confined in the dungeon—"

"No! I want to stay with his lordship."

She started toward the dais, but two of the soldiers grabbed her arms and held her back. A look of rage passed quickly across Randall's features, and Elissa wondered if it was directed at the woman because of her outburst or at the soldiers because they had dared lay hands on her.

"Take them away," Elissa ordered. "And see that sufficient guards are placed."

Randall marched out stoically in the midst of the soldiers. Clara was carried kicking and screaming from the chamber. Her cries could still be heard after the doors were closed. Elissa glanced once more at Lord Roric. His face had become a mask, but he could not hide the hurt in his eyes.

Edgar looked up at his mother and she nodded.

"Is there any other business to be brought forward?" he asked.

No one spoke up.

"Thank you, my lords, ladies, and gentlemen," Geoffrey said.

The doors were reopened and everyone filed out, except for Deward. He came toward Elissa as she, the prince, and the lord marshal descended.

"Those two may be more dangerous now than they were as fugitives," he said.

"Yes, I know," Elissa admitted.

"He could be . . ." Deward began, then looked down at Edgar. He smiled at the boy, who smiled back. "He could be quite a king one day," he finished.

"Yes, I will," Edgar said eagerly.

"But now it is time for your supper," Elissa said. "Go on up to your room and let Nurse take off your finery."

"I want to wear it awhile longer," Edgar said, warming her heart with a smile.

"Well, all right. Be careful not to get food on you, though."

"Yes, Maman."

He sped off toward the stairway, the guards keeping close.

"Now, Uncle. What were you about to say?"

She turned toward the banquet hall. With so many of the men and their ladies dressed up, she had decided they should all dine together.

"Only that if he tries to escape . . ." He shrugged.

"And you think that could happen without any repercussions?" she asked. He said nothing. "I am in hopes that it might not come to execution."

They looked at her in amazement.

"How can you do otherwise?" Geoffroy asked. "We have needed an excuse to be rid of him and it practically falls in our lap."

"But we need Roric. If we destroy Randall, we will lose him, too."

"I am not so sure. Roric needs the support of the monarchy as much as the monarchy needs him."

"Not at the moment," she argued. "The monarchy—this monarchy—is shaky at best. Until we are more readily accepted by everyone, from peasant to the highest and strongest noble house, we are not on firm footing."

They fell silent as they entered the hall. Servants rushed around preparing the tables, setting out large ewers of drink and bowls of dried fruits. The hunters had been very successful and there would be venison and boar and onions boiled in their juices. Elissa made a mental note to send platters to each of the prisoners, hopefully part of a softening up of their antagonism toward her.

Lady Margaret spotted them from halfway across the hall and came bustling up.

"Everything is nearly ready," she said.

Her eyes glittered and her face was flushed. This was her strong suit, something she loved to do, and Elissa had already seen how happy she was to be near her husband. She had herself told Margaret that Randall was returning as a prisoner, but the young man was her stepson. She loved him, of course, she had said, but there never had been a bond between them, no matter how she had tried. It was not her fault that his mother died shortly after giving him birth. Nor was it her fault that Roric had been unable to give her children. Ah, well.

Elissa smiled. Having this cheerful woman in the castle was a treat. Hopefully, she would help Roric to cope with the days ahead.

The atmosphere during dinner was a strange mix of gaiety and solemnity. No one dared not to come, but Roric and a few of Randall's friends left early. Margaret bustled around, directing servants and urging everyone to eat. She rushed over when her husband rose to leave, said a few words, and he leaned down and kissed her cheek. Clearly, they were still fond of one another. How fortunate they were to have grown old together.

As conversation rose and fell all around, her mind wrestled with the problem of what to do with Randall. He was Ethelred's cousin and a powerful man in his own right. There must be a way to either ensure his loyalty, or establish a truce between them. But there was nothing she knew of that she could offer him. Not even herself, for she had come to realize that his assault on her was more an attempt to dominate her than an expression of any passion.

He had always been jealous of Ethelred, wanting everything the king had. Probably he had wanted the king's wife for the same reason. Was there anything else that had belonged to Ethelred that she could give to Randall?

Oh, it was all impossible. He had killed a royal guardsman, a crime punishable by death. But it was the Privy Council who would judge him. Would they be able to find him guilty?

Job suddenly appeared at her elbow, startling her.

"A messenger has come," he whispered so that only she could hear.

Not another one, she said to herself. He handed her a note, but she waved for him to keep it.

"Excuse me, gentlemen," she said and rose.

She followed the chamberlain through the kitchen and into the new office she had just set up. A young retainer sat waiting. His livery was not Alboran. He leapt to his feet and bowed as soon as they entered. She moved to the chair at her desk and motioned for the stranger to sit. Job followed, handing her the note when she had settled down.

She broke the wax seal and unfolded the paper. The handwriting was elaborate, the signature unexpected. The page was full, but one paragraph was the most telling,

I am sure you have received reports of the forces my husband has gathered in the capital, she read. *My younger son and I have taken the field against King Verald, He will soon send that force against us. We have chosen our field well and can hope for a positive outcome. You need only worry should we lose, for then we would also lose a certain letter. Perhaps it would be in your best interests to send a contingent of your army to help ensure it does not fall back into unfriendly hands. Should you decide to assist us, come yourself to receive the letter. Thank you in advance for your support. We queens must support one another above all.*

Enclosed with the letter was a letter of marque granting her and those who accompanied her safe passage into Ravelin and within its borders.

Elissa sat back. So, the letter had moved to someone else's control. She read the rest, which briefly sketched a plan, and then reread the signature: *Marie, Queen, Ravelin.*

Turning, she ordered Job to give the messenger whatever food and drink he needed and a place to stay until there was a response for his queen. Thanking the young man once again, she returned to the banquet. The minstrels still played and everyone was enjoying the food. She told Geoffrey that they needed to meet later and asked him to tell Deward. She ate a little and watered her mead to keep a clear head. No one must suspect that anything was amiss, but she often felt Geoffrey watching her.

It was late when everyone was finally sated. Some of their lordships, with their heads on the tables, snored. Elissa signaled for their retainers to help them to their rooms, said good night to those still able to stand, and went to her own rooms to freshen up a bit.

"That damnable letter," Geoffrey said hotly when she told him the news. "Will we never hear the end of it?"

"It would appear that we can, if we agree to help Queen Marie," Deward said.

"How can you even think of doing that?" Geoffrey looked over at Elissa. "Are you considering it?"

"Of course."

"You cannot. Don't you see?"

"I see only that we have been given a chance to rid ourselves of this letter," she said. "And we can be rid of King Verald at the same time."

"But at what price? The killing of another king? Don't you see how that might give others the idea that a throne is there for the taking?"

"That risk has always been there."

His attitude puzzled her. She had expected he might oppose their aiding Queen Marie, but for reasons other than this. In fact, she had expected he would object more to risking Alboran soldiers to save her reputation.

"Have you changed your mind about supporting me as regent, my lord?"

He looked up at her then at Deward, with an air of confusion. When he looked back at her, that confusion was gone, replaced by decision and a touch of sadness.

"No, I have not changed my mind, your majesty," he said. "If we are going to do this, I suggest we act quickly and quietly."

"What about the Privy Council?" she said. "Should we tell them anything in advance?"

"Since they know about the buildup of Verald's army, we must," Deward said.

"They will rant and rave," Geoffrey said. "But I think they will accept a reconnaissance mission."

"Then we are agreed that I will go?" Elissa asked.

"I rather think they will expect it," Deward said.

Geoffrey nodded curtly and left the room to begin the preparations. First thing in the morning she would send Marie's messenger back with their response. She went to sleep wondering how the letter had come into Queen Marie's hands.

~ 24 ~

The temperature dropped with each mile they traveled northward. At least no more snow fell. That would have slowed them and made Elissa more uncomfortable.

She could not be much more uncomfortable. She would never get used to the cold.

The messenger from Queen Marie left a day ahead of them. Before he passed over the border, he was to have delivered a letter to Captain Bergerson, telling him to prepare his men to move. Although he might have guessed, she and Geoffrey would tell him their destination.

She left the arrangements and leading their little group to Geoffrey, who insisted on accompanying her.

"Who else do you have in mind?" he had asked. There was no good reply, of course. "And if you get yourself killed in Ravelin, I might as well die too, or become a hermit," he had added. It was difficult to admit, but there was great truth in that statement. Their futures were now interdependent.

When they broke camp that morning, he had told her they should reach the border headquarters by afternoon.

Once they had left Winfield behind, his mood had changed. For the better, she was glad to notice. His was a warrior's heart and tending to day-to-day details of government must often have been difficult for him.

Suddenly a challenge rang out in the forest stillness.

"Halt! Identify yourselves," a man's voice shouted.

"Stand easy, soldier," Geoffrey said from the front of their party. "I am Geoffrey, marshal of Albor, here to see your captain."

A moment of silence, then a soldier carrying a spear stepped into view from a small clump of dead bushes in front and a little to the right of them. He moved a little closer. His clothing was white with brown streaks and he had been completely invisible until he moved.

"I recognize your badge," he said. "I do not know any of these others."

"Before you sits your queen, soldier. Surely you recognize her badge, too."

The man's mouth dropped open in amazement.

"Yes, sir. I do, sir." He bobbed up and down from the waist a couple of times. "Would you like for me to guide you to the camp?"

"I know the way," Geoffrey said. "Remain on guard here."

The man saluted and they rode on. The way ahead led up a slight hill. At the top, they found several small cabins and more soldiers. A few stood at the edge of a cliff staring across into Ravelin. Others lounged around. One of these spied the party approaching and went running to one of the buildings and pounded on the door.

By the time they were within the camp, a man came out of the door, buckling on his sword. He smiled and Geoffrey waved.

"My lord!" the man said. "It is good to see you."

"And you, Captain. It has been a while since our last little skirmish."

They came to a stop and Geoffrey jumped down to shake the man's hand.

"It has, indeed."

Elissa got down off her horse. She stretched her legs, working out muscle cramps and stiffness, then looked around at the camp. The cabins were only slightly better than lean-tos and she doubted that any had a fireplace inside. If she were lucky, there might be a small circle in the floor surrounded by stones just under a hole in the roof through which the smoke escaped. It was possible these cabins might be warmer than a tent at night, but not by much.

The captain was offering her his own cabin for the night. She accepted.

The soldiers who had accompanied them moved toward a corral where they dismounted and began unsaddling their horses. Elissa was unsure what to do, but was saved from further guessing when Geoffrey called one of the men to take her horse and his to the corral and feed them.

The next priority was for the soldiers to eat. They all sat at tables around a central fire and ate venison that had been killed just recently, and hard brown bread.

"It's the best there is," Bergerson said. "Which is good since there is nothing else."

Everyone laughed as if it were an old joke they had all heard many times before. They had only mead to drink and that was rationed carefully, either because there was little in stock or because the men had to be alert at all times.

But if they were that careful about the mead, why would they not be careful about the smoke from their fires? Surely anyone a few miles to the north could see it as it curled into the sky.

The captain saw her studying it.

"Are you concerned about the smoke, majesty?" When Elissa nodded, he laughed. "Do you think they don't know we're here? If you look just over yonder"—she turned to look where he pointed—"you'll see the same from their side of the border."

Sure enough, smoke billowed from another hill a mile or two away. Then she spotted another and another.

"They have anywhere from three to five separate camps

over there," he explained. "Same as us. As long as we see each other, it seems like we know everything is okay."

He smiled and finished sopping up the meat juices with a piece of bread. She listened as they all talked about past campaigns and the life of solitude here on the border. Shortly after the sun went down, several of the men lit lamps and headed off to different cabins. Men who had been on watch were replaced by others. It seemed that the camp ran of its own accord, but Bergerson kept his eye on everything.

Soon, Elissa retired to the captain's cabin, which was slightly larger than the others. Geoffrey and Bergerson followed to help her get settled in. Besides two cots, there were a small table and three stools. The captain lit the small lamp on the table with a brand from the fire outside then did the same to a fire already laid in the center of the floor. As she had suspected, a hole in the roof drew out the smoke. They sat at the table and one of the soldiers brought them each a mug of mead. The captain thanked him and sent him off to bed.

"Now, my lord, What is this all about?"

"For reasons I cannot discuss, the queen has agreed to help Queen Marie of Ravelin in her attempt to take the throne from King Verald. She intends to place her younger son on that throne."

"And be the power behind him?" Bergerson snorted. "Women should not mess in such things as this."

He looked at Elissa, embarrassment showing on his face.

"There are good reasons, my friend."

"Well, my men are ready. As am I."

"I knew you would be."

They talked then of where the queen of Ravelin awaited them, the best route to take, and how long it would take. The winter was a difficult time to move large groups, but they knew that early spring would be worse with all of the mud from the thaws making roads impassable.

"If we get there as quickly as we can, will we be in time?" Bergerson asked, almost as an afterthought.

"Only if our intelligence is good and Verald truly has not yet left his capital. Otherwise, all of this may be futile and we could be walking into a trap. However, we have every reason to believe the queen is not playing us false."

"I can't for the life of me figure why Verald would go at all, to tell the truth of it. Not at this time of year."

"I suppose it would not be a good idea to let such a challenge go unanswered. And if the roads are as good as they seem . . ."

"They've been improving," Bergerson said. "Those two have been at each other's throats for years, though." He shook his head.

Soon, they all went to their cots. Elissa found it impossible to sleep. *We could be walking into a trap,* she kept thinking.

The fire cast shadows on the flimsy walls and she shivered. The fire gave off no warmth that she could feel and even less cheer. She knew the one thing she could do to try and guarantee some success in this venture, but she was still afraid, and even more so at the thought of doing it by herself. However, the only risk in that was to herself. Without the knowledge she could gain, everyone else was at risk, too.

Closing her eyes, she called on the Lady. "Protect me," Elissa whispered. The coils of light looped around, warming her. Their glow seemed to hold promise, chasing away fear.

Elissa moved into the night, able to see more than would normally be the case. She did not know this country, but she did know where Marie was supposed to be headquartered. She whispered the name, Crendon, and thought of the queen and open space. She turned the shadow cast by the fire and stepped through. It was the largest single jump she had ever made. The landscape moved under her feet as if she flew in the air. The night moved toward morning. When everything settled down, she found herself outside the walls of a castle. Light shone through a few windows and she chose one.

The room proved to be a bedchamber but no one was there. She chose another. On the third try, she found herself in a room with several people planning, discussing, arguing. At one end of the room sat the only woman. The respect they showed meant she could only be Queen Marie of Ravelin.

Having heard that Verald repudiated her as his wife, Elissa had come to believe that she must have looked old before her time, or perhaps never was beautiful. However, this was a woman of great beauty. Her smile would melt the hearts of most men. Her frown would make them do anything to win back her favor. It was impossible to guess her age, and just as difficult to believe that she had two grown sons.

At that moment, Marie listened to the men, most of them soldiers, as they argued about tactics and how Verald would deploy his own troops when they finally met. The youngest man of the group leaned against the wall near the queen, listening, too. However, he seemed not to care about the discussion. In only a moment of studying his face, Elissa knew that he was Marie's son.

That he was not interested in the plans that might put him on the throne was surprising. Yet, the disdain in his expression when he looked at his mother might explain that. Perhaps his father's attitude toward her had influenced his. Or it might be that he blamed his mother for his father not favoring him.

Whatever the truth might be, it was a problem best left to them. Elissa had enough of her own. And at that moment, her own mission was more important.

"We need more bowmen," a very large man was saying. "Verald will come at us with as many mounted soldiers as he can muster. I've heard he has even hired some mercenaries from Thulia."

"He has hired no one," another man spoke up. "He thinks our numbers are small and we will be easily overcome."

"He is not far wrong in that," a third man said.

"Plinus," the large man cut in, addressing the second speaker. "You can't know what Verald has or has not done."

"Not directly," Plinus said, grinning. "But her majesty does."

The men looked toward her and she gave them a small smile. A few of them smiled back.

"I still have a few friends in the castle," she said. "However, it has become more difficult for word to be sent out."

"What we really need to know is when the king plans to move against us," the large man said.

"Not for two more days, Gregory," she said. "They had some . . . uh . . . difficulties with various preparations. Even though my father will not be joining us here, he delayed them that much."

"You are certain they will come?" Gregory said.

"Yes. They have very strong reasons to come. I have seen to that with the help of my son." She looked over at him. "Don't sulk so," she scolded. "You will be king more quickly this way than with your friend, Niall."

He scowled at her, but said nothing. It suddenly occurred to Elissa how fortunate she was that she would not have to marry this young man, who clearly had been warped by his strange childhood.

They talked awhile longer and at last the meeting broke up. Elissa guessed that it had been called to go over their plans one last time. Only Plinus, Galen, and Marie remained. At first, Elissa guessed the older man was her advisor in this venture, but the look that passed between them when everyone else had left made her believe they were lovers.

"Are you certain the border guards have been alerted that our friends are coming?" Marie asked.

"Most certain."

"Good. It would be a shame for them not to get here in time because of an error like that."

"A great shame, indeed."

She smiled up at him, then glanced at her son.

"Galen, go on to bed. There is nothing more to do tonight."

"You promised to find out about Niall."

She sighed. "I know I did. But there has been no word as yet. I promise I will let you know as soon as there is news."

The young man stalked out of the room. Marie and Plinus were quiet a moment after he had gone.

"I think his friendship with that Niall was an unhealthy one," Plinus commented.

"I am sure it was. But his lordship will bother no one again."

"And the letter you got from him will guarantee the Alboran queen's coming to our aid?"

"She and her entourage left Winfield three days ago, headed this way." She stood up and put her arms around his neck. "I am so very glad you are here."

"I know," he said. His arms went around her waist and drew her to him. They kissed.

"When this is over, we will be married," he said.

"I told you I have no interest in marrying anyone," she said angrily. "No man will ever hold sway over me again."

They began to argue loudly. It was time to leave. Elissa felt that she had the information she had sought and more: Marie had not lied and Lord Niall was probably dead. And she did not wish to be a witness to their personal conflict.

Elissa tried to think of the camp on the other side of the border. Willed herself to flee there where her body waited. But their anger beat at her, their words and voices confused her. It was as if she was being physically assaulted. Every shout struck her. Anger pulsed through the chamber, forming a barrier. She had felt Tommy's pain when she found him, but it was nothing like this.

She tried to scream, but could make no sound. Her knees buckled and she fell to the floor. "Lady, help me." Blackness enveloped her.

It was early morning and Geoffrey jerked awake. He sat up, staring around in the darkness. Like any good soldier, he woke up quickly and was alert. Only the red coals of the fire gave off any light. Someone had cried out. Yet Captain Bergerson still slept. He could hear the captain snoring in the deep silence. No echo of the shout. Must have been a dream.

He slipped from under the blanket, too disturbed to go back to sleep. Going outside and away from the cabin, he relieved himself then stood looking at the stars overhead. Strange how their light could seem warm in a summer sky and so cold in the winter. He shivered. Speaking of cold, he would feel much better back under the blankets. But he wanted to check on Elissa first.

As quietly as he could, he walked over to the captain's cabin, opened the door, and went in. The fire was low and he put a couple of logs on the coals. As he got to his feet, he glanced over at Elissa. She had thrown the blanket back, which was not like her at all. He had never known anyone to suffer from the cold as much as she did.

He went to her cot and pulled the blanket back up around her shoulders. As he did so, his fingers brushed her cheek. Her skin was cold as ice. He felt her forehead. It, too, was cold. Her hands likewise.

"Your majesty, wake up," he said softly, shaking her shoulder.

There was no response.

He hesitated a moment then slid his hand under her clothes to feel her shoulder. So very cold. He leaned down to listen for her breathing. Not a sound.

Dead? How? No, he would not allow that. She must be all right. She must be. He shook her hard by the shoulders.

"Wake up!"

Elissa came to herself slowly. She lay facedown on the floor, the cold from the stone penetrating her clothing. She felt so cold all over. The argument had gone on and on. The last thing she remembered was when Marie slapped Plinus. The very last thing.

A new sound filled the room. The two of them were in the huge draped bed, making love. Theirs was a very strange relationship, she thought as she rose to hands and knees.

She must get back before she was missed. All she wanted now was to be warm.

"Lady, please help me," she whispered.

Thinking hard about the camp and the cabin, she moved

away at last. But when she was sure she was back in her own body, everything was as cold as before. Worse, she could see nothing. Surely there were coals on the fire.

"She can't be dead," someone said in the darkness.

Oh, no! With no one to watch over it, had her body died? She was gone too long. Or the cold had been too much.

Suddenly, she felt that she was choking. She put a hand to her throat, tried to swallow. She coughed instead, wracking her whole body. Hands grabbed her arms and pulled her to a sitting position. Her breathing became easier, broken occasionally by more coughing.

"Get some water," a familiar voice ordered.

In a moment a cup was held to her lips.

"Just a little," the voice told her gently.

She sipped, managed to swallow it. The moisture seemed to soothe her throat. Strong arms holding her upright held the only warmth she could feel.

She opened her eyes and found that she could see at last. Over Geoffrey's shoulder she could see small flames from the fire. Lit by that fire was Captain Bergerson's face. Fear distorted his features.

25

"I don't understand," Bergerson said. "One moment she seemed dead. The next she is sitting up and talking."

"It is pretty simple, really," Elissa said, her mind racing. "All of my life, I have had difficulty with the cold. If my body becomes too cold, I go into a very deep sleep. My breathing nearly stops and it seems that I am dead. The king and I decided not to tell anyone. We took extra precautions to make sure I was always warm. It does seem to happen mostly at night, when the temperature drops so low. I scared him once or twice in the night, but he knew what to do to revive me."

She looked straight at Geoffrey.

"Somehow you knew instinctively what to do, my lord," she said. "I am grateful."

"Didn't you think that once the king was dead, someone else should have been told?" he asked. "You might have died."

"My uncle knows and that is one reason I have kept him close to me since Ethelred's death. I was afraid to tell anyone else."

Geoffrey nodded, apparently ready to accept the explanation. She glanced at the captain, who simply seemed relieved.

She smiled at him and nodded. Geoffrey sat down on the cot beside her.

"Should I keep an eye on you the rest of the night?" he asked.

"If you can keep the fire as warm as possible, I should be all right."

He nodded. Bergerson went back outside and Geoffrey put more wood on the fire. She closed her eyes, trying to compose herself for sleep. The second cot creaked as he lay down.

His concern for her was almost palpable. That helped her to finally drop off to sleep. When Geoffrey awakened her at dawn, she wanted to protest loudly, but did not dare. She accepted that it was necessary, no matter how unpleasant.

Bergerson brought her warmed and watered mead followed by hot gruel of some kind. It looked awful but actually tasted good, having been sweetened with honey and wine. Warmed and feeling more awake, she left the cabin with her two companions. The soldiers who were to accompany them stood by their horses. Their own mounts stood ready as well.

"Gentlemen," she said, "now we will find out if the pass Queen Marie sent us works."

She got up on her horse without assistance and the captain led the way down the hill. The air was icy in spite of the bright sunshine. Elissa found herself shivering every so often, blaming it as much on the experience of the night before as the cold temperature. Never again, she vowed, would she try that by herself.

The morning was quiet except for the crunch of the horses' hooves in the snow and the crying of some bird in the distance. They were all tense with the knowledge that their first test would come soon.

It happened just after they had crossed the small stream that marked the border between the two kingdoms. There was no bridge, but the stream was very narrow and shallow. The water ran so swiftly that it had not frozen over, although ice played around its edges.

They had all cleared the water when the challenge came. A soldier stepped out of some bushes into their path, crying, "Halt!"

The guardsman looked over the safe conduct Geoffrey showed him. No other soldiers were visible, but she was sure they were there somewhere. Probably with arrows ready to fly from bows if the strangers showed one sign of aggression.

They knew this would not work if Verald had sent word not to let anyone from Albor cross the border, but he should not have any idea they were on their way to assist his queen, even if he had spies in the court at Winfield. Unless such spies were very high placed, of course.

The Ravelin soldier proved to be a bit suspicious and Geoffrey patiently told him that, with the royal safe conduct, he must let them pass. And no, he would not say what their mission was as it was a matter of serious diplomacy.

Grudgingly, the guardsman at last decided to let them pass. They rode on north, but it was some time before Elissa no longer had the urge to look back.

Late the fifth morning, Queen Marie's camp was in sight. For Elissa the last two days of the journey had been grueling. Camping in the open at night, and the deep bitter cold, had left her limbs feeling numb much of the time. But she had asked for few special favors. She wanted to know as much about a soldier's life as she could, without killing herself. However, the lord marshal checked on her often during the night and made every effort to make sure she was always warm.

During the day she had often ridden beside the captain, engaging him in conversation. She tried to display enough intelligence that he would not dismiss her out of hand, but also enough womanly ignorance, so that he felt good about explaining things to her. Especially relating to battles. Because of the high reputation of its army, Albor was at peace with its neighbors more often than it was at war. Still, there were occasional border skirmishes or internal matters to be taken care of, and he experienced many of those.

Sometimes during these conversations, she would feel Geoffrey watching her. When she would look over at him, he would smile. He understood that she was making friends with the good captain, calming his doubts, and he approved of her methods.

Now, they sat their horses, Geoffrey on her right and Bergerson on her left, looking over at the encampment surrounding the small castle. It looked very large and there must be hundreds of soldiers.

"Why would Verald come to them instead of making them come to him?" she asked.

"He cannot stay in his castle and let this army roam around the countryside," Geoffrey said. "He must show his people that he is not afraid. Especially not of a woman and his own son. I am sure Marie was counting on that and it looks as if she chose her ground well."

"Why?"

"The river protects her back," Bergerson said. "The cliffs protect her on the left."

"But doesn't that also mean she has no escape route?"

"There are probably boats on the riverbank just in case."

"So Verald must enter the site from one of two directions," she said.

"Yes," Geoffrey said. "And on the left, there is enough cover for an ambush. She will probably post some archers there."

"What will prevent Verald from just laying siege to the castle?"

"Marie's forces will be in the field rather than inside the castle. He will have no choice but to fight."

They looked over the terrain for a few more minutes. It was difficult for her to imagine how different things would be once Verald arrived.

They passed through the castle gates amid much excitement. The queen met them at the stairway leading into the main hall.

"Welcome to Ravelin," she said. "You are most welcome."

"Thank you, your majesty," Elissa said. "Is there someone who can show our men where they are to billet?"

The man beside Marie motioned for someone to show them and groomsmen came forward to hold the lead horses while their riders dismounted. The queen led the way up the stairs, followed by the lord marshal of Albor, his captain, and Elissa.

Marie led them to a small room just off the great hall. She sat in the same chair Elissa had seen the night before. The door closed behind them.

"Welcome to Ravelin, your majesty," Marie said. "We welcome your assistance in this venture."

"Thank you, your majesty," Elissa responded. "We also welcome your assistance."

She tried to make her tone as neutral as possible. She had not liked the woman the night before and liked her even less now. Her feelings would have been difficult to explain. She was sure they had nothing to do with the fact that both Geoffrey and Bergerson were now staring at her in open admiration. Or that Marie seemed not to notice their admiration. A cold passion flowed from this woman, and for the first time, Elissa did not blame Verald for wanting nothing to do with her. She was dangerous and scheming.

They made introductions all around. Marie was accompanied by Plinus and Galen. Out of the corner of her eye, Elissa watched the younger son. He looked so much like his mother.

"Would you like refreshments before we begin discussing the battle plans?" Marie asked.

"That would be most pleasant," Elissa said.

Marie turned to Plinus, instructing him to have their things taken to the rooms assigned to her guests.

"I have had a suite prepared for you so that you can all stay together," she explained. "I hope that is satisfactory."

"Most satisfactory," Elissa said.

"Good. If you will follow me into the dining hall."

The meal was pleasant, and although they did not rush through it, they did not tarry either. Afterward they retired to the same meeting room where servants had set up tables and chairs. They sat around the larger table, drinking wine, while the coming battle was discussed.

"Verald should arrive tomorrow," Plinus said. "We expect him to attack the day after. He has gathered an army of nearly a thousand men. Our own force here numbers almost eight hundred."

"We brought eighty-five," Geoffrey said.

"We will be nearly evenly matched, then," Plinus said. "Although we may have the advantage of the battleground itself and most of the better warriors have sided with us. Verald had to search high and low to find enough experienced soldiers to lead this army of his. Many of them are not as experienced as he would like."

Elissa spoke up. "There is the small matter . . ."

". . . of the letter," Marie finished for her.

Elissa bowed her head slightly, Marie held out her hand and Plinus handed her a folded piece of paper.

"This is the one you refer to, I believe," she said.

Elissa took the paper, unfolded it, read the beginning, and checked the signature and the broken seal. It was hers and it was the original.

"Thank you," she said.

She placed it inside her jacket, intending to burn it the moment she returned to the suite. Strangely, though, its contents no longer seemed so threatening. More than anything, she just wanted to be rid of the thing.

Later, they ate supper in the meeting room as they continued discussing the battle plans. It was very late when they were shown to the suite assigned to them. None of them was ready to sleep and they sat in front of the fire. Elissa had finally asked if there was any mead, and a full ewer had been left in the sitting room along with one of wine. They drank sparingly.

"Does their plan suit you?" she asked both of her companions.

"It seems well thought out," Geoffrey said.

"It would be better if they had a larger force, though," Bergerson added. "Good thing they chose a defensible position."

"I thought the same thing, but I'm no expert," she said.

"I would feel better if you stayed out of the fight," Geoffrey said to her. "The outcome of this battle is too uncertain and Albor cannot afford to lose you."

"I do not—"

"He is right, majesty," the captain said.

"Gentlemen, I want to learn what it is like to be a soldier." Their expressions were grave. She sighed. "All right. I will stay back, but I will enter the fray if I think it either necessary or advantageous."

They nodded, glad to have that much of a concession. For a while she asked questions, trying to get some idea of what to expect in a battle, but especially why Verald would come at all. They explained that Marie kept contingents out all the time, harassing his outposts across the countryside.

Eventually, they all grew too sleepy to go on. They said good night and went to their separate bed chambers. For the first time in what seemed too long, Elissa was warm enough and went right to sleep.

When she woke early the next morning, she felt better than she had in a very long time. The physical exercise of the trip and the exhausted sleep had chased away barely remembered dreams that often haunted her days. She lay listening but could detect no sound outside her chamber. She rose from the bed, hastily slipping her feet into slippers, and wrapped the cloak around her.

She padded to the window and looked out. Not only was it too early for bright sunshine, but the landscape below was completely hidden by grey fog.

Had another storm moved in? If so, would that delay the arrival of Verald and his army? She hoped not on both counts.

More than anything she wanted this whole affair over and done. She wanted to be back in her own castle, overseeing her son's kingdom, and sleeping in her own bed.

She looked over at the bed she had just left. Sleeping in a strange bed did have some advantage, she must admit. A servant entered. He bowed to her, went to the fire, and added more wood. In moments, there was a blaze going. After he left the bedchamber, she got the letter from the jacket pocket. She had forgotten the night before, but in the morning quiet, she held the letter in the fire until it caught. Laying it on the uppermost log, she watched until it was consumed, then scattered its ashes with the poker.

She moved into the sitting room, where the fire had also been revived. She stood in front of the renewed fire, turning to warm herself on all sides. Just as the man came out of Geoffrey's chamber, a woman servant entered bearing a tray with ewers of wine and mead, and three goblets.

She set the tray on a side table and curtsied. "Your majesty, Queen Marie invites you and your companions to breakfast with her in the small dining room."

"Thank her majesty and tell her we will be glad to join her."

She poured a little of the mead. It was watered, but warm, and tasted very good.

The manservant came out of the captain's chamber and, having finished his duties, bowed to her and left. Soon both of her companions came into the sitting room, stretching and yawning but fully dressed.

She told them they were invited for breakfast downstairs and went to dress. It took a bit longer than usual because she had forgotten to ask for a maid to help.

"Shall we find breakfast?" Geoffrey asked. "I am starving."

"Certainly," Bergerson said. "Afterward, I will check on my men."

After they had eaten, Marie and Plinus took Elissa and Geoffrey on a tour of the castle. The whole time Ravelin's queen kept looking at her guest as surreptitiously as possible.

"I am sorry," she said at last. "But is your hair—"

"Short?"

Elissa swept the hat from her head and shook out her hair. She smiled at Marie and turned so that she could see the back.

"I see that it is. Do your people not object?"

"Most of them do not know. I have a hairpiece that I wear much of the time. But it's too difficult to pin in place by myself."

"Is there a reason for this?"

"My sword master insisted."

"I see."

Elissa was certain Marie did not understand that, but was too polite to ask further. For some reason, she took pleasure in not offering to explain further.

The tour continued until nearly noon. Crendon was older than Winfield, but it had been endowed with all the luxuries the new generations had come to expect. Originally, it consisted of only the central square building, three stories tall. In later years, small buildings had been added then surrounded by a wall. The village that had grown up around had been gone for over a generation.

Just after noon, they found Bergerson, and they all mounted their horses to take another look outside the walls. Several feet of snow still covered the ground, but the footing was surprisingly good. Still, the going would be a bit cumbersome and slow.

"This," Plinus said, indicating the wide field, "will be the main battleground. However, we will have archers placed in the woods to the east. Verald's forces are due to arrive this afternoon and will be tired from the march, but they will attack the next morning. From the north."

He pointed to the end of the field opposite the castle. There were woods there, too, but a much thinner growth. With space for their tents but protection from the prevailing west wind, it would be a good place for Verald to set up his camp. Not that they would stay there very long. If he won this battle, he would stay in the castle. If he lost, he and his forces would be scattered across the countryside. If Marie and her forces won, she would immediately send troops to take over the castle in the capital. While that happened, Elissa intended to be well on her way home.

The last thing they were shown was a line of boats along the riverbank behind the castle, just as Geoffrey had predicted. Plinus explained that although they did not expect to be beaten in this battle, it was always a good idea to have an escape plan. Elissa counted twenty boats; each could carry about ten people. Not everyone would escape.

It was midafternoon when they returned to the castle. Marie invited them into the dining room for mead and wine. They had just settled down when a messenger was brought in.

"Verald and his army have arrived, it would seem," Marie announced. "We fight tomorrow."

Elissa's heart leapt into her throat and she swallowed hard. Captain Bergerson looked grim, while Geoffrey's expression remained pleasant. Maric and Plinus both looked eager. So far there had been no sign of the possible future king.

∾ 26 ∾

The next morning proved as foggy as the day before. It muffled sounds while, at the same time, carrying them a great distance. Standing on the roof walk, Elissa wished that the parapet was not quite so high. She had put on the male clothing she brought with her, further confusing her hunters.

She stood at one merlon watching and waiting, while Queen Marie stood at the next one. These two were placed right in the center of the parapet, giving them the best view from the roof. It seemed to take forever, but eventually the rising sun burned off the fog. At first Elissa could see nothing of the men whose voices had carried across the field from the other side. However, she could see the rebel forces lined up almost below her in front of the main gate.

The edge of fear she had expected to feel was blunted by a sense of excitement. It was galling to be on the roof watching and waiting, but she had promised to stay out of it, unless she was forced to fight somehow. Imagining that happening was even more difficult as she looked over the proud soldiers.

She made out Geoffrey, who wore Queen Marie's colors in this fight. All of the Alborans were given tunics with the same colors. Officially, they were not even there. Nor was she.

During the night she had considered just gathering up her own soldiers and quitting the castle. Even if that were honorable, however, it would be impossible with Verald blocking the main road into the valley and Marie's archers already set in the woods to the east.

Finally the fog thinned and she could just make out a few figures across the way and some of the banners hanging limply from the staffs. It was extremely cold, and horses and men on both sides breathed out a bit of their own fog.

A trumpet sounded from the other side and everyone began moving forward in a body. Somehow she had expected the beginning to be more dramatic, yet from the pounding of her heart, this was dramatic enough. The horses, bred in this country, stepped high through the snow. The snow itself was packed amazingly hard with slick spots that could catch one unawares. These men knew what they were facing. The distance between the two forces decreased slowly.

Suddenly, a small troop broke off from Verald's main army. About twenty men leaning over their horses' necks urged their mounts into the woods on the east. Arrows began flying at them and a few were struck. Only one man fell.

Meanwhile, a shout rose from the main body and their comrades increased their pace to a run. With another great cry, Marie's forces also rushed forward. Within moments, the two groups began to merge.

Elissa tried to keep her eye on Geoffrey, but the skirmish to the east occasionally drew her attention. The main battle was a kaleidoscope of color and metal flashing in the morning sunlight. Men shouted and horses screamed. After a time, she could detect a rhythm as one force pushed the other back momentarily, only to have their opponents rally and push them back.

The ground was already littered with fallen men, both wounded and dead. The horses sometimes shied away from stepping on a man, throwing their riders off balance.

Another horn sounded and the two sides broke away, returning to their original positions. Other men ran out and began removing the casualties, not seeming to care on which side they had fought. Their task was just to get them out of the way.

Elissa spotted Geoffrey in the milling crowd below and breathed a short prayer of thanks to the Lady. Then the horn sounded and they were off again. Not long after they engaged each other, the horn sounded and foot soldiers began running onto the field from the north. The gates opened in the castle wall, and more foot soldiers poured out. For a time, the sound of steel striking steel was the clearest element of the fray.

Then the number of casualties again required a halt as those that carried on sometimes tripped over their bodies, but no horn sounded. The battle was too fully engaged for them to break off.

Shouts came from the woods as the fight continued there. It was impossible to tell who might carry the day in that fight. In fact, Elissa was surprised that the archers had held on so long.

Then she spotted a small group break from those same woods, headed for the castle gates. She counted twelve wearing Verald's livery. There was a good chance they outnumbered the guards left at the gate.

She rushed for the stairs at the corner of the parapet and started down just behind two of their guards. She heard the swish of Marie's skirts behind her.

"You better stay here where it's safe," Elissa said.

"I wouldn't miss seeing you fight for the world. Go on!"

Under her breath, Elissa called her a foolish woman, but this *was* her castle, after all.

She ran down the stairs to the first floor, then out into the center courtyard. The gates were wide open!

Three guards struggled to push them. She ran to help but the troop closed on the opening. Some guards outside challenged them, slowing them down, but several rode on. The guards had gotten one gate closed, but could not reach the other as two horsemen dashed through.

As they passed, a horseman slashed at the guard beside her

and he fell to the ground. The horses could not stop immediately, and she kept pushing as the other two guards finally helped her. The invaders wheeled their horses. A third got through and the gate slammed closed behind him.

One man stayed long enough to lower the bar into place. Elissa drew her sword and turned to face three enemy soldiers. One horseman charged straight at her. He swung his sword at the guard who had run up, ignoring her. The guard ducked the blow and the horse would have gone on by them, except she slashed at the man as he passed. She had cut his thigh.

The third guard joined them. Three on foot against three on horse.

The same horseman galloped toward her again. She waited until he was nearly in striking distance then dropped flat to the ground. She poked at the horse's back leg with her sword point, catching him in the forelock. The horse bucked and kicked out with its back legs. The man lowered the sword to grab the reins with both hands, and pulled on them, trying to get the animal's head up and stay in the saddle.

Elissa heard others fighting around her but she concentrated on this one. She could only hope that the guards were able to do their part.

She got to her feet, crouched, and moved toward the still bucking animal from behind. The man did not see her, but the horse tried to dance away sideways. Its legs moved too quickly for her to catch the other leg in the same way. She swung the sword so that the blade sliced the animal's rump. It reared and bucked, lashing out with its rear legs. She just missed being kicked in the head. Instead she received a glancing blow on her left shoulder.

This time the soldier was unseated, falling so that the horse was between him and her. She tried to move around it, but it pranced side to side because the man still held tightly to the reins. A small trickle of blood stained the dirty snow from the second wound and Elissa's shoulder began to ache.

The man finally looked under the flailing hooves and saw her. He got to his feet, his gaze not leaving her face, and he released the reins. Finally free, the animal galloped to the other side of the courtyard.

Standing at his full height, Elissa realized how big this man was. This was going to be a very different fight from the one with Randall's champion. This one was taller and his arms were long so he had reach on her. And from the scar on his face, she would guess he had a lot more experience.

He stepped toward her, holding his sword casually. Suddenly he bounded forward, striking overhanded. She countered with her own blade. And countered again as he swung his blade quickly and smoothly. He was good, better than she. Her only hope was to find a weakness. She had found her own. Every blow brought pain to the injured shoulder. If this kept up, her whole arm would soon be numb.

She backed up, trying to take the sting out of his blows and gauge his style. And stay alive.

She tried to attack, but he was just too strong. He kept coming at her, until he tripped on a small piece of wood that had been left lying in the snow. His sword tip dropped as he regained his balance. She swung high, forcing him to raise his blade, then dropped the tip and lunged forward.

He looked as surprised as she felt, for her blade had pierced his abdomen deeply. His own forward momentum had pressed him against it.

He looked at her in disbelief, and tried to raise his sword, but only managed to slide the tip in the snow where it had fallen. She tried to pull her own blade free but when she did, he stepped closer. He reached out with his free hand trying to grab at her. She stepped backward, maintaining the distance between them. He let go of his sword and grabbed her blade with both hands. It had become slick with his blood and his hands slipped. She pulled with him and it finally came free. He stayed on his feet another moment, then dropped to his knees. She got only close enough to pick up his sword and throw it out of his reach.

"I thought I had you," he said.

"I did, too."

He looked at her intently as his hands pressed against his belly, trying to stop the flow of blood.

"You're not a boy."

"No."

"Damn you."

"I am sorry."

She did not know what else to say. Was there some kind of code in a case like this?

Quickly, she glanced around the courtyard. The other two horsemen had been overcome—one dead or dying and the other wounded and a prisoner. Marie stood off to one side from where she must have watched the whole thing. She smiled and mouthed the words "Well done."

Some distance away, the wounded horse limped around in circles as if the pain was too much for it. She hoped it was not too badly wounded. That would be too much.

She sat cross-legged in the snow beside the man as he died. She was still there when Marie's troops returned in victory. She sensed Geoffrey beside her rather than saw him.

"He's dead," the marshal said.

"Yes, I know."

"Come, your majesty. Let us see if you are wounded anywhere."

"I had to stay," she said as he lifted her to her feet. "No one should die without someone there to see it."

"I know."

He led her to their suite and Marie's physician came to check her over. The shoulder was already turning purple and there was a cut on her side that she had never felt until then. He put a poultice on the shoulder and stitched up the cut. A maid appeared to undress and wash her. She drank some warm mead and soon after went to bed. She did not sleep as well that night.

They stayed at Crendon for two more days. They met with Marie and discussed the aftermath. Verald had survived the battle and was on his way back to his castle with a small number of his soldiers. Marie sent a troop after him. If they overtook him, it would make matters so much easier.

It was also discovered that her precious son, Galen, was the one who had left the gates open. It seemed that he was still trying to earn his father's favor in spite of everything. Marie seemed undecided about whether she would still support his bid for the throne, which she had engineered in the first place.

No one seemed to know where his older brother was. It was not known for sure whether he had even taken part in the battle. Perhaps the queen's plans would depend on finding and talking with him.

The day after the battle, Elissa went out on the battleground itself. Bodies still lay there awaiting burial. Dogs sniffed around the carcasses, but most of them were being kept away. She wanted to ask Geoffrey if other soldiers and warriors experienced this letdown feeling after a battle, but somehow she did not think they did.

He hovered around, worried about the effects the fight seemed to have had on her. He said little, but fussed about her eating and drinking enough and staying warm. That was the real problem. She could not stay warm enough.

The horse she had wounded was going to be all right, it turned out. She had not done it serious harm. Horses did not deserve to suffer just because men could not get along.

The night before they left for home, Geoffrey and the captain sat with her before the fireplace in the sitting room of their suite. They had eaten a final supper with the queen and her nobles, who were preparing to march toward the capital the next day. Bergerson and the remainder of his command were going with her.

"I know you have been concerned about me, my lord," she said after conversation had waned. "Are you afraid now that I might not be able to lead our kingdom during my son's minority?"

"Yes, I am somewhat."

"You think I haven't the stomach or I am not tough enough."

"You have to admit that you have seemed a little unbalanced."

She chuckled at the word "unbalanced."

"I know I have not been quite myself," she said. "But I understand the necessity of warfare and such. That does not mean I have to like it."

"Perhaps you will not have to face it again."

"That isn't very likely now, is it?"

"Not in this world."

"I know."

～ 27 ～

Snow melted in the afternoon sunlight. Still, spring was a long time coming. Perhaps this year it would not come at all. Perhaps winter would last a whole year and warmth would be a thing of the past, a memory of what had been.

Memories were traitors, reminding Elissa of what had been and creating hope that what had been good would return.

Now she wished that the smell of death would leave her. She had heard that such a smell could linger for a very long time. She had not been born when soldiers from the north poured south, killing and plundering, taking anything the king might want, but people had always talked about it. Ah, how she missed the warmth of her home. That thought led inevitably to thoughts of Ethel. Maybe she could come home now if she wanted to. She was a princess and should be beside her brother. But Edgar was making friends with his cousin and two other boys who had moved into the castle with their fathers. He would neither want his sister around nor suffer her bullying.

Elissa smiled in spite of the sadness in her heart. All of these changes meant that her children were growing up.

"Are you ready to come away from the window, niece, and get some work done?" Deward asked.

At that moment, the door to the chamber opened and Geoffrey walked in. A messenger had come for him nearly an hour ago, and he looked saddened by whatever news was brought to him.

"Are you all right, my lord?" Elissa asked. "I would guess the news from home was not good."

"My wife grows worse," he said in a subdued voice. "The physicians can do nothing for her. But they say she could live this way for many years."

"In a day or two, you should go home and see her."

He looked over at her. The pain in his eyes made her ache for him. She wanted to put her arms around him and comfort him. Yes, she loved him. However, there was little she could do about it. Now or ever.

"Yes, thank you, your majesty. I should go to her."

He loves her still, she thought. *Yet he has feelings for me. It is a complicated world.*

She could not risk a relationship with a married man. And one of the things she admired about him was his devotion to his invalid wife. It was so hopeless.

"I will not stay long," Geoffrey was saying. "Just long enough to—"

"Stay as long as you need, my lord. Just remember, we have need of you here, too."

They looked into each other's eyes for several heartbeats. Deward broke the spell.

"So, can we get down to work?" he asked loudly.

"Yes, of course," Geoffrey said.

"Good. There is something we must decide on as soon as possible. What are we going to do about Lord Randall?"

"What can we do?" Elissa said in exasperation. They had been discussing this problem off and on for days.

"That is precisely what we must decide. What are our options?"

"The ideal solution would be for him to honestly and permanently pledge to support me and my children. We also need his support in order to assure the support of his father."

They sat in silence, each wondering and hoping, but no one coming up with a good idea. Elissa stifled a yawn.

"I am tired, gentlemen. Let's consider all of this again tomorrow."

They agreed and all three went their separate ways. She was tired. But she could not go to bed until the one question was solved. A possible solution occurred to her at the last moment. She sent one of her guards on two errands, while the other followed her to her apartment. Edgar had gone to bed quite some time ago and she resisted the urge to peek in at him.

Cein, her new maid, was stirring the fire in the sitting room when she entered. The girl was chosen by Margaret, Roric's wife, who had been busy while Elissa was gone. The castle already ran more efficiently. Clara was still in the dungeon, and the new girl was young and in awe of her mistress. She was also very good with a needle and had a lovely singing voice.

"Majesty," she said and dropped a curtsey.

"Good evening, Cein. Go down to the kitchen and find an ewer of wine and one of mead, would you? I have another meeting tonight. Once you have delivered them, find someplace to stay for a while."

"Yes, majesty."

She curtsied again and hurried off. Now the question was, who would arrive first?

She got two swords out of the cupboard and stood them in their scabbards beside the fireplace against the wall. Then she collapsed into one of the chairs in front of the fire and stretched her feet toward the fire. Actually, if it were not for the two major problems facing her, she would be quite content. But there would always be something. She was sure of that.

A knock came on the door.

"Enter," she called.

The guard had returned from his errand. He escorted Lord Randall inside and started to close the door.

"Wait outside," she told him. He hesitated, looked unsure.

"It's all right. Lord Randall and I want to talk for a while."

Her husband's cousin looked at her suspiciously. His hands were tied in front of him, and as soon as the guard left, she untied him. She expected his hands around her throat any moment as she turned her back on him and returned to her chair.

"Be seated," she said. "We will have some wine in a moment."

"What do you want?"

"I want you to sit down."

"I'd rather not."

"Oh, don't be a fool, Randall! How can we possibly talk with you standing there like a jousting dummy." His brow wrinkled in anger. "We must solve this situation between us somehow. Now, sit down. Please."

Slowly, he moved to the other chair and sat. He rubbed his wrists where they had been tied and looked into the fire. Cein knocked and entered, carrying two ewers. Her mouth dropped open when she recognized the visitor.

"Set them down," Elissa said.

She placed them on the sideboard, curtsied, and left hurriedly.

"Wine or mead?"

She went to the sideboard and poured herself some mead. The girl had already warmed it. How she could have done that so quickly was a new mystery.

"Wine."

She poured for him and carried the goblet to him. She took a deep drink, letting the warmth spread throughout her body.

"Now what?" Randall asked.

"You have heard about my trip to Crendon, I assume."

"Yes."

"Ravelin is now experiencing a civil war. It will not last long, whichever side wins, but their kingdom will suffer. I do not want Albor to go through the same thing. You and I can avert that possibility tonight. Just the two of us."

"How?"

He had been glancing at the two swords ever since he sat down. She pointed to them now.

"We can fight for the regency."

He grinned, but would not look at her.

"Or we can decide to work together for Albor and for the memory of Ethelred."

He snorted.

"Your father has sworn to support me and my children and I believe him. Ease his pain at the thought of losing you."

"He gives up too easily."

"He realizes that the position he already has is nearly as great as being regent and much less restrictive."

"He can do whatever he wants. And so can you. But I will not give you my blessing. I won't fight you, either. I am sure you have instructed those guards outside to dash in here and kill me if there is any sign of trouble."

Elissa went to the door and opened it. The captain of the guards had come as she requested.

"Take Lord Randall back," she said to the captain. "He is to leave in the morning for his own castle. Nowhere else."

"But it isn't livable!" Randall protested. "The renovations have not been finished. Much of the furniture is still stored away."

"It is livable enough." She turned back to the captain. "Notify his wife that she may join him there if she wishes. Set guards within the castle. Have plenty of food brought in but leave no horses or other riding animals."

She turned to face Randall. He had gotten to his feet, glaring at her.

"Damn you!"

He threw the goblet of wine to the floor. Thinking that he was going to throw it at the queen, the captain had stepped between them. He then called in one of his men and they again tied Randall's hands.

"I will send further instructions on his household," she said as the three men approached the door.

"You will regret this!"

"I already do, my lord." He tried to pull away from his captors. "Oh, do go peacefully."

They led him away as he shouted invectives. The remaining guard kept a bland expression as if nothing had happened around him. She closed the door. In the morning, she would have to tell Randall's father that she had banished his son to his own castle until the Privy Council decided what should be done with him.

Midnight had passed and Elissa composed herself comfortably in her chair. Deward sat near, watching. When she told him what she wanted to do, he expressed strong disapproval. But seeing that she was determined on this course, he agreed to stay with her.

Randall had been gone more than two weeks. In that time the Privy Council had debated his fate. All except Roric and the queen. She had presented the case against him and gave the problem to them to decide. Roric had begged off, knowing he could not possibly sanction his own son's execution. All along she had suspected they would not be able to reach a decision. He had been one of them too long, and the proof against him was not strong enough to convince them.

She and her children could not continue with this danger hanging over their heads. She had been prepared to take this step and the moment had come.

Closing her eyes, she went through the ritual of asking for the Lady to watch over her. The strands of light engulfed her. She now had a better feel for traveling in this manner and she went straight to Randall's castle.

One wing of the first floor was blocked off for their living quarters. It consisted of a small dining chamber, three bed-chambers, the kitchen, and another small room. She had allowed his cook and two servants to join him there.

She found him asleep next to his wife. Standing next to the bed, looking down on them, courage deserted her for a moment.

She took a deep breath and sat down on the edge of the

bed. Neither of them stirred. She leaned down and put her arms around him. For a moment nothing happened, and she feared that either she did not remember how, or it only worked with a person who was already dying.

But then, she felt it. His essence flowing into her. Life draining from him. Her whole being tingled. His eyes opened and he tried to push her away, but his hands just passed through her. He tried to struggle but he was weakening.

"Goodbye, my lord," she whispered in his ear.

"No," he whimpered.

Soon, he was empty of life. She sat back and looked at him one last time. His eyes stared upward, through half-closed lids. His face was pale. She stood and willed herself into the courtyard. Just before she left for Winfield, his wife screamed.

᧞ EPILOGUE ᧞

The funeral was planned as a grand affair, befitting a nobleman of Albor. Elissa insisted that it be held in the main chapel at Winfield and that the king's cousin be given every honor he was due.

Randall's body lay in state in the chapel for three days after his son performed the sin-eating ceremony. All that time, Roric roamed the halls of the palace like a restless ghost. He grew gray and haggard so very quickly.

Everyone gathered in the chapel, where he would be interred in the family crypt under the altar. Roric stood with his wife on one side, and his grandson on the other. People's expressions ranged from sadness to disbelief. Everyone had whispered about how young the king's cousin was. About the feud with Elissa, now regent. She had tricked Cein into telling her about the rumors running rampant within the castle.

Some people believed she had something to do with his death, but hadn't a clue how. As the patriarch intoned the ritual, some stole glances at her. She was amazed to see one wife make a sign against evil. Several of the lords saw it, too. They could not help looking from the lady to the queen. Nearly as surreptitiously, she blew a kiss in the woman's direction.

There was a sharp intake of air by those few who saw the whole exchange. Lord Witram stared at her. She smiled at him and bowed her head slightly. Realization showed in his eyes, his open mouth.

Later, when she made her way across the courtyard back toward her own apartment, she spied a violet peeping from the snow. A sign of spring at last.

Later that day, both Roric and Geoffrey took their leave. The former needed time to mourn the loss of his son. He assured her that he knew she had nothing to do with it, that the physicians had declared the cause was not poison. Which meant, of course, that he *had* suspected her.

The lord marshal was going home at last to see his wife, whose health continued to decline. He would be missed, but they all needed a break from the work.

Deward came to her late that night.

"Have you learned anything?" Elissa asked her uncle the moment he appeared.

"Not yet. Nothing in the books."

"There must be something we can do!"

"I am sure there is. We will just have to wait for word from the other teachers."

"I cannot wait much longer. I feel him inside my mind. I think it may drive me mad."

Deward reached over and took hold of her hand.

"There is a way to get his spirit out of you. We must be patient until it is found."

She tried to smile, but the attempt failed.

"We now know the price for this kind of magic," she said.

Deward nodded and continued to hold her hand. With nearly everyone gone, she could stay in her apartment until the remedy arrived.